THE NIGHT SHIFT

A SAM POPE NOVEL

ROBERT ENRIGHT

GW00685325

For my Mum.

CHAPTER ONE

'Not guilty. You are free to go.'

Chris Morton smiled smugly as he stood up, the verdict a wild case of injustice. He could hear the victim and her family weeping on one of the benches behind him, surrounded by the murmurs of the disgusted witnesses. The judge had hesitated before announcing her verdict, her disgust at the justice system evident on her face. The jury, meekly making their way to their own exit, refused to make eye contact with him. He stared at them all, basking in their nervous twitching.

He had gotten away with it.

His lawyer, his name of little consequence, ran a hand through his thinner hair and then offered it to him. Chris sneered, knowing that the sleazy man had gotten him off on a technicality.

The woman was intoxicated due to excessive drinking. That was what he had presented to the jury, with her toxicity reports showing she had just over the required amount to be considered inebriated. That and an unfortunate sexual escapade at university which had ended up online had not only caused her family to weep with shame, but it had also planted a seed of doubt in the jury's mind.

There was no doubt in Chris's mind.

He had raped Catriona Crouch.

And he had gotten away with it.

His ill-fitting suit sat over his podgy frame, his gut pressing the buttons of his shirt apart like an open crisp packet. His bald head was shiny with sweat and he grinned a yellow, jagged smile as if he were warning off potential car parking.

His lawyer scrambled to collect his papers before scurrying down the courtroom, eager to dodge the family of the victim and the inevitable angry press.

Chris didn't care.

He was a free man.

As he turned, he caught Catriona's eye, her anger overwhelmed by fear, which caused Chris to twitch with excitement. Before he could smile any further, he noticed Mark Connor sat a few benches back. The man screamed East-End gangster, his shaved head sitting atop a stocky frame that was clad in a leather jacket. His knuckles were well sanded from years of bare-knuckle boxing and debt collecting.

He worked for Frank Jackson.

As did Chris.

Swallowing nervously, Chris tried to button his blazer, the material struggling across the gut that spilled over his belt. Working for Frank Jackson had been the best thing to ever happen to him. Years had been wasted on construction sites and bouncing nightclubs. It was the consequence of dropping out of school early and diving headfirst into a life of drugs. After years of breaking the law just to get his next fix, Mr Jackson had dragged him from it and allowed him to break the law for a living.

Chris was a pusher. Dressed up to be a high-level security guard in one of Mr Jackson's strip clubs right next to Upton Park station, Chris would ensure that the 'higher clientele' had constant access to the best 'product'. Where Mr Jackson got the product, Chris wasn't too sure. But asking questions was beyond comprehension. Many of Chris's co-workers and similar subordinates in the other families had gone missing for asking the wrong question.

Or for crimes such as his. Seeing Mark Connor wasn't a good sign for Chris, as it meant Mr Jackson wanted to see him. Chris knew, from being one of the men called to arms, that when someone in Mr Jackson's crew stepped out of line, there were violent repercussions. Mr Jackson wouldn't let this crime go unpunished.

His reputation wouldn't allow it.

Mr Jackson was known as 'the Gent'. His reputation for excruciating violence was only preceded by his strict code of conduct. An untucked shirt, a stray curse word, and you would find your pay docked or fingers broken.

Raping a young woman; Chris suddenly didn't feel like such a big man anymore. With a nervous smile he approached Mark, who rose from his seat like an exploding volcano.

'Hello, Mark.'

'Chris.' Mark's voice was as powerful as his tree-like arms. A silver chain hung around his neck, overlapping the collar of his blue shirt. 'Follow me.'

Chris obliged, following the hulking man through the courtroom towards the exit, each step rocking the benches. The courtroom had emptied, apart from a few members of the family, who stared daggers at him. Beyond that, a couple of reporters finished their notes and lastly, just by the door, a young man with short brown hair and a strong jaw was staring rigidly ahead. Chris managed to make eye

3

contact with him as he passed, the man's brown-eyed stare catching him off guard.

It was as if the man knew him.

Shaking it off, Chris pushed his way through the doors and into a stream of activity. Reporters had huddled around the failed legal team, asking them their true thoughts of the British justice system. Whilst they answered diplomatically, Chris flashed them his rotten grin.

A firm hand clamped onto his shoulder like a Rottweiler and led him towards the exit.

'This way,' Mark's voice boomed, hatred lacing each word.

Eventually they pushed through the doors of Southwark Crown Court and into the London sunshine. Instantly, the busy roads roared to life, the sound of the never-ending traffic bouncing off the buildings that shot towards the blue sky like rocket ships. The sun bounced off every window, the city twinkling majestically.

At the bottom of the concrete steps was a black Range Rover, which would undoubtedly have Brian Stack in the driver seat. Brian, like Mark, was one of Mr Jackson's most trusted advisors. And like Mark, he was bald and brutish too.

They were affectionately known as 'the Mitchell Brothers', on account of being follically challenged East-End hard men.

Except these two didn't just act tough.

Every story that hung around the East End like a rising fog was true.

Mark approached the car first, pulling open the back door and arching his neck towards the seat. Chris offered a weak smile and entered, sliding across the smooth, white leather seats. A bucket was positioned in the footwell, causing him to place his feet either side. Mark got in next to him.

The door slammed shut.

They joined the traffic.

Mark swung a vicious punch that crushed Chris's stomach.

He arched forward in pain, his lunch instantly jetting out of his mouth and into the bin, which suddenly made a lot of sense. The pain was sickening and Chris struggled for breath, the fear shaking his body.

Was this how Catriona had felt when he had pinned her against the barrels in the nightclub warehouse?

'He better not get any sick on my floor, son,' Brian stated, indicating and turning onto the road that cut through Bermondsey.

'Don't you worry,' Mark assured. 'If he does, he'll be cleaning it up with broken fingers.'

The Mitchell Brothers laughed and Chris squirmed uncomfortably. After a few moments, he felt his breath slowly returning to him. Mark stared out the window, letting the silence sit terrifyingly between them like a third wheel. As they approached Canada Water Station, Chris let out a small sigh of relief, as they were heading back to his.

His mind started racing, wondering how much money he could pull together and how quickly he could disappear. He knew a few people who might be able to help him, but it would be tricky.

He had never been the most reliable or friendly.

The idea of all his chickens coming home to roost began to ironically mock him, until Brian made a sharp turn, cutting off a passing car and shooting down a main road to the sound of a furious car horn.

Mark chuckled. 'Mr Jackson thought it would be best if

you stayed in one of his facilities this evening.' He turned, flashing a gold-tooth-dominated grin. 'Just so he knows where you are.'

Chris sank in his chair, his flabby gut straining against the seat belt. He wanted to be home, where he could drink or smoke a spliff—maybe even arrange for a prostitute to celebrate his freedom, provided that Marco hadn't cut him off after sending one too many of them back with a bruise or two. Now, as they cut through Peckham towards one of Mr Jackson's 'High-Rises', he could only think about the soul-destroying wait before he was punished.

'You're pretty quiet,' Brian noted. 'Mark, why don't you see if he's okay?'

'Good idea, Brian.' Mark turned his massive frame, his leather jacket squeaking against the seats. 'Chris, what is bothering your fat self?'

'Fuck you.'

He immediately regretted it.

Mark raised his eyebrows mockingly. 'Well that wasn't very nice, was it Brian?'

'No it wasn't.' Brian flashed an enthusiastic grin in the rear-view mirror. 'What do manners cost again?'

'I believe they're free.' Mark turned back to Chris, staring threateningly. 'What does Mr Jackson always say about manners, Chris?'

Chris swallowed hard, bracing himself for the incoming pain. His words stuttered from his unwashed mouth.

'M-m-manners don't cost a penny.'

'Correct.'

Another clubbing blow, this one catching him dead centre of his diaphragm. Trying desperately to breathe, Chris wheezed like a punctured airbed. Mark sat back, flexing his meaty fingers from their fist, and watched as

Peckham slowly dissolved into Dulwich and they cut through the beautiful park. As the leaves rustled on their branches, families and dog-walkers filled the streets. Chris, taking sharp, careful breaths, envied their freedom.

His own was turning into a nightmare.

Brian slowly brought the car to a stop outside a large, six-storey building. The brickwork was new, giving off a slick, white sheen. Floor-to-ceiling windows dominated each floor, many with their curtains drawn. A gazebo reached out above the entrance like a protruding lower lip. The glass automatic doors were framed by beautiful plants.

It looked like a private hotel, where only London's elite were invited.

In reality it was a haven for criminals to escape, to live, and to indulge. Many of the clients were well-respected, established figures that not only helped shape the city, but also ran it. Mr Jackson, with his courteous manner and his insistence on class, was doing his level best to bring an element of decorum to the criminal underworld—despite what went on behind the doors once they closed.

This was where you came when you wanted to really be yourself.

'Right. Fuck off,' Mark said as they came to a stop.

'Language,' Brian insisted.

'Apologies.' Mark turned to Chris. 'Go and check in. Then stay there until we come to you. Mr Jackson still isn't sure whether he wants to see you in person yet.'

'Look, I'm so sorry.' Chris began to cry, his pathetic tears running over his acne scars.

'Now, now. Don't beg.' Mark smirked. 'You'll have plenty of time for that.'

Chris reluctantly left the car, trudging through the door which slid open, giving way to the marble entranceway. At the desk, a nameless blonde lady welcomed him, handing him a key and telling him the room with which he had been allocated. The security guard, who made the Mitchell Brothers look like Smurfs, glared at him as he ambled to the lift. Up to the fourth floor and he walked down the warmly decorated hallway. Each room would be occupied, with scenarios playing out that would see many people arrested.

Vile sex acts.

Horrifying violence.

The High Street.

With an abject sigh of resignation, Chris slid the card into the lock above the handle, pushed open the door, and stepped into the room. A massive bed welcomed him, opposite a beautiful oak cabinet. Above, mounted on the white walls, was a fifty-inch TV, with surround sound speakers clinging to the ceiling corners like spider webs. The bathroom housed a lavish bath and walk-in shower, with a sink built into the marble unit.

Very classy.

He would never have been able to afford this in a million years.

A letter was lying on the bed, his name scrawled across it in beautiful handwriting. He opened the envelope and retrieved the thick paper and began to read.

Chris.

Please take this evening to relax. I will be there to see you tomorrow.

Mr Jackson.

. . .

Along with the letter, the envelope contained a small card with an escort services number as well as a bag of cocaine. Chris knew what was coming. He had seen it before. He would likely take a beating, with Mark undoubtedly chuckling as he knocked seven shades of shit out of him. He'd be relegated to some menial job for a while, like cleaning out the wanking booths in Mr Jackson's gentlemen's clubs.

And he would likely be kept away from women for the next few years.

All of that sounded a lot better than the alternative. He wasn't quite ready to be fitted for his concrete boots just yet.

As the afternoon faded to a glorious, warm evening that was framed by a pink sky, Chris found himself slithering across the bed, waiting impatiently for a knock on the door. The bag of blow was half empty, a few lines of it already beating his brain into a frenzy like a pro boxer on a punching bag. He was lying in just his boxer shorts, his grotesque, sweaty body jiggling as he scrambled across the sheets to the mini bar. Eagerly draining his seventh bottle of beer, he was doing his level best to forget about what awaited him the following day.

Tonight was going to be about him.

He wanted to feel powerful again, like he did when he had Catriona held against the barrel, thrusting against her as she wept for him to stop.

He had demanded a brunette from the escort service, and he hoped to hell she was as liberal as he was going to be.

He also wondered if she could take a punch.

Shooting another line up his nose, his eyes widened with excitement as knuckles rapped against the door.

She was there.

With an erection building in his shorts and a lifetime of inadequacy bubbling inside his drug-addled body, he bounded across the room, ready to unload on this poor, unsuspecting hooker.

He opened the door with a smile.

He caught a glimpse of the metal bat as it swung directly into his face.

Everything went black.

CHAPTER TWO

Earlier that morning, Samuel Pope was lying on his bed, the covers kicked to the surrounding floor, waiting for his alarm to go off. As the sun began to creep through the gaps in his blinds, followed by the first tweets from the early birds, he watched as the minutes changed on the digital clock that sat atop his bed side table.

Next to it was a half-drunken glass of water, his watch, and the recent novel he had been reading: *To Kill a Mockingbird*. Underneath the book was the folded photograph.

Wearing just his shorts, his toned body lay alone on the double bed, the rest of the room decorated with a metal rail for his shirts and trousers, a small chest of drawers for his underwear and T-shirts, and a wash basket.

The room lacked a woman's touch.

His entire life had for the last three years.

Thinking about that moment caused him to sit up in frustration, his body telling him once again that he had slept barely a wink. As he pushed himself out of his bed, the clock hit five a.m. and he slammed a hand on top before it could begin its irritating chirping. He wished he could reach out his window and do the same to the birds.

Sat with both legs draped over the side of the bed, he reached a scarred hand out to his mobile phone, clicked the button for his voicemail, and waited for the monotone lady to introduce his message.

'Hey Dad.' He smiled as his son's voice raced to meet his ears. 'I miss you. Mum says you are going to be away for a while. I understand, but I wanted to see you. I have some new books to read with you. I'll speak to you soon, Dad. I love you.'

The message ended and he leant forward, one hand reaching up and rubbing his eyes, the gentle moistness of tears seeping through.

He missed his son.

He missed his wife.

With a deep sigh, he looked at the meaty book that adorned his bedside table, knowing he would have to force himself through it to make good on his promise to his son.

His Jamie.

He walked through the hallway of his adequate two-bedroom flat, the walls bare and empty, holding no memories or secrets.

If his walls could talk, they would have nothing to say.

He relieved himself in the modest white bathroom before trudging back to the spare room, which was empty, save for a weight bench and a punch bag. Forty-five minutes later he emerged, sweating heavily, and the boxing bag swinging like a rack of meat headed for slaughter. After showering, he combed his short, brown hair into a side parting and then shaved, removing the stubble that had sprouted up like unwanted weeds. As the steam from the mirror cleared, he saw himself.

Lucy had always said he was handsome, but he had never been vain. He had a strong jaw and deep, brown eyes that burrowed into people. His hair was neat, with the temples slowly starting to grey as he approached his thirty-eighth birthday. As he was approaching middle age, he knew he was in great shape.

It was the military regime.

You could take the boy out the army but couldn't take the army out of the boy.

He scowled. He had been taken out of the army.

The two bullet holes at the top of each pectoral muscle had scarred to two white eyes. He remembered little.

The stone room.

A sudden hesitation.

The barrel of the gun pressed against his back before the burning sensation, followed by darkness.

That was years ago—when he was a soldier, ready to come home to his family. Now, he walked robotically through life, his empty apartment, and his repetitive job.

He dressed, a black T-shirt and jeans, and then made his way to the kitchen for his breakfast.

He had booked the day off from his job, his boss laughing at the idea of him finally taking some holiday. His ID badge loomed at him from the kitchen counter where he sat, the Metropolitan Police logo proudly in the corner.

As he shovelled the porridge into his mouth, he wondered what it would have been like to have finished the training and become a police officer. After serving for ten years in the army, it would have been great to have a sense of purpose once again, with orders to follow and a well-adhered-to chain of command.

Life didn't always work out the way you planned it.

The silence of his flat, the absence of his family, would attest to that.

As he marched to the front door, he stopped for one moment to scan an eye across his front room. There was a sofa, which had been left by the previous occupant, the leather torn and beaten. A wooden desk was pressed against the far wall, with a lamp and a number of files neatly placed to one side. Opposite was his bookshelf, which was slowly filling up as he kept one of the two promises he had made to his son.

Again he scowled, refusing to allow himself to be drawn back into the misery, where he struggled so badly to find the light switch.

His eyes landed on the small table near the door.

A row of medals stood neatly, all of them earnt in the heat of battle. Each one was in a decorative case, handed to him by a senior-ranked officer with the utmost gratitude. A number of them were for saving the lives of his squadron, watching over them from the scope of his rifle. One of them was for placing a bullet between the eyes of a man that was on the FBI's ten most wanted list.

All of the relics to a life that had long since slipped away.

Today was a day when he was reminded of who he used to be.

Of who he had promised he wouldn't be again.

With his head lowered almost in shame, Sam opened his front door and slammed it shut behind him, heading off into a city that hadn't woken up yet.

He spent the day sat in a coffee shop just to the right of Southwark Underground Station, a small business doing its best to battle the continuous wave of chain coffee shops. The journey into central London wasn't too bad; his small flat just outside of Maidenhead was near to the train station. With the new generation unable to afford the astro-nomical prices of London properties, the rail companies saw extreme profit margins in the neighbouring counties.

The UK economy.

Where the rich get richer by providing even less.

As he ploughed through the book, surprisingly finding he enjoyed some parts, he slowly saw the deep morning fade, the incredible rush of London bursting into life wafting through the door like a continuous conga line. Young professionals bought extraordinary flavours of coffee, the mark-ups painting a wide smile on the proprietor's face.

The UK economy.

Where the rich get richer by providing even less.

As the day rolled into the afternoon, he finally settled up, paying for his coffee and breakfast roll before strolling through the cultured streets of Southwark, daring himself to take in a museum.

Willing himself to find a new hobby.

Whilst today wasn't what he would call a hobby, he knew he couldn't get distracted.

This was a duty.

His life of orders and fighting for the flag was out of sight in his rear view, but today was a reminder of what he used to be.

Of what he would always be.

As the trial resumed at Southwark Crown Court, he watched as the disgusting Chris Morton sat in his chair, his gut pressed against the desk and a look of pleasure on his face. In the rows between him and the vile rapist, he saw the victim, a shivering woman who had been through hell and was about to be dragged back through by her ankles. Her family were protectively around her, trying their best to hold together the pieces before she shattered.

Because of Chris Morton.

Sam had seen the file as he placed the case files into the selected evidence boxes, his role as a senior archivist in the police headquarters in Victoria giving him access to plenty of information. Usually he tagged and bagged, or shipped boxes into the vast corridors that sat one level below ground, a labyrinth of crimes.

A tapestry of the horrors of London.

Although his wife leaving three years previous had

ended his desire to be a police officer, he had eventually found solace in the darkness of the archive rooms, still finding a place to serve but away from the public eye.

Away from all eyes.

As he watched the foreman of the jury stand, anxiously twiddling his fingers as he gave the judge a 'not guilty' verdict, his jaw tightened with anger. Once again a technicality had been weaselled out of a nightmare, and that justified a rapist walking free.

The young woman, Catriona, burst into tears. Her mother was sick on the floor. As the room emptied amidst a symphony of moans, murmurs, and slams of the gavel, Sam sat still, his hands rested on his knees. With his back straight, he locked his eyes onto Morton with the same precision as he had moved a sniper scope.

He watched.

The vile man looked unclean; his hygiene, like his suit, was ill fitting. He watched as Morton ignored his lawyer, who scurried down the aisle with his hand covering his face in shame. Sam watched as Morton caught a glimpse of a large, muscular man in a leather jacket, and he made a mental note that he wasn't the only one who was there for business.

For Morton.

The judge retired to her chambers and Morton, with less swagger than before, eventually wandered towards the door, heading in Sam's direction. With every step, Sam could feel his knuckles whitening. He had read the file, the terrifying account of how Morton had held Catriona by the throat, threatening to cut her open as he had violated her.

Sam turned and stared directly into Morton's eyes.

As Morton, with his image to protect, tried to return the look with venom. But Sam knew his unblinking stare would win out. There was nothing about Morton that scared him. When he cast his mind back to Iraq, watching as two jeeps full of Taliban soldiers headed in his direction, armed to the teeth with nothing but death for company, none of the London underbelly scared him.

Morton scrambled through the doors and into the foyer, and after a few moments Sam followed, stuffing his hands into his bomber jacket and strolling unnoticed as just another civilian. Hands stuffed into his pockets, he was just a curious citizen.

No one knew what he really was.

As he watched Morton enter the Range Rover, driven by what he assumed was Right Said Fred on steroids, he hailed a taxi and followed, handing the man two fifty-pound notes to follow them, four cars back and without questions. The driver obliged, only speaking when he tried to strike up a conversation.

Sam ignored him until he gave up, gently thumbing the vacant slot on his wedding-ring finger and sending a painful jolt through his heart. The skin had long since healed from the indent caused by the years it proudly wore that silver band.

'Hey, fella,' the cabbie eventually said, snapping him back from his pleasant memories. 'They're stopping.'

'Just keep going.'

They rolled past, the flow of traffic giving Sam enough time to memorise the building and the street name. He caught a glimpse of a nervous Morton shuffling out of the car, wincing in pain and pressing a hand to his stomach. Sam afforded himself a smile at what he assumed wasn't a pleasant journey.

When he returned later that night, he carefully scouted the road from the alley on the road opposite. London shot to the sky, every building racing its neighbour to the moon, which was slowly beginning to invade the pink dusk sky. He had changed, now wearing black jeans, boots, and his black bomber jacket. Stuffed in the pocket was the bala-clava; just holding it reminded him of the 'need-to-know' missions from years before.

The ones that were nowhere near the books.

In his right hand he gripped the taped handle of the metal baseball bat. In his left he held up a single-lensed binocular, scouting the front of the building and watching as the security guard stuck regimentally to his rounds.

Sam was aware that this building belonged to Frank Jackson, one of his rumoured High-Rises that were strictly off limits according to the police briefings he had ducked into or the cigarette smokers who congregated near the windows of the archive rooms. He gathered that there were a lot of greased palms willing to look the other way.

Well not tonight.

A black car pulled up out front and left just as quickly, a scantily clad brunette stepping out and dropping a cigarette butt on the floor as the guard trotted out to greet her. They spoke for a moment before she headed in, her high heels clicking on the pavement as he sparked a cigarette to life and slowly headed to the alleyway that framed part of the building.

Taking a deep breath to calm himself, he thought about the two other times he had done this. He thought of the sense of right and wrong, the line between them slowly vanishing as the world fell further into the darkness.

He thought of the moments he had held his breath, closed one eye, and pulled the trigger.

Now was that moment.

Sam shot forward.

He crossed the road silently, a black blur as he pulled down the balaclava to conceal his identity. The bat made a sickening clang as it connected with the back of the guard's thick skull. He watched the man collapse forward with zero compassion, doubting the security guard of a criminal hideout was a good Samaritan.

He slid through the double doors silently, the blonde receptionist and escort locked in discussion in an Eastern European language. Before they could scream, Sam lifted a finger to his lips and pointed the baseball bat at them. Frozen on the spot, he kept the bat held up as he approached them.

'Morton. Room number.'

His words were laced with venom, but the eagerness with which she gave up the information told him that she didn't exactly approve of the clientele. The prostitute told him that she was there for Morton, which caused Sam to smile.

Morton would be expecting a knock on the door.

Saving the woman from an undoubtedly horrible experience, he demanded both of them go into the back room and wait five minutes before calling for help. The hooker waved him off before lighting another cigarette. The receptionist seemed almost grateful, nodding as a tear dragged a line of mascara down her pretty face.

He ascended the lift to the fourth floor and slowly and silently moved down the hall, keeping his knees bent and his back against one of the walls. Behind one of the doors he passed, he heard a woman moan loudly—undoubtedly a hooker indulging some scumbag in whatever debauched fantasy he had.

He approached Morton's door.

He tapped gently.

Angry stomps raced towards the door, and as it swung open, he swung upwards.

The bat connected directly with the bridge of Morton's nose, shattering it and then exploding down his pasty, naked chest. The cartilage ruptured, blood gushing downwards like an opened dam. Morton squealed as he stumbled back into the room, hands clasping his face as he howled in pain. Sam darted into the room, kicking the door shut behind him. Morton lunged forward in sheer anger, his eyes wild and his face a crimson mask.

Sam jabbed the bat sharply into the flabby gut, driving the air out of the rapist and watching him double over. Then, as if going for a home run, he swung the bat upwards, connecting fully with the sweaty, bloodstained skull.

The noise was sickening.

Morton—all seventeen stone of him—left the floor, flopping backwards and crashing through the oak cabinet and rolling onto the floor, his back covered in splinters. With his brain rattling around his head, Morton woozily tried to get up, only for a firm boot to catch him in the chest, sending him falling backwards into the side of the bed.

After a few more moments of dazed movement, he gave up.

Sam stood in silence, watching as Morton tried to process what had happened, his face a car crash of blood, broken bones, and missing teeth. As he breathed, his nose gasped for air like a dog's chew toy.

'Who the fuck are you?' Morton's words slurred together. Sam squatted down in front of the beaten criminal and pulled off the balaclava, locking on the same scowl he had in the courtroom. He watched as Morton searched his mind before realisation set in.

'You,' he said accusingly. 'You were there today.'

'Yup.'

'Do you know who the fuck I am?' His words were followed by sprays of spit and blood.

'You're Chris Morton,' Sam said calmly, standing up again and gently handling the bat. 'And you raped that young girl.'

Morton started chuckling. 'I was found not guilty.' He watched nervously as his attacker lifted the bat. Suddenly, before he even knew it, the bat crashed down on top of his foot, shattering his ankle and snapping the foot forwards and shooting a bone through the skin. He roared in agony.

'You ruined her life.'

Another swing and Morton felt the bones in his left hand fall to dust. Suddenly, the pain began to fade as his rotund, battered body began to slowly relinquish itself to shock. As tears streamed down his face, he slowly spat a few more words out.

'I did it. Okay. I did it.' He lifted his hand, a pathetic final glance of hope. 'Please have mercy?'

Sam lifted the bloodstained bat once more, looking from the metal to the man at his feet. He thought of the young woman whose life would never be the same again.

Of the injustice of the system set up to protect her.

How much mercy was she shown?

Morton's head dropped forward as he slowly began to lose consciousness.

Sam lifted the bat once more and coldly responded.

'No.'

Morton felt the bat crush into his testicles before he blacked out from the pain. Sam Pope hung around for a few more moments, ensuring he handed the rapist exactly the sort of sentence he deserved.

By the time the receptionist had called for help, the security guard had returned to the front desk, staggering like a drunk with blood caking the back of his suit. A few more henchmen turned up, with the hooker screaming at them in her native tongue and them all rushing to Morton.

They found him on the floor.

Both ankles and knee caps shattered.

Both hands crushed, with the elbows shattered inwards, the bones jutting out of the skin like crooked teeth.

His testicles were smashed to a bloody pulp and his face was crooked, the jaw hanging loosely and exposing bloody gums where his teeth used to live.

He had been brutalised.

As they stared in horror, Sam dumped the bat in a recycling bin in the car park of a large Sainsbury's before turning his black bomber jacket inside out to a maroon colour, then heading down the steps of the nearest Tube station and into the depths below, leaving behind another night of blood and chaos.

Another night of justice.

CHAPTER THREE

The Metropolitan Police Headquarters was alive with activity the following day. The hub, sat on the side of the Thames, a stone's throw from Westminster station, had long since been a tourist hotspot. Despite the pleas of the government and officers themselves, tourists loved to get a snap in front of the triangular 'New Scotland Yard' sign which sat proudly outside.

Behind that, the glass pavilion led into the building where dozens of specialist teams worked in unison to protect the city of London as well as the country itself. With the Ministry of Defence occupying one of the neighbouring buildings, it was one of the safest places to find yourself. It was where Samuel Pope found himself passing through that morning, head down for the usual silent trip to the archive facility.

A few of the regular officers regarded him with a look of confusion; this impressively built man had shut off all social conventions and was seen as a bit of an oddball.

One to stay away from.

It was just how he wanted it.

As he wandered through the offices, nodding a few curt

hellos to those who did offer a greeting, a sudden twinge of jealousy ricocheted through his muscular body. He had wanted to serve, ever since he had been honourably discharged on the grounds of his injuries. But after everything that had happened, he now found himself walking a different path instead.

His handiwork was the talk of the office, with a few officers discussing the rumours of Morton '*getting exactly what he had coming.*' Sam afforded himself a smile as he passed through the corridor and into the archive waiting room, where officers stood impatiently, waiting for one of his co-workers to retrieve their necessary files.

'Morning,' Sam muttered, weaving between the small collective of uniforms.

One of them stepped back, his shoulder ramming into Sam's and knocking him off balance.

Another officer giggled.

'Ooops.' It was Officer Harding, a real 'lad' who had two more testicles than he had brain cells.

Sam ignored it, knowing the other officers knew about why he hadn't continued his police training. His lack of judgment would haunt him forever, and just as he thought about turning back and showing Harding just how outmatched he would be, a cough echoed over his shoulder. He turned, seeing his boss, Des, stood behind the security glass with his hands on his hips.

The officers went quiet.

'Sir,' Sam offered, reaching for his pass that swung from his neck on a Met Police issue lanyard.

'Pope. What are you doing here?' His manager was a short, podgy man who pushed his glasses up his nose after every sentence. 'You have an appointment.'

'Sir, I'm fine,' Sam protested.

'If I recall, it wasn't optional.'

The two of them stared at each other before Sam

pushed his satchel through the glass for his manager to store and sighed. Turning back, he heard a few sniggers from the officers.

'Off to see the shrink, eh?' Harding muttered.

Sam stopped, smiling to himself. He would have loved to take Harding apart and expose him as the same old 'big man' that walked around wearing their badge like a sign of their toughness. Compared to the things Sam had seen overseas, the man was a fluffy kitten. Ignoring the goad, Sam headed back to the hive of activity, watching as uniformed and suited men and women buzzed around the office.

With a heavy sigh he made his way back up to the ground floor before heading into the lift to the second. Once there, he ventured down the corridors, his well-polished shoes clicking against the tiled floor. On the cork notice boards that framed the walls was a tapestry of leaflets, ranging from neighbourhood watch to how to deal with sexual assault.

An index of crime and how to handle it.

Eventually he came upon the door and stopped. He looked down at his neatly ironed white shirt, the sleeves rolled up to the elbows and a navy tie dangling like a clock pendulum.

It could have been a police uniform.

It should have been army camouflage.

Suddenly he felt an ache in his chest, the two bullet scars pulsing out a painful memory like ripples on a lake.

With a deep sigh he knocked on the door, waited for the friendly voice to welcome him in, and then entered.

———

Downstairs in the main briefing room, Inspector Michael Howell was watching, arms crossed, as the chairs before him slowly filled up with officers. It always struck him how eclectic the Metropolitan Police Service was and gave him a sense of pride for his years of service. There were large, world-weary veterans, their idea of justice being a slightly firmer hand and a slightly more discriminating eye. The new recruits, all trimmed beards and tattoos, optimistic that they could change the world for the better. Different cultures and ethnicities, gay, straight, men, women—all of them the same under the black and white brush of the Metropolitan Police.

Taking a seat four rows from the back was the one person who filled him with the most pride of all.

His nephew.

PC Jake Howell.

Inspector Howell cast his mind back to the moment his sister had told him of her son's intentions, leaning on her brother to deflect the interest with horror stories. She had wanted him to become a lawyer, and with the grades he had accumulated, a life of further education was a real possibility. As he met his then fresh-faced nephew for a pint to dissuade him, he couldn't help but share the thrilling stories of his career.

The years spent on the armed response unit, zipping through the city locked and loaded.

The cases he had cracked whilst working for CID, the five murders he had solved and the sex trafficking ring he had helped bring down.

With no kids of his own, he had always felt a special bond with Jake and, despite the occasional glare from his sister, watching him pass out as a police officer was the proudest day of his life. Watching him take his seat amongst his colleagues and the inappropriate banter, he realised how much he missed being out on the beat.

It had been over six years since he was promoted to his highly respected ranking and over a decade and a half since he was out on the beat. Age had caught up with him; he could feel the slackness of his muscles now, his once tall, built figure a lot slimmer as Father Time slowly picked away at him.

His hair was thinner, like a soft blanket of snow on his head. His reading glasses sat on his nose, their necessity ever growing.

Inspector Howell, not long for retirement.

As he stood, arms folded, staring into nothingness whilst his mind wrestled with his stellar career and unfortunate aging, a voice brought him back to the room.

'Sir?'

It belonged to Detective Sergeant Colin Mayer, a brutish man with forearms like slabs of meat, a temper as explosive as Vesuvius, and his nose so far up every authority figure's arse he could list their lunch habits.

Mayer stepped to the side, revealing everyone stood to attention, arms straight by their sides, chins proudly lifted. Beside him was another man, younger, clean shaven, and clearly nervous.

Howell smiled before addressing the room.

'At ease.' Howell spoke calmly, a trait he was well liked for. 'It's great to see so many of you in here today. As you know, this Sunday is the London Marathon. It's one of our busiest days of the year and we are required to provide a strict and visible presence. Now many of you may question why someone wants to run twenty-six miles, and you know what? I don't bloody blame you.'

A few chuckles bounced around the room like an echo as Howell continued.

'But whilst their jobs will be to get from start to finish, our job will be to ensure that the runners, organisers, and of course the wonderful people of this great city who come out to support the event, are able to do so in complete safety. I know I don't need to remind anyone in this room that we live in dangerous times. Our threat level remains high and we have reason to believe that there could be a terror attack this coming Sunday. As always, we pray for the best but prepare for the worst.'

All of the officers' eyes were glued to him, watching as he commanded the room with the effortless authority that had evolved over many years of steady stewardship. The door to the briefing room opened slowly. A man slid in silently, dressed in a sharp grey suit with a yellow tie, which his trim frame filled nicely. His black skin showed no signs of age, but the grey hair that framed his head and chin caused Howell to place him in his fifties. He nodded a respectful apology for interrupting and took a seat.

Howell didn't know who he was, but he certainly held the aura of a man of importance.

Clearing his throat, Howell returned his attention to his officers. 'So before we go through the teams and shifts for this weekend, we have Detective Sergeant Mayer and Detective Constable Williams from the Counter Terrorist Team to go through the protocols for this Sunday'— audible groans rose throughout the room— 'and I *expect* you all to show them the same courtesy and attention as you have shown me.'

Mayer stepped forward, his dark three-piece suit strapped to his body like a straitjacket. He shook the inspector's hand and thanked him audibly. Addressing the room, he spoke with passion and conciseness, a man clearly in charge of the situation. Despite his weaselly penchant for cosying up to those in power, Howell had to admit that Mayer was good at his job. As the officers scribbled notes in their notepads, and DC Williams struggled with the laptop presentation, Howell snuck a glance to the back of the room.

The mystery man was sat casually, one leg flopped over the other, watching intently.

Who was he?

Howell also caught a glimpse of his nephew, studiously noting down every word. He smiled with pride, turning back to the front and allowing the rest of the presentation to filter into his mind. When it was finished, Mayer reiterated that he was their person to contact. Howell rolled his eyes at the power grab, quickly stepping up, thanking Mayer, and ushering him to the side. Howell thanked his team for their attention and wished them luck on Sunday.

'Dismissed.'

As the officers slowly filtered out of the room like a clearing fog, Howell noticed the latecomer still sat in his chair. Howell thanked Mayer and Williams, who soon vacated, before striding purposefully through the chairs. As he approached, the man stood, buttoning the top button of his well-fitted blazer, and extended a hand.

'Inspector Howell?'

Howell nodded as he accepted.

'DI Adrian Pearce. Department of Professional Standards.'

'DPS?' Howell exclaimed with raised eyebrows.

'Yeah. We tend not to go by that as people think I'm delivering some pointless item they bought on Amazon.'

Howell chuckled. Already he liked Pearce and could see why he would be working in a unit that needed to gain trust quickly. After the humorous moment passed, Howell stood straight to impose his authority.

'What is this about?'

'I'm just doing some routine checks. There was another attack on a criminal last night—Chris Morton. You may have heard.' Pearce scanned the room; Howell could see him making mental notes. 'He was found beaten half to death last night just hours after his NG.'

'I heard.' Howell shook his head. 'Nasty business.'

'It certainly is.' Pearce strolled across the room, closing

the door to the briefing room. A few officers shot a curious glance in his direction, but his stare through the glass soon sent their eyes wandering.

'Wait. You think it's one of my men? A police officer knocking off rapists?' Howell shook his head in disbelief.

'Not necessarily.'

'Please do tell.' Howell folded his arms, his go-to show of authority.

Pearce smiled politely, undeterred by the act and understanding of the man's offence. 'I'm not here to question the integrity of you or your team. However, I would like to speak to a few people who may have had access to the information that told them who, when, and where.'

'This is preposterous. We have criminals out there and you're here looking into my men…'

'I'm here doing my damn job,' Pearce snapped, catching Howell by surprise.

An awkward silence hung in the air before Howell unfolded his arms. He was a loyal man, but he knew that Pearce wouldn't be bothering him if he didn't have a lead.

'Any people in particular?' he eventually asked, his fingers sliding under his glasses and massaging the bridge of his nose.

'I have names. I'd like an interview room set up, no cameras, no recording. No peeking through the mirror.' He flashed a grin. 'This is just preliminary discussions. Not a witch hunt.'

Howell sighed, stepping forward and looking out over the rows of desks, his officers bounding about busily, all ready for the challenge of the London Marathon ahead. He didn't like it one bit.

'These people are good officers,' he offered one more time. 'Of that I have no doubt.' Pearce joined him by the glass. 'I'm not here to speak to them.'

Howell turned, his white eyebrows shooting upwards with surprise. 'You're not?'

'No, sir.'

'Then who?' Howell asked, his eyes searching for answers as Pearce turned with another warm, perfectly white smile.

'Tell me, Inspector. How much do you know about Sam Pope?'

CHAPTER FOUR

All he could see was the sand. Miles and miles of it, frosting the entire landscape with its drab shading. The sun beat down, the horizon line wriggling restlessly in the heat. On the cliff faces that surrounded the large, open caverns of the Afghanistan landscape, Samuel Pope watched intently. Whilst the odd pocket of land sprouted a beautiful, close-knit group of trees, huddled together like a halftime team talk, the rest of the world looked as dry as his throat was.

It had been seven months since his deployment, his third term out in the deserts, but this time it was different.

This time, his orders had been to clear the path for Operation Hailstorm to pass through.

It wasn't just off the books.

It wasn't even acknowledged.

Crouched on the cliff face, he had hollowed out his surrounding area to allow for movement. Draped in a dust-covered sheet, he simply blended into the cliff face.

The long, powerful forty-six-inch nose of his Accuracy International Arctic Warfare rifle was shrouded in long, looping weeds that concealed its murderous intent. Attached to the high-power, bolt-action chamber that sat motionless across the rocks in front, Sam felt his hands naturally slide around the stock of the impressive killing machine, adjusting his body so his line of sight was brought up to the Smidt & Bendter PM II Telescopic sight.

He watched the sandy road that had been worn into the terrain, a wild rabbit hopping across the roasting stones, the image as clear as day from over eight hundred yards away.

He had sat there for over seventeen hours.

A small ditch to the side of his spot was filled with piss which had long since warmed up. The sweltering heat consumed his sheet, even though the inner lining was designed to keep him cool. Sweat dripped down the back of his neck, underneath the camouflaged T-shirt, pooling with the rest that clung to his spine. Other droplets had slithered down his face, revealing a trail of his skin amongst the mud and face paint.

He waited.

The air was windless, the heat grabbing it with both hands and choking the oxygen around him. To the west, the city of Kabul rose proudly into the horizon line, the bricks skewed by the blur of heat. A city of innate, rustic beauty, constantly under the terror of ISIS. Unlike their American brothers, who constantly batted the word 'freedom' around like a ping-pong ball, he did believe they were there to help. He wasn't naïve—there were certain agendas that were above his rank and grade—but he knew the ultimate outcome would be bringing an end to a reign of terror that the rest of the world was just turning its back on.

He had come across the sceptics many times—Lord knows that too many of Lucy's friends were critical of his job. Whilst they thought he and the army were sticking their nose into situations that didn't concern the UK, he saw it as being one of the few people to take the fight to those who prey on the helpless.

The people of Afghanistan couldn't fight back.

That was why he was there. To fight on their behalf.

But as he sat in the continuously rising heat of his hideaway, staring down the barrel of his gun, he had begun to have his own doubts. Project Hailstorm was beyond a 'need-to-know' basis.

It was the most secretive protocol he had come across in over a decade as one of the military's elite marksmen. All he knew was that 'Alpha Unit' would be passing through these co-ordinates within a two-hour timeframe.

Likely pursuit.

Lethal force necessary.

As he contemplated the integrity of such a mission being carried out in such secrecy, his radio crackled gently below his chin.

They were inbound.

Suddenly, the air roared with the sound of cracking, guns unleashing a flurry of bullets that ripped through the tranquil road. The jeep hurtled around the corner. He could see Corporal Murray at the wheel, his tanned forearms wrestling with the steering wheel as he tried to stay on course. Beyond him, in the back, he could see three men lying prone and a lot of blood.

Something had gone wrong.

Very wrong.

Before he could even contemplate the whooshing sound that echoed through the sky, the RPG rocket hit the back wheel of the jeep, sending it flipping into the air amongst an explosion of car parts and stones. As the jeep rolled twice over and came to a clunking stop on its side halfway down the embankment, Sam clicked the evacuation button on his radio, sending an immediate request for help. Following the trail of the crash with his scope, he saw an unidentified soldier, the body snapped in half and a streak of blood from where his leg had been separated from his body.

Another limb lay estranged from Private Griffin, who was screaming in agony as the blood pumped from the sleeve where his arm used to be.

Corporal Murray wriggled free from the driver's seat, as if he had been dipped in a vat of red paint. Clearly shocked and dazed from the crash, his arms were shaking as he fumbled with the clip of an SA80 Assault Rifle, his fingers frantically snatching at the metal.

The roar of two more cars shook the road, the burnt stones shaking as the dusty pickup trucks raced into view, the ISIS soldiers stood proudly on the back, one of them with an empty rocket launcher resting over his shoulder.

'Stand down, Pope,' a voice crackled over his radio. 'Evac in agreed location. ETA three hours.'

Without moving anything other than his left arm, he clicked the button to respond.

'Negative, we still have men alive. Targets closing in. Permission to engage.'

'Negative, Sergeant. Those men are KIA. Do not engage. I repeat, do not engage.'

Sam recognised the voice. It was General Ervin Wallace, a portly gentleman who, despite being resigned to command due to shrapnel, was as vicious as they came.

He was in charge of Project Hailstorm, and Sam didn't doubt one bit that it was his penchant for violent resolution that had gotten him the job.

Humans were expendable.

The enemies more than his own.

It wouldn't be until twenty-four hours later, when the bomb that 'Alpha Unit' deployed had levelled seven streets and a children's hospital, that he would realize just what was happening.

But then, as he watched ten men loading their weapons, ready to turn his friend into a game of target practice, the chain of command suddenly meant very little.

'Fuck this'.

The blast of the gun echoed around the entire opening, bouncing off the hill faces and the surrounding broken cliffs. The bullet whipped through the man's skull so fast he was flung backwards off the truck, his scalp spraying into a red nothingness. Before his comrades could react, Sam snapped the bolt back, the bullet casing clinking out onto the surrounding stones as he aimed, aligned, squeezed.

Another roar from his gun.

The bullet blew out the side of one of the men's skulls before ripping straight through another's chest.

Both men dropped to the ground, dead instantly, as the rest of the men took cover behind the other vehicle. A few of them randomly shot into the cliff face, hoping to stop the invisible death that awaited them.

After a few moments one of the ISIS soldiers, who appeared to be in his early twenties, bravely stood up to spray a sweeping round in Sam's general direction.

The bullet whistled neatly as it left his rifle before tunnelling a hole through the young man's skull, spraying the surrounding stones with brain matter.

As the group took cover, he knew it wouldn't be long until they called it in and an Apache helicopter was levelling the entire cliff face with enough firepower to destroy a small country.

In that moment he decided to flick his radio, hoping beyond hope that the upturned jeep, which was slowly being engulfed in flames, hadn't been completely destroyed.

'Murray. Murray, receiving?' he uttered quickly, keeping his eyes firmly on the scope that had the insurgents pinned down. He hadn't been able to watch as Murray, under the realisation that Sam had disobeyed command and was keeping him alive, had removed his fellow survivors from the wreckage.

They now lay, in varying amounts of agony, down the side bank. Murray, drawn by the crackle of the radio, snuck his way back to the truck, his rifle in his hand.

'Pope. You crazy bastard.' He chuckled. 'Not looking good here.'

'Do you have any grenades?' Sam asked, his eyes fixed on the car as a few of the men had heard the radio.

'Negative.'

'Any ammunition?' A bead of sweat dropped over his eyebrow, onto the scope. His body remained motionless.

'I have one box with seventeen clips.' Murray sighed. 'Get your arse out of here, mate. Just promise me you will find Becky and tell her what happened.'

Sam cut him off angrily, telling him they were leaving together. As he explained the idea to him, he fired a warning shot at the car, keeping the bloodthirsty ISIS crew behind it. Murray called him a madman at his suggestion, but he soon obliged, sliding to the side of the overturned jeep and lancing the petrol tank with his combat knife.

The petrol drenched the row of bullets that sat in the box. Slowly, he crept to the side of the jeep and Sam let off another warning shot, causing the enemy to cover once more before screaming profanities in a language that only meant death to him.

Murray then hauled the box back, and with all his might he hurled it towards the car. As it spun towards the group of them, the petrol leapt off it in wild, suicidal splashes.

Sam sat up, pushing away the sheet and squinting in the unrelenting sunlight.

He had one shot.

He took it.

The bullet hit the box with such a force, causing the ignition that detonated the gunpowder.

The entire box exploded, taking the car and the seven men with it in a blaze of metal, rubber, and body parts. As the remains of the explosion rained down, Murray hijacked the other vehicle, loading his men into it slowly before hurtling back towards base.

Sam had watched him go, his heart racing as he scanned the roadside. Blood and bodies littered everywhere.

The road was a genuine highway to hell.

Ignoring the furious voice on his radio, he took one last sweep of the area before packing away his rifle and making his way across the sun-drenched cliffs to his extraction point.

———

'So how did disobeying those orders feel?'

The soft voice of Amy Devereux, sat on the chair with one slim leg overlapping the other, her pencil skirt pulled tightly against her slender frame. Her blazer was hung on the hook behind her office door, allowing her slim arms to escape through the sides of her green sleeveless blouse. Resting on her lap was a notepad, a pen clasped in her well-manicured fingers. Her blond hair, cut into a neat bob, sat atop a strong face with prominent cheekbones.

Amy was a certified therapist, but as he sat on her 'sharing sofa', Sam wondered if maybe a few of the guys faked their traumas just to try and catch a glimpse up her skirt. He had to admit, she was a very attractive woman, and he had spent more time with her than any other woman since Lucy had left him.

When she had to leave him.

'Sam?'

He turned his head at her second prompt, scanning his immediate memory for her question.

'It was the right thing to do.'

'But it must have been hard—ignoring direct orders from a superior and willingly attracting gunfire.'

'Not at the time.' Sam shrugged, his well-rounded shoulders leaping upwards. 'Look, I know you probably think that soldiers just follow their orders like robots. But in the heat of the battle, when I saw my friend facing the hard goodbye, I acted. I got reprimanded and I was soon off the team.'

'Project Hailstorm?' She arched a thinly tweezed eyebrow, knowing the question would fall flat. Samuel Pope didn't speak of the alleged Project Hailstorm.

'Look, Ms Devereux…'

'Mrs,' she corrected, noting Sam's eye flick to her wedding ring, which shimmered alongside the jewel-encrusted engagement ring.

'Apologies.'

She lifted a hand in acceptance.

'I know service in the military can cause serious prob-lems for some people—the world not quite fitting when they return, like a photo that is constantly out of focus. But I am fine. I am proud of the work I did serving this country.'

Amy smiled warmly, her brown eyes panning around her quaint office. Sam sat on a leather sofa, the black faded to a dark grey and signs of wear-and-tear in abundance. Between them was a coffee table, where a box of tissues sat alongside a bowl of sweet-smelling potpourri. Behind her was her desk, which was enough for her laptop and more pertinent files.

The entire room was framed by shelving units, filled with either folders or books. On the walls, several certificates were framed and displayed proudly.

'I have no doubt you were an impeccable soldier, Samuel. Your record speaks for itself.' She placed her pen down and adjusted the small, frameless glasses that sat on her slightly curved nose. 'But that isn't why you are here, is it?'

Instantly she could see him shudder, a horrible memory dancing down his spine.

'We've already spoken about that.'

'Yes, several sessions ago.' She remembered the pain of the conversation. 'We spoke, but didn't deal with it.'

'I have dealt with it.'

'How?' Her question slid through him like a knife through butter. Sam suddenly had flashbacks to swinging the metal baseball bat, the satisfying crunch as Morton's shins shattered. He thought back to Jason Marlow, who he had hung over the bannister of a stairway until he was on the cusp of death before bringing him back from the dead.

The brutal assault of these criminals.

That was how he was dealing with it.

After a few moments of silence, Amy adjusted on her seat, straightening her skirt before speaking. 'How did Lucy deal with it?'

'She left.' Sam spoke quietly, eyes down. 'I don't blame her.'

'Why?'

'Because I did too.' Sam tapped the side of his head. 'In here.'

Amy nodded, making a note of the tear threatening to slide over Sam's eyelid. This was the furthest she had gotten to him in seven months. She had read his file. She knew what she was taking on when she had agreed to the mandate that he needed to be monitored.

He needed help to deal with the blame he had self-imposed.

Sam took some deep breaths, regaining composure over a body he usually had regimented control of. He trained daily, was a picture of health, and was widely regarded as the top sniper the UK had seen for the past few decades. Despite the two scars that reminded him of how close he had been to death's sweet release, he knew they would welcome him back. Even just as a tutor, to help guide the next harbingers of the sightless death.

But he had made a promise.

'How's the reading going?' Amy asked, revisiting the previous notes regarding his newfound reading habits.

'It's going all right,' he offered meekly with a forced smile.

'Still on *To Kill A Mockingbird?*'

His nod confirmed it.

'What do you think?'

'It's okay. Bit heavy.' He chuckled. As did Amy.

'Are you enjoying it?'

Sam leant forward, his muscular arms pressed against his shirt, his hands clasped together. She noticed he no longer wore his wedding ring. That part of his life had long since gone. With a deep sigh he turned to her, a look of defeat in his eyes.

'What does it matter?'

With that, the big hand of the clock above the door fell upon the hour and Sam pushed himself to his feet. With purposeful strides he headed to the door, ignoring Amy as she called out that they would meet the following Thursday. Stepping out into the hallway, he closed the door behind him, leaning back against the cold, white wall. The pain clawed at him—the reason why he was expected to attend these sessions.

He couldn't deal with the fact that he couldn't hold his wife anymore or see his son. That much he knew. What he was slowly starting to find out was...

He didn't want to.

CHAPTER FIVE

It was turning into a hell of a morning.

No sooner had Sam returned to the archive office than Ash had told him that the inspector had summoned him. With raised eyebrows, Sam had once again left the archive room, navigating his way through the hyperactive head-quarters to the inspector's floor. As he walked, his mind raced to the assault of Morton, if he had left any clue or lead.

He had been so careful.

As he ascended the stairs, he drew a few sneers from some passing officers, his reputation as a silent loner clearly preceding him. As with all of them before, he ignored them completely, arriving at the correct doorway and entering. The blast of noise was surprising, clusters of offi-cers gathered around flip charts and computer desks as they prepared for the London Marathon on Sunday. He drew a few unwelcoming glances, Officer Harding shooting him a look of disgust from across the room before the pounding footsteps of Inspector Howell approached.

'Mr Pope?' Howell offered, a friendly hand reaching forward.

'Yes, sir.' Sam took it, shaking it firmly.

'Wow. Quite a grip. Sorry to interrupt your day, but I have a gentleman who has asked to speak with you.'

'Who is it?' Sam asked, following Howell as he led him across the bullpen.

'Pearce. DI. From Department of Professional Standards?'

Howell flashed a glance at Sam, who shrugged. 'Internal Affairs, essentially.'

'And he wants to speak to me?' Sam asked. 'What about?'

'You'll have to ask him, son.'

Howell led them through the office and out into the far corridor. The walls shimmered under the halogen lights that stretched across the ceiling, the walls covered in noticeboards and fliers. A couple of plain-clothed officers ventured down, both female, and both of them gave Howell a respectful greeting. One of them smiled coyly at Sam, who felt his cheeks flush as he looked away. Instinctively his thumb stroked his wedding-ring finger, the feel of only skin another reminder that he needed to move on.

Eventually Howell came to a stop in front of a grey door before turning to Sam with a look of apprehension.

'I don't know what he wants, but these guys are the lowest of the low. They know the struggles we have to keep people safe and they are looking for any excuse to take down one of their own.'

Sam shrugged again. The senior officer's frustration was abundantly clear and he suspected, due to the concern he had, that maybe there were one or two corners being cut in the department. With a gentle raise of the eyebrows, Sam turned and knocked on the door.

'Come in.'

The voice had a welcoming quality to it and Sam pushed open the door into a dimly lit interview room, complete with the tried-and-trusted two-way mirror. Under the main light was a wooden table with a seat situated either side. Rising from the one furthest from the door was DI Adrian Pearce, with a pearly white grin and an exuberant handshake.

'Mr Pope.' He wrenched Sam's arm with surprising gusto. 'DI Pearce. Please, take a seat.'

He ushered Sam to the nearest chair before returning to his own. Sam obliged, smiling politely at the cup of water Pearce had placed for him. As Pearce sat, he lifted a mug, downing the remnants of the coffee. Both of them could feel the harrowing stare of Inspector Howell through the glass. Clearly a tactic, Pearce sat casually in his chair, lifting the manila folder and flicking through it as Sam watched patiently.

'What's this about?' He eventually broke the silence.

'Last night, a man named Chris Morton was brutally assaulted. He suffered several internal injuries, a severe head trauma, several broken bones, and completely destroyed genitalia. He is currently at Kings College on life support.' Pearce stared Sam straight in the eye. 'Morton had been on trial yesterday for an accused rape but was found not guilty by the jury. It seems someone didn't agree with the decision.'

'It's a dangerous world out there,' Sam said, shaking his head.

'It is, isn't it?' Pearce narrowed his dark eyes, small cracks folding in at the edges. 'You of all people would know that, wouldn't you?'

'I have a clear idea.' Sam spoke calmly, refusing to break the eye contact.

Pearce smiled before dropping his eyes to the open file before him. 'Your service record is extraordinary, I'll give you that. Three tours in Afghanistan, two years off the radar—I'm assuming some sort of covert team—several medals, over sixty confirmed kills. Fuck me, it's like sitting with Rambo.'

Silence sat between them. Pearce was sure that Howell's jaw had dropped open at the burst of information about the highly trained killer working in the archive room. After a few moments, Sam took a sip of water and then spoke.

'I'm very proud of my record, sir.'

'So you should be. You don't talk about it though, huh?'

'It's nobody's business but my own.'

'But you were quite the asset, weren't you. Highly trained in covert operations, moving undetected and striking cleanly and quickly.'

'From hundreds of yards away. With a rifle.'

'Hmmm.' Pearce pulled his lips tight. 'Moving on, it seems that just over three years ago, you attended Hendon to become a police officer. Your file is even marked with the superiors' comments about fast-tracking you to AR, put those firearms skills to good use. But then you dropped out?'

'Yes, sir.'

'Why?' Pearce slapped the file down on the table, clearly agitated by Sam's lack of nerves. 'I spent some time early in my career on Armed Response. Hell of a job. Right up your alley with your background. So why'd you quit?'

'Personal reasons.'

'Personal reasons?' Pearce repeated sceptically.

Sam nodded. 'Enlighten me?'

'Do you understand what "personal" means?'

'I think so. It means you don't want to tell me. Which is fine, we can approach this a different way. Tell me, what do you know about Chris Morton?'

Pearce leant back in his chair, casually draping one leg over the other. Both men refused to fluster.

'I know there was a substantial amount of evidence that he raped a young woman and that he got off on a technicality. And, from what you told me, he's been banged up pretty badly.'

'Why were you at the courthouse?' Pearce asked, his tone suddenly hardening.

'Is it a crime to attend a public courthouse?'

'Pretty convenient, don't you think? You being there, and then he is found beaten to a pulp later that evening?'

'Are you accusing me?' Sam asked, returning the tone. 'Do I need a lawyer present?'

'Merely speculating.' Pearce flashed an unfriendly smile. 'Do you want to know what I think?'

'Not really.'

Sam's response was ignored.

'I think someone knew exactly what they were doing. Someone who had access to all the files pertaining to the case, someone who knew where he was and where he was taken to, and someone with the skill and training to infiltrate a known criminal hotspot and systematically take him apart in a matter of minutes.' He glared across the table at Sam, who didn't flinch. 'Seven weeks ago, a Jason Marlow was found with every finger broken, along with both wrists and several ribs. He said he had been jumped by a gang, but when we investigated his injuries, we found he had been hung for several moments, with the attacker loosening the rope just before death. Sound's nasty, right?'

'It's pretty messed up,' Sam agreed.

'Four months ago, two members of the O'Riordan Gang were found, severe head trauma and several broken bones. Do you know what links all of these men?'

'They all got what they deserved?' Sam shrugged.

'All of the casefiles pertaining to their cases passed

46

through this office. Funnily, it's your name on the log books.' Pearce slid a sheet of paper across to Sam to prove his point. 'Explain that.'

'Okay. You do know I work in the archiving office, right? This is just my job.'

'You know what I think?' Pearce said, his eyes locked onto Sam like a homing missile. 'I think you're working a night shift.'

Sam tossed the paper back across the desk at the smug-looking Pearce.

'I think these people all got off because we have a flawed justice system. And instead of looking at that, you've been tasked with looking for someone to blame. Now don't get me wrong, I know what people think about me. They don't like me, they think I'm a crazy ex-soldier and all that bollocks. Whatever. I couldn't care less. But if you want to start poking into my past and my record to try and make your little theory stick, then I have a problem. So instead of spending all this time trying to find out what happened to these people and accusing me of this nonsense, why don't you direct your effort at the fucking system that let them off in the first place.'

Pearce sat still for a few moments, his eyes flicking to the mirror, knowing full well Howell would be applauding that speech. What frustrated him most was the complete calm that Samuel Pope had maintained throughout.

The man was well trained.

'I'm not looking for someone to blame, Pope. I'm looking for the man who is responsible.'

'And I fit the bill, right?'

'Well...' Pearce began. 'You have the necessary training. The necessary access. Your "personal reasons". I'd say you wrote the damn bill, son.'

Sam stared at him blankly before also casting an eye at the mirror. 'Can I go?' he eventually asked.

'Absolutely. I won't stop you,' Pearce said, lifting himself off his chair and motioning to the door. 'Somewhere to be?'

'Yeah, my job.' Sam stood as Pearce approached. Pearce was an inch or two shorter than Sam, with a slowly forming gut that threatened to ruin a trim physique. 'Maybe you should start doing yours, sir.'

'I'll be seeing you,' Pearce uttered quietly as he extended a hand. 'Soon'.

'Can't wait,' Sam responded, ignoring the handshake and yanking open the door. The brightness of the corridor crashed in like a wave and Sam ventured out into the busy office. Pearce sat on the edge of the table, a smile slowly wrestling control of his face. A shadow loomed from the hallway as Howell stood, hands on hips.

'Well, that was embarrassing.'

'Did you know about him? About Pope?' Pearce asked from his seated position.

'I knew he was ex-army but just figured he was a little bit PTSD is all.'

'Personal reasons?' Pearce flicked his eyebrows up in a show of frustration.

'Did you not read his full file?' Howell asked with surprise.

'I only had his army record and his police training file. HR wouldn't let me have any more until it became more prominent.'

'Well I can see why with him.' Howell shook his head.

'The PTSD?' Pearce asked with interest, pulling his pad from his pocket.

'It's not my place to say,' Howell responded sadly. 'Mrs Devereux has pages on him.'

Pearce scribbled down the name and was sure it was riddled with spelling mistakes. Suddenly he could feel his instincts tingling; his gut, which had served him well on a number of cases, was telling him that there was more to Samuel Pope than he was seeing.

Howell let out a dejected sigh, shaking his head sadly as he turned to head back to his office.

'Sir?' Pearce asked, getting his attention.

'What is it, Detective Pearce?'

'Is there something I should know?' Pearce stood, knowing he was treading on thin ice. The scowl that now greeted him told him it was close to breaking.

'There are some things that people, even those who have done and seen what Samuel Pope has, just can't come back from.' Howell shook his head one last time, a combination of sadness and anger. 'My advice, Detective Pearce. Leave that man alone.'

With that, Howell stomped out of the interview room and was swallowed by the brightness. Pearce slowly sat back down on the edge of the desk, circling the incorrectly spelt name that he hoped would provide him some answers. He turned slightly, lifting the manila folder and thumbing through its contents. An exemplary military record along with top marks in his police training.

A man who was heavily trained in combat, both hand to hand and from devastating range. A man who was discharged after two close-range bullets were put through his chest.

A man whose marriage and life had evaporated in the last few years.

As always, his gut was telling him there was more to it, especially as those years corresponded with the recent attacks. The last thing the Metropolitan Police Department needed was a rogue vigilante, with more tactical nous than the entire armed response put together.

With a firm sigh, he packed the sheets of paper back into the folder and left the interview room, marching back through the office and a sea of sceptical eyes and muttered curse words. Howell's final words echoed in his mind.

'Leave that man alone.'

Sadly, after years of hunting down dark parts of the Met, Pearce knew that he couldn't do that.

CHAPTER SIX

The streets of London were bursting at the seams, like an overstuffed scarecrow. As the civilians lined the concrete jungle, their pathways were blocked by the mapped-out fences that laid out the path of the marathon. A yearly event that drew the eyes of the watching world, over forty thousand runners would take to the streets, finally seeing the results of their training plans.

Each barrier was covered with an advertisement banner, a highly paid advert for a company sponsoring the event in the hope of gaining a few more clicks to their website. Behind each metal railing, people crammed their way to the front, some of them cheering and supporting friends and family members, many others just taking in the carnival atmosphere.

Some of the most successful long-distance runners in the world were participating, with the UK's champion one of the few heading the pack, miles ahead of the struggling crowd of office workers who had been duped into running the marathon on behalf of a charity. As they reached the halfway point and their bodies were near breaking point, they were all probably willing to just donate the total sponsorship themselves. But the streets were lined with eager civilians, many of them with their homemade banners, cheering on their loved ones for this life-changing moment. At various checkpoints throughout the city, popup food stands eagerly hoovered up the extra custom as several musical acts took advantage of the self-promotion, entertaining the people of the great city.

Derek Earnshaw was approaching mile seventeen when he felt the first twinges of fatigue, his body willing him to give in to the tiredness. As the Head of City Planning, he was one of the few government officials actually running the race, which had become as ingrained in British culture as afternoon tea and crumpets. At fifty-seven years of age, Derek had been on a rigorous training regime, using his substantial salary to pay for a personal trainer and top-of-the-line running gear. Running for a charity dedicated to helping the homeless, he couldn't help but see the irony.

But the mayor had been adamant that they were shown to be caring, putting themselves through four or five hours of pain to help those who spent a lifetime in it. But as he rounded another corner he saw signs for Canary Wharf, the money-making centre of his great city. The beautiful roads were lined with tall, shimmering glass buildings that burst with light on the cool spring morning. As he passed the large HSBC building, he turned down one of the shut off roads, passing the Tube station as he did.

The watching crowds all cheered.

He smiled, knowing that he did everything he could to make this city better for them. As the pain of fatigue began to bore into his side like a termite, he thought back to the meeting he had had three weeks previously: the angry gentleman who wanted to erect two more high-rises in the centre of the city, one of them right in the heart of Canary Wharf.

With his reasoning suspicious and details at a premium, Derek had rejected the proposal, arguing that he didn't feel the intentions were as innocent as they appeared. The next evening, as he had walked through a dark car park to his car, a masked man had approached him, threatening him with physical violence if he didn't relent. After scaring Derek almost to tears, the masked attacker shoved him to the ground and took a piss on his briefcase.

As he had cowered in the dark, listening to his personal possessions being sullied, he noticed the four separate knives that stuck out of each tyre.

That was when he had informed the police, who had taken an interest in the case, assigning a keen young officer to begin digging into the shell company that had originally approached him. As he tried to regulate his breathing and his pace, he made a mental note to check in with the young officer when he was back in the office, to discuss the progress.

'Keep up, Derek.' A playful voice broke his concentration.

He spun his head to the right to be met by the joyful smile of Chris Bolton, one of the few other high-ranking city officials running the iconic race. Chris was a big man, who had lost over three stone training for the marathon alongside him. Chris was a high-ranking judge who specialised in property law. Apparently the very same people had approached Chris after Derek had shot them down, with an envelope of cash and promises of future benefits should he rule in their favour.

Unluckily for them, Chris Bolton was as straight as they came, with his dedication to the law seeing the two men being ejected rapidly. Despite their threats of retaliation, Chris was fortunate enough not to have faced the same humiliation as Derek.

'I'm flagging,' Derek admitted, sweat bouncing off his head.

'Just stay with me, mate.' Chris beamed, his cockney accent sneaking through. 'We'll go at a slower pace.'

Derek smiled thankfully as they slowed their pace slightly, watching as a few super-fit youngsters shot by, their bodies tighter than their apparel. They turned left, breaking onto a long road that headed back out of Canary Wharf and back down towards London Bridge. The pavement was a sea of colour, bright T-shirts and waving hands as the public roared them on. As the tall buildings slowly began to pass them by, the sun burst down upon them, bathing them both in a warm glow. The city twinkled before them.

Chris sighed appreciatively.

'Hell of a city, eh?' he offered, his flabby body bouncing with each heavy step that slapped the concrete.

'It sure is,' Derek replied. And he meant it.

Despite the pain that was shaking through his legs with each step, and the constant screaming of his lungs, he realised how much he loved the city of London. How it filled him with pride to not only be running through it for a cause that could help the less fortunate, but how he served it every day, ensuring the safety and integrity of the city.

As he ran side by side with someone who felt the exact same way, Derek felt a second wind channel through his body, a newfound determination to keep going.

To continue to serve the city with pride.

Just as he was about to turn and tell his friend that it was almost the perfect morning, he saw a bright flash as they approached London Bridge Station, followed by a horrifying roar. As the bomb went off, Derek heard some terrified screams before everything went black.

PC Jake Howell watched with great interest as the runners raced past. With his hands comfortably tucked into the front of his met vest, he smiled at the arse-kicking he would have received back at Hendon. During his training, the supervising officer had drilled into all of them that they shouldn't get caught with their hands in the front of the met vest, as it left them susceptible to an attack.

As Jake watched the kids reaching out for high fives from the runners, cheerful people making new friends as they cheered on the selfless runners, and the sun washing all of it in a soft warmth, he couldn't have felt further from danger.

His fiancée, Cheryl, has been annoyed that he had signed up for the extra shift, complaining that she hardly ever got to see him and that it felt like she was planning the wedding on her own. When he told her how much the overtime came to, he joked that he would be paying for it on his own. She had laughed and they had made love not long afterwards, their passion still as hot as ever, even after six years together.

He had met her in his early twenties, much to the constant jibes of his friends, who rubbed their promiscuous lives in his face every chance they got.

It didn't bother him in the slightest. He pitied them.

Whilst they went out every weekend, trying their level best just to get a woman to talk to them, he was usually snuggled up on the sofa, his arms around the most beautiful woman he would ever have the luck of meeting.

He couldn't wait to marry her.

His radio crackled, HQ with their routine check-in. He gave them the all-clear and went back to watching the city move together, with the runners in sync with the cheers of those on the sidelines. He knew his uncle had worked this shift countless times, and it was one of the reasons he had wanted to be selected for it.

It had been one of the best days of his life when his uncle had told him that he had personally seen to it that he would be on shift for the London Marathon. Although he had been partnered with PC Harding, the party atmosphere and beautiful weather had more than made up for it. Besides, Harding had made it clear he wasn't fussed about spending time together, having walked off to 'grab a coffee' some half hour ago. Jake was sure he would find him in a bar somewhere, chatting to a young lady and feeding her line after line of bullshit.

He could never be like Harding—not when he had his uncle's reputation to live up to.

Jake smiled as he took a few steps forward. Knowing that his uncle had taken an interest in his career filled him with pride. He knew where he wanted to end up: working cases for CID and becoming a highly decorated detective just like his uncle. He also wanted to get married and have a few kids, hoping one of them would grow up wanting to emulate him just as he had his uncle. A big cheer pulled him back to his duty; a smiling runner, drenched in sweat, waved as a big banner was unfolded by those nearest the railing, the name 'DANIEL' painted on a big sheet.

Jake smiled.

He loved this city.

Keeping it safe was the best thing he had ever done with his life.

As he began to wonder what life would have been like if he had accepted the chance to undertake a degree in media technology at Kingston University, his eyes met those of a hooded man about ten people back. Not wanting to racially profile, Jake couldn't help but be alarmed by the quickness of the man's turn and hurried dash into a nearby alleyway. Whilst reprimanding a young black man on the grounds of 'being shifty-looking' was likely to see him end up attending a cultural diversity lecture, Jake remembered the vow he had taken to protect the city and the people who inhabited it.

Being accused of racism was a price he was willing to pay to ensure their safety. Careful not to raise alarm, he slid his hands back into his met vest and casually headed towards the alleyway, smiling politely at the locals who let him through. One young child looked at him with complete awe, causing Jake to blush slightly in the cheeks.

He remembered looking at his uncle in the same way when he had arrived at his school wearing his full uniform. Jake had been the coolest kid in his class after that.

He smiled and tipped his hat to the young boy, making a note to return and speak to the young boy's parents, hopefully making a lasting impression too. As another batch of runners struggled past, PC Jake Howell entered the alleyway, scanning his eyes over the faded brickwork of the adjoining buildings.

A few large metal bins stood to one side, surrounded by black bags and an appalling stench. Bright letters ran across the walls, the local graffiti artists tagging their names on the brickwork, foolishly thinking it bought them any kind of status other than 'criminal'. Jake began to wonder if he should have radioed Harding, the idea of entering the alleyway alone was starting to seem potentially foolish.

He soon breathed a sigh of relief.

The man had gone.

As PC Jake Howell turned, he suddenly came face to face with the hooded man, whose wide eyes relayed pure fear.

'I'm sorry,' he begged, his eyes watering.

'Sorry?' Jake repeated, trying his best to maintain his calm demeanour.

'They made me.' The young man's voice trailed off

silently, as the scuffing of shoes echoed from behind him as the group approached. They were the last words PC Jake Howell would hear, as he would be discovered as one of the fatalities of the bomb that obliterated the London Marathon.

CHAPTER SEVEN

The next forty-eight hours became a blur.

The fallout of the bombing shook every layer of the British economy. The media whipped the country into a frenzy, with the idea that a family day out could be targeted enough to ensure panicked parents pulled their kids from schools. Companies saw a drastic increase in absence for the following Monday and Tuesday—especially those who were based in the capital. Each paper, regardless of political standing, hammered home that the UK was a country under attack, that every action should be treated with extreme suspicion.

Angry civilians protested out the front of Westminster, signs demanding that the government retaliate and putting ever-growing pressure on the Prime Minister to stand up to the extremists.

The blame was of course laid at the doorstep of ISIS, the terrorist cell who were all too happy to accept the offer, their reign of terror ever increasing as the world watched in horror. Sure enough, social media played its part, with videos of people in the crowd showing the harrowing moment the bomb exploded, with many of them not realising the irony in their pleas for people not to panic.

The police commissioner gave a damning statement, declaring she would find those responsible and bring them to justice, a rallying cry that would no doubt only help her tenure.

The world needed to hear those words.

The British public demanded action.

On Wednesday morning, three days after the country was subjected to what the rags were insensitively calling the 'Marathon Massacre', Sam found himself shaking his head at the vile newspaper. With their usual class and dignity, they had laid out a number of gut-wrenching photographs, including one of a young girl crying in her father's arms, with blood splattered across her face. Another image they had posted, to the usual uproar in the oversensitive world of social media, was of a young man strapped to a hospital stretcher, his right leg missing.

Sam had seen similar during his lifetime, remembering the night when Private Miller lost his leg to a car bomb on the streets of Kabul. The smell of burning flesh was as clear to him that morning, stood in the archive room, as it was on the sandy streets of the Afghan city, the screaming from the public as the vehicle exploded, wiping four people off the earth instantly and changing the lives of seven others.

Miller was nineteen years old, crippled by a war that had started before he had even hit puberty. And because of it, he was forced to live his remaining years with the scars of war all too prominent. The last Sam had heard, Miller was running a very successful digital marketing company, was married, and had a beautiful daughter.

War had changed Miller just as it had himself.

Only Sam wasn't sure it was for the better.

As he perused the paper that Des had brought into the

office, he overheard the two officers waiting in the archive waiting room, both of them complaining to Sam's colleague that she was taking too long and they were going to miss the briefing. Sam, who had been at the office since seven a.m., popped his head into Des's office to realise he wasn't there. Quickly, he followed the two officers as they gratefully took their folders before marching hurriedly back to the main offices. The briefing room, which only a week before was filled with the excitement of another glorious day in London, had turned deathly silent. The spectre of the day loomed large, especially as the passing out photo of PC Jake Howell was proudly displayed in the centre of the whiteboard at the front of the room. To the side of it, a heartbroken Inspector Howell stood, the usually triumphant stance replaced with a man that looked like he wanted to implode. His shoulders hunched and his eyes were darkened, the lack of sleep evident of a man who had not stopped grieving. He didn't even look up as the final officers slid in through the door, taking the final two seats. Other officers were stood to attention at the back of the room, as if casually leaning against the wall would be disrespectful to the recently departed.

Samuel Pope managed to catch the door before it closed, silently holding it open and sliding into the room. A few curious glances came from the nearest officers, but with the room as quiet as a library, no one dared break the eerie silence.

Sam's eyes fell upon Inspector Howell and he instantly felt the man's pain. Sam knew more than anyone what it was like to lose someone close, that feeling of helplessness that the grief slaps on you like a straitjacket. It wrenches your body inwards, daring you to try to escape and mockingly squeezing you tighter as you try.

He could see in Howell's eyes that he wasn't yet at the point of anger.

Next to Howell stood DS Mayer, his eyes relaying nothing but sheer fury. As leader of the Counter Terrorist Unit, he had been in charge when the Marathon collapsed into anarchy. Whilst everyone else in the room was busy mourning the loss of their colleague or nephew, Mayer had been mourning his prospects of promotion, determined to turn the tragedy into his own twisted career ladder. Mayer's eyes locked onto Sam's and he easily conveyed a 'what the fuck are you doing here?' with a glare.

Sam ignored it, stuffing his hands into the pockets of his navy trousers, the sleeves of his white shirt rolled up to just below the elbow. His eyes scanned the room, years of training that had become automatic long ago, every detail being absorbed and memorised. He counted forty-seven officers, eight detectives, and four sergeants.

Another six stood to his left, three more officers to the right.

Howell and Mayer stood at the front.

Then, to his complete surprise, Sam saw DI Adrian Pearce stood in the far corner, hands tucked into the pockets of another well-fitted suit. Pearce locked eyes with Sam, giving him an accusing nod, which Sam returned graciously. Why Pearce was there, Sam didn't know, but he was sure it wouldn't be too long before he found out.

Before Sam could analyse the distance between himself and his recent tormenter, Mayer stepped forward, running a meaty hand through hair that had long since given up the ghost but had neglected to tell him.

'Right, quiet down,' Mayer demanded, his dark eyes locking onto an officer in the front row. 'Now.'

Sam could feel every officer's sphincter tighten with fear. Mayer was known as a brown-noser, but he also threw his considerable weight around with the younger officers. His reputation as a boxing champion in the Met Police during his beat days preceded him. Inspector Howell stepped forward, every movement taking considerable effort, along with a deep breath. The heartbreak was written across him like a billboard.

'As we know, at eleven fifty-two on Sunday, an explosive device was detonated just after mile seventeen of the London Marathon, just here in the London Bridge area'— he pointed to the large map of London which decorated one of the whiteboards— 'claiming the lives of six civilians and one officer…'

The entire room felt heavy with grief as the likable inspector swallowed back tears, his throat closing slightly with sadness. He let out a deep breath and turned back to the other whiteboard, his teary eyes falling upon the youthful face of his deceased nephew. Sam watched as many officers bowed their heads in respect. Howell tried to speak up again, but his words once again caught in his throat. Surprisingly, DI Pearce stepped forward, placing a hand on Howell's shoulder and ushering him towards the corner. A number of officers watched on with intrigue, many of them unfamiliar with the smooth-talking internal investigator.

Mayer took his cue with glee.

'Let's not piss about. An officer, Police Constable Jake Howell, was one of the victims of this disgusting attack. The phrase 'one of our own' has never been so apt. Inspector Howell, as I have said in private, my condolences to you and your family during this horrible time. I'm sure all of the officers in this room extend the same courtesy.'

Sam watched Mayer milk the room, with many officers mumbling their condolences to the inspector, who had mentally checked out. Pearce stood, arms folded, watching the DS as he stood powerfully, hands on hips.

'As head of the Counter Terrorist Unit I failed in my duty to protect this city and its occupants, and that will never be something I will be able to scrub from my conscience. But what I can do is promise that we will find the fuckers who did this and we will bring them in here kicking and screaming so they can look this man in the eye.'

Mayer pointed a finger at Howell, who peered at the room with desolate eyes. Once again he tried to muster some words, but grief tightened its grip on his vocal cords yet again. With an apologetic nod of the head, he opened the door at the far side of the briefing room and took his leave. A few of the younger officers dabbed a tear or two away. The hardened veterans watched with a stoic acceptance, all of them making silent promises to find justice for Howell and his family. Sam watched all of them, catching the eye of PC Harding, who scowled in return. Mayer let the silence slowly tilt towards awkward before addressing the room again.

'The reports are on their way back from the morgue as we speak, which means we can start contacting the families and allowing them to start making their arrangements. I will be devising a specialist task force to start rattling some damn cages, and hopefully kick down some doors.' A few veins rose to prominence as Mayer's temper began to surface. 'I want these fuckers found and I want them found today. I will be in touch personally once my team has been selected. To everyone else, knock on every door you can, chase every lead, and let's not let Officer Howell's bravery be for nothing.'

A number of audible agreements filled the air before the Metropolitan Police Force burst into life, all of the officers filtering to the doors. Sam held the door open, getting nothing but the odd look and a crass comment from Harding for his troubles.

Just as he was about to exit, DS Mayer stomped past, stopping a few inches from Sam. The DS was broader than Sam, but the years had begun to pad together around his midriff. A few inches taller than Sam, the DS scowled into his eyes.

'Just for the record, this is police business. Next time you interrupt or intrude on an official briefing again, you're going to need more than a fucking shrink to fix what I will do to you.'

Mayer barged past, ensuring his mighty shoulder slammed into Sam's, knocking him a step back. Sam responded with an eye roll, taking a few seconds to play out a scenario where he systematically took the DS apart in a matter of seconds. It was only the calm voice of DI Pearce that brought him back to reality.

'I reckon he would put up more of a fight than Morton.'

Sam smiled, gently shaking his head as he turned to face the DI. 'I wouldn't know.'

'Really?' Pearce asked insincerely. 'See, I beg to differ.'

'Oh yeah?'

'Yeah. And very soon, I'm going to start connecting dots.' He leant in close, a few inches from Sam's ear. 'Do you know what will happen then?'

'You finally complete your dot-to-dot book?'

Pearce chuckled, raising his eyebrows. Despite the rumours and stories of Sam Pope being an oddball, he certainly had a sharp wit and quick response. Delving into his military career, Pearce had begun to piece together a picture of Sam Pope that no one else seemed to have noticed. Observing him in the office, he had seen every officer either regard him with disgust or ignore him completely. He was a ghost, hiding in plain sight and in the thick of everything. With his undoubted reconnaissance skills, Pearce was sure that Sam Pope knew more of what was going on than the commissioner herself. As Sam stood before him, Pearce took a friendly step back, nodding a friendly goodbye.

'I'll be seeing you, Pope.'

'Can't wait.'

Sam left the briefing room and marched through the office. Every police constable was either deep in conversation or clattering their fingers across their keyboards. The entire Metropolitan Police Service was on alert, their focus on the brutal act of terrorism that not only sent a shockwave of fear through the entire country but had claimed the lives of seven people.

Including one of their own.

As he passed through the office, he noted the position of every officer, their likely escape route and pathway to him and the calculated time of response. He made mental notes of how many desks, what was on them, even what colour the coffee mugs were and where they sat. All the information scrolled through his brain like the credits at the end of a movie, building not only a clear image of what was in front of him but several likely scenarios and the best course of action.

It was what he had been trained to do.

What he had put into practice, the many years he spent out of sight, silently killing without leaving a trace.

As he neared the door to the corridor to return to his job, he caught a glimpse of a morose Inspector Howell slumped in his chair, his desk a myriad of files that he was clearly ignoring. DS Mayer stepped to the door, giving Sam one last glare of hatred before slamming the office door shut, clearly looking to score some brownie points off his grieving superior.

Sam shook his head and stepped out of the noise and into the corridor, the office behind him buzzing faintly like a bee trapped in a bottle. As he approached his office, he was reminded of the bombings in Afghanistan—the sheer terror they bring and the helplessness that follows.

The destruction.

The death.

Knowing it had happened just a few miles over the Thames caused his body to shake. At first he was sure it was anger, the usual reaction any patriotic person has when they see their homeland under attack. He then thought it was fear, the scars of war reopening and allowing the PTSD to finally catch up to him.

But it was neither of them. As he entered the archive office, nodded a greeting to Des, and walked towards the recent stack of files, he knew what the feeling was.

It was guilt.

Sam felt the guilt rise up inside of him as he lifted the files and began to wander through the rows of filing units. Placing them into their expertly marked locations, he knew what he was doing. He was ignoring the call to look further into the bombing.

To use the skills and training that country had provided to find out who the hell took a shot at it.

As he filed away the large manila folders, he also shut away the call of duty.

He was no longer that man anymore. He had made a promise to his son.

Fighting back a sudden wave of emotion, he steadied himself and went back to his job and begrudgingly left the Metropolitan Police to do theirs.

CHAPTER EIGHT

The following morning, Sam Pope went for a run to clear his head. Rising before five a.m., he slipped on his running gear and headed out, his feet slapping the pavement as the world slumbered around him. As he ran, his mind raced to the previous Sunday, when during the iconic London Marathon, a terrorist attack had broken the capital and spread fear like wildfire. Remembering the brutal explosions during a raid in Kirkuk seven years previously, he could only sympathise with the civilians who would never outrun that memory.

Every second of his ordeal stayed with him.

And he had had training. Lots of training.

A milk float lazily hummed down the road, the milkman nodding at Pope, who smiled back, surprised to see the profession still in existence. In a world full of one-click purchases and being able to pay with your watch, seeing a milkman felt like a throwback. As his pace quickened, so did his thoughts.

A young police officer and six civilians had been killed, wiped off the world like dust in the wind. Their families had been rocked by the cruelty of the world, their lives pulled apart like wet paper. For the other dozen who had suffered severe burns and loss of limbs, he had witnessed many a fellow soldier go crazy after not adjusting. The media was always willing to roll out the centrefold for a soldier who had been injured in the line of duty, who had gone on to do incredible things—his friend Miller being one of them.

But they tucked the horrors of war, the ones the other soldiers returned home with, out of sight. The public didn't need to know their struggles, how their lives had been wrecked by serving bravely for a fight that wasn't their own. As sweat poured over his chest as he reached his third mile, he could feel it sliding across the bullet scars, his own personal reminder of those horrors.

Eventually he turned a corner and picked up the pace, pushing his body through the final mile as he raced through Maidenhead town centre, through the windy streets lined with the high street shops. With High Wycombe and Windsor easily commutable, the town centre was slowly becoming a ghost town. More and more shops were closing down, with old banners strapped across dirty windows, the rooms behind derelict and dark.

Finally he returned home, instantly hopping into the shower and allowing the water to splash against his hair, splashing down his back. His mind was racing again.

Every inch of him wanted to do something.

He had been trained by the country to be an effective defence mechanism, with the skills and abilities to strike back against any enemy, foreign and domestic. Knowing a young man who had proudly served his country as he had was senselessly murdered was gnawing at him like a toothache. The previous acts of retribution, the brutal assaults that had DI Pearce sniffing around like a lost puppy, they had been in the face of grave injustice.

He turned the tap off, steam rising from his wet body

as he exited the shower and quickly dried off, brushed his teeth, and then raced into his bedroom to throw on his neatly ironed shirt and trousers. As he selected a tie, his mind flashed back to Jason Marlow and how he had dropped him over the edge of the stairway and choked him to within an inch of his life.

Sam thought about taking to the streets, using the same kind of tactic to find out who the hell had bombed the city.

Who had killed that police officer.

Just as his mind began convincing him to act, his eyes fell upon *To Kill a Mockingbird* on his bedside table.

He felt the guilt rush through his body like a tidal wave.

Sam slowly finished tying his tie before taking a seat on the edge of the bed and reaching out to the book. He ran his hands over it, remembering the promise he had made to his son.

Suddenly, the emptiness of his flat became very prominent, the absence of Lucy and Jamie growing like a sinkhole. How he longed to hear his son playing in the other room, crashing his toys together in some bizarre imaginary storyline. Or to smell Lucy's perfume as she sat at her dressing table, running straighteners through her blond hair.

Those days had gone.

He lifted his phone, sighing deeply as the idea to call Lucy was immediately rejected by his brain.

His family was broken, and he was sure it was because of who the war had made him. How it had changed him.

As he held the book, Sam thought back to a happier memory, safe in the knowledge that not all scars of war were physical.

———

The sun was making a rare appearance, bursting through the clouds as the British summer threatened to actually happen. Sam sat on the bench to the side of the adventure playground, his hands sat on his lap and a smile on his face. The playground was a hive of activity, with kids racing around in every direction, their cries of excitement batting back and forth like a tennis rally. Parents huddled together on the picnic benches, tables covered with bags of food, and the world was alive with happiness.

This was what he had come home for.

Lovingly, his eyes followed the smooth legs of his wife as she walked by, rolling her eyes with faux annoyance as their son raced towards the swings.

Just watching Jamie run, with his delicate prance, filled Sam with pride.

At five years of age, Jamie was starting to show signs of being a prodigy. Not the most athletically gifted or confident, the boy loved books. He was already reading at a nine-year-old level and his school work had already received recognition from his teachers.

The boy was smart and Sam was thrilled that he had seemed to have inherited more traits from his mother than himself.

Thinking back to his own childhood, Sam had never been one for studying. His father, a strict military man, was constantly being redeployed, meaning Sam never spent more than a year at a school.

It was hard to be a good student.

It was even harder to make friends.

Jamie scurried across the park, stopping every few feet to flash his pearly white smile at Lucy, who dotingly followed. He watched as his wife moved effortlessly towards the swing Jamie was now clambering onto, feeling his heart jump with love. They had been together for over ten years, married for six, and he had loved her more every day since. Whilst he had been pinned down in an abandoned warehouse in Iraq by two snipers, he had spent the entire time clutching her photograph.

She had always made him promise he would make it back.

He always did.

Jamie was sat in the swing, his little fingers gripping the chains *until his knuckles whitened, and he called to Sam, urging his dad to join them. With a grin, Sam pushed himself up, walking with a little discomfort across the park. He hadn't long since been released from hospital, his chest still flaring with pain regularly, and the stiffness in his shoulders told him it was a long road ahead.*

As he had lain on that bloody concrete, with two bullet holes still smoking from his chest, he had thought of his family.

His gorgeous wife and his beautiful son.

The very image he was seeing now.

With a smile he joined them both, his wife wrapping her arm around his waist and offering him a concerned look which he immediately batted away. Nothing was going to stop him from pushing his son, who shrieked with happiness as he was launched forward. As he came rushing back, Sam ignored the aching as he reached out and gently pushed his son again, watching him rise and fall in the sunshine.

It was that moment then, with his wife by his side, lovingly watching him bond with his son, that he had made a silent promise to them both. That he wasn't going to go back to the man he had been.

The world had trained him to be a killer. Then tried to kill him.

He promised them both he was done.

And at that moment, as the world allowed him to spend those precious moments together as a family, he had truly meant it.

———

Sam was still thinking of that memory when he arrived at work, walking through the building like a ghost, with no one offering a 'good morning' or even a courteous nod. Quietly he dropped his bag off in the archive office before making his way to his weekly meeting with Amy. He scoffed at the idea of having mandated therapy to deal with his life. Sam had eliminated targets that had caused deaths to thousands, had over sixty confirmed kills, with over double that on a strictly 'need-to-know' basis.

He had a decade of war bubbling inside him.

Yet Amy Devereux, as lovely as she was, was expected to piece together the shattered remains of a life that he had valiantly fought for.

Despite his misgivings, Sam appreciated the chain of command, and despite not finishing his training to become a police officer, still held the idea of rank very highly. He had lived his life reporting to duty, obeying the chain of command and carrying out his orders.

They had ordered him to therapy.

Begrudgingly, he obeyed.

As he hopped up the stairs, a couple of officers trudged past, one of them casting an uneasy eye over him before disappearing round the corner. The terrorist attack had the entire building rocking, with Mayer hunting down anyone he suspected of, as he so eloquently put it, being 'stood around with a thumb up their arse.'

Sam wondered where the case was, how many leads they had, and how close they were to catching those responsible. He didn't like Mayer, a view that wasn't uncommon in the station, but he respected how much the man wanted the bomber found. Sam had refused to look into the file, to allow himself to get swept up in it, but now, as he watched another officer burst out into the corridor on her mobile phone, demanding someone give her information, he could feel that sense of duty rising within him.

He fought it back, realising that his need for therapy may not have been as outrageous as he had once thought.

Especially with DI Pearce tracking him. Sam needed to keep a low profile, and ripping the city of London apart to find out who had tried to do it themselves wasn't the best idea.

Amy Deveraux's door was closed, the metal slide pushed to the side to reveal 'Engaged'. Slid the other way, the message was a lot more welcoming. With a few minutes to spare, Sam idly wandered down the corridor, hands stuffed in his pockets and trying to listen to any intel he could.

He already knew how many officers were in the main office, noting every detail as he had walked to his meeting.

He knew how many were set for the regular patrol from a quick glance at the rota boards.

Sam had memorised every detail, from the number of mugs left next to the coffee machine to how many of those officers had their ASP and pepper spray attached to their belts.

He had spent his life doing it—evaluating every scene, filtering those details, and devising whatever strategy he needed. Today, in the Metropolitan Police HQ, the only strategy was to follow orders, have his therapy session, and report back to work like a good little soldier.

The days of harnessing that intel so he could deliver a bullet to the centre of a skull were long gone.

The sound of Amy's door opening caused him to turn and then instantly step briskly to the corner, out of sight. Peeking round the corner, Sam watched in shock as Officer Harding stepped out, forcing a smile before stomping off in the opposite direction. He whistled joyfully, an undeserved swagger on his heavy frame as he passed a female officer, whom he leered at, before pushing through the double doors and disappearing into his shift.

Sam waited for a few moments, trying to fathom why someone like Harding, who revelled in the boisterous nature of his job and treated everything like a pissing contest, had been to a mandated therapy session.

Shrugging at the bizarre sight, Sam took a deep breath and headed towards the door, preparing himself for another hour of painfully yearning for his family.

CHAPTER NINE

That Saturday morning, nearly a week after the horrific blast had ended his life amid a city living in fear, Police Constable Jake Howell was laid to rest. In a service at his local church, grieving friends and family sat in tears as the vicar ran through the usual service, offering peace through his religious words and the hope that Jake would be happy in the afterlife. The church itself was full to capacity, the sadness of a jovial young man being snatched so cruelly clearly affecting many.

They all came to pay their respects.

Sat at the front, grasping the hands of his weeping sister, was Inspector Michael Howell. Wearing his police tunic, Howell took to the podium to read a small speech about the pride he had for his nephew, the struggles he had with his sister who didn't want him to be a police officer, and the heroic death that would not be in vain. Whilst all of his speech was met with tears, Howell felt disconnected from it all; the grief had taken a bizarre stranglehold on him and he felt nothing. His eyes scanned the room, but he felt like he was on the outskirts, witnessing those who loved his nephew grieving through frosted glass.

The weight of guilt felt heavy on his shoulders.

As he came to the final sentence of his speech, he felt his voice crack, the sadness rushing up through his body like volcano, and he began to sob. As this triggered more weeping inside the church, Howell felt determined to complete his tribute, speaking once more of how proud Jake had made him before patting the coffin that sat at the front of the room. Before him, rows of pews were filled with black-clothed loved ones and people he didn't know. The walls of the church were a drab grey, the monotony broken up by the stunning stained glass windows. Wooden beams arched across the roof, which echoed with the sadness of the mourning crowd.

The vicar reassuringly patted him on the shoulder as he returned to his seat, before turning and saying a silent prayer to the shiny wooden coffin. With a gentle nod, he pressed a small button, a curtain drawing around the body, which would then be respectfully taken to the crematorium behind the church, for Jake to be cremated. As the curtain slowly crawled around the edges of the coffin, Howell felt the tears fall down his world-weary cheeks, the finality of his nephew's tragic death becoming too apparent.

The vicar's soothing voice did little to quash the wave of sadness that swept the room as the coffin slowly faded from view.

'Father, thank you so much for your grace and your goodness, for your message of hope, for this man's life and how it was spent. We pray that we might all aspire to live as well as Jake did. We thank you that he is now safe in your presence. And we pray that today you fill us with faith and guide us along our way so that we might end up in the same place when it is our time.

'In Jesus' name, amen.'

A resounding 'amen' echoed back before Jake's favourite song, 'Hey Joe' by Jimi Hendrix, filtered through the speakers as Howell led his sister through the aisle and back out to the front of the church. As they passed through the large wooden doors, they stopped, their mouths open with shock.

Over fifty uniformed police officers stood, dressed like Howell in their tunics. They lined the pathway on either side, and at the command of a senior officer, all of them raised a white-gloved hand to salute.

Howell choked back more tears.

His sister beamed with pride.

They walked through the respectful corridor, with Howell nodding his appreciation to each officer who stood to attention. Beyond the officers, a small crowd of other mourners had ventured to pay their respects. Howell didn't see anything but blurred faces, his vision obscured by the tears and the grief. He failed to spot Samuel Pope, a man who, until recently, had been nothing more than a quiet man behind a glass screen.

As he helped his sister into the car that would take them to his nephew's wake, Howell took a deep breath, said one final goodbye to his nephew, and promised him his death would not be for nothing.

———

The old, crooning voice of Neil Diamond struggled through the speakers that hung overhead as Sam patiently sat, his arms crossed and resting on the table. The pub, the Old Crown, was a traditional 'old man' pub, filled with uncomfortable furniture, money-stealing fruit machines, and enough local ales to keep the regulars happy. The décor was dated, with random black-and-white pictures of the good old days only hammering home the pub's status as a relic.

Still, at least you could have a conversation and actually hear it.

Just as Sam began to focus on the nearest dreary painting of an old market square, Theo Walker returned to the table, his meaty hands wrapped around two glasses. Setting a gin-and-tonic in front of Sam, Theo took the seat opposite, necking a long sip from his pint before settling down and smacking his lips with satisfaction.

'Cheers,' Sam mockingly offered, lifting his glass.

'Cheers', Theo repeated, their glasses clinking before he took another sip. The foam rested along his lips, even more noticeably due to Theo's black skin. His cropped hair faded as it ran down the sides of his skull, merging into the neatly trimmed stubble that framed his strong jaw. He still looked every bit the soldier he had been back when he and Sam had served together, his light blue shirt wrapping tightly around his muscular frame. After a few moments of silence, Theo rested his dark eyes on his former comrade. 'What's up, Sam?'

'Nothing.' Sam took a nervous sip, his social skills having left the same time his wife did.

'Come on, man. You can talk to me.' Theo offered a pearly smile. 'The shit we been through, you could tell me anything.'

'That is true.' Sam chuckled.

'How's things, man? You heard from Lucy?'

Sam sighed and shook his head. 'Not for a while. She's got her new life now. They're expecting.' Sam took another sip. 'Jamie always wanted a little brother.'

'Look man, don't do this to yourself.' Theo spoke with the same authority that had made him one of the most respected and trusted medics during Sam's tenure. 'What happened, happened. You can't go back in time, you can't change the past. So let it be. You can't sit here and wallow. That isn't the Sam Pope that I know.'

Draining the remains of his drink, Sam offered another

with a raise of the eyebrows. Surprised at the speed, Theo shrugged and went about demolishing his own pint as Sam approached the bar. By the time he had returned, Theo was gently placing an empty glass onto the rickety wooden table between them. They clinked again and took another sip.

'How's work?' Sam asked with genuine interest.

'Really good, thanks. A few of my guys got together and they decided to start a dance group.' Theo beamed proudly, which sent a small twinge of envy through Sam. Since being honourably discharged, Theo had dedicated his life to working with underprivileged and wayward kids in the East End of London, tackling some of the most toxic and poverty-stricken estates in the country. With gang culture rife on every street, Theo had built up a lot of respect with many of the gangs, with surprising results. It didn't surprise Sam at all. Despite being a great soldier, Theo was a born healer and Sam had witnessed him bravely risk his own life to save others. Whilst working with street gangs to forge a better path for the next generation wasn't exactly a firefight in an abandoned factory in Iraq, it was another battle for Theo.

Sam wondered if maybe his own quest for justice could be considered a public service too. Smiling, he brought his mind back to the conversation.

'You're not teaching them, are you?' Sam asked with a cheeky grin. 'I mean, they want to improve, don't they?'

'Hey, screw you. I got some moves.' Theo chuckled. 'How about you—how's work?'

'I'm not sure.'

'You're not sure?'

'Everyone is on edge since Sunday,' Sam began, his words tailing off. 'That young officer, I knew him. Was a good kid, actually. One of the few.'

'I'm sorry.' Theo shook his head, recounting the

reports he had read on the senseless act.

'We had his funeral today. I think that's why I needed a drink. Seeing someone die in the line of duty, you know how it is.'

'Yeah. I do.'

Silence hung between the two of them, their minds casting back to morbid memories of fallen friends. Suddenly, Sam felt his eyebrows furrow into a frown.

Theo looked at him with caution. 'Sam?' he asked tentatively. 'What's wrong?'

'I just feel like something about it all is off.'

'What do you mean?' Theo took a nervous sip of his beer.

'I looked over the initial report of the bombing and it said that PC Harding was at the scene and he saw Jake go into the alleyway. Other eye witnesses only place one officer in the vicinity of the area, and that was Jake.'

'Sam…' Theo tried to cut in, knowing where it was going.

Sam ignored him, allowing his mind to race. 'Then I saw Harding at a mandated therapy session, which—trust me—is the last thing someone like him would do. He didn't seem remotely interested. Then today, at the funeral, I caught him twice joking around with other colleagues.'

'Sam!' Theo exclaimed purposefully. 'Just stop it.'

'What?'

'Look, I know what you're doing. Okay? I looked the other way when you told me you were hunting down the odd gangster or beating the shit out of a rapist. After what happened, I understand why you have no faith in the justice system and you want to take things into your own hands. I didn't approve, but I could understand.

'But this is crazy. You are second-guessing how a fellow police officer is dealing with his grief? You, of all people, should know just what that can do to a man.'

Sam looked sullenly at the glass before him, twisting it slowly with his fingers.

'The guy might be a prick, Sam, but it doesn't make him a criminal. This isn't your fight. None of them have been your fight and they never will. Besides, you promised your boy wouldn't kill anymore...'

'I haven't killed anyone,' Sam interjected, without looking up.

'Good. Keep it that way.'

Again, they sat in silence, the intensity of the conversation causing Theo to finish his beer and make his way to the bar. Sam knew he was right.

He was looking for a reason that wasn't there, something to make sense of a world trying to tear itself apart. Ever since that night, he had been lost. Only when he began scanning the archives for potential miscarriages of justice had he begun to deal with his grief. With every gangster or sex offender that he had brutally attacked, he had begun to feel like himself again.

Like he had a sense of purpose again.

But now, as he sat on a worn-out chair in an old, forgotten pub, he knew the only friend he had was right.

There was no 'night shift' needed for this one.

Theo returned with the drinks once more, the smile breaking across his face telling Sam the conversation had come to an end. As he placed the drink down in front of him, Sam looked his friend in the eye.

'I love you, Theo.'

'Fuck off.'

Both men started chuckling as they clinked their glasses together and settled in for the evening to take a more pleasant turn.

Stuffing his hands into his pockets to battle against the surprising spring chill, PC Harding impatiently sighed. Head to toe in black, he looked like a burglar, but he knew it was best to be able to blend into the shadows on the off chance a drunken idiot somehow stumbled up to see the city. It was past three in the morning, and from the top of the seven-storey car park he could see the entire city of London, bathed in shadow. The busy centres such as Camden Town and Leicester Square never slept, even during the week, where most bars were full way into the early hours. From his vantage point he could see Walthamstow Central Station, the cage locked shut across the front and the streets surrounding it bereft of people.

He felt entirely alone.

Alone and not in control.

They had told him where to be at the Marathon and he had obliged. They had told him to go to the therapy sessions and he had obliged. They had told him to meet them here at two o'clock and now, an hour later, he was stood, wondering just how far down the rabbit hole he was going.

Nervously he looked around; nothing but darkness and the whistling of the gentle breeze. Looking out over the city once more, he took a deep breath of the fresh air, closing his eyes, and begging himself to get some clarity.

He was a police officer.

He knew he shouldn't be accepting money, regardless of who was paying it and who else was on the take.

He had to do the right thing.

At that moment, a wave of content washed across PC Harding as he told himself that he was going to march into the nearest police station, identify himself, and tell them everything.

How he knew when and where not to be during that fateful minute of the London Marathon.

How he knew that Jake Howell was not going to live beyond that day.

How none of it was an accident.

Suddenly, Harding heard the scuffle of footsteps behind him, and as he turned, he felt the vice-like grip of powerful hands grab him from either side. The two men, their faces covered by masks, struggled for a few moments as he tried to use his large frame to fight back. But they had him, and a swift right hook to the ribs from one of them smashed the air straight out of him. As he collapsed to his knees, he hurried his body to catch its breath, the air struggling into his lungs in short, sharp intakes.

A third set of boots appeared before him, but before he could bring his eyes up to try to identify who they belonged to, a black sack was roughly drawn over his head, the back pulled tightly to arch his head backwards. A mouth hole was cut into it, exposing his mouth, which he drew open to scream for help.

Instantly a bottle was shoved into his mouth, the burning sensation of vodka hurtling down his throat, threatening to drown him as he gasped for air. He felt the alcohol dribbling over the sides of his mouth, dousing the front of his jumper and splashing across his jeans. The dampness was soon joined by a fresh batch of urine as PC Harding realised what was happening.

The alcohol kicked in pretty quickly, a near-litre of vodka sloshing around in his body and turning his brain to mush.

The city of London suddenly turned on its side before rushing past him.

In his drunken state, PC Harding had no idea he had been thrown off the top of the car park. Nor did he feel anything, as his body collided with the pavement, shattering his spine and sending his life into eternal darkness.

CHAPTER TEN

The following morning, the Metropolitan Police was in anarchy.

Every avenue of media was reporting on the apparent suicide of the partner of PC Jake Howell, with their media officer working round the clock to douse the flames of fear. The city was watching as a terrorist attack was ripping through the heart of the very body designed to protect them.

With the threat level firmly in the red, the government was now being pressured to deliver some kind of placation, something that would remove the fear from the city of London and show the world that they were prepared to fight back.

That their city was safe.

PC Harding's death had hit the office hard. Despite his boisterous and at times offensive behaviour, a death of a colleague always hung around the Metropolitan Police Service like an ethereal fog. Every officer wanted to fight back, offering whatever they could to the cause to find the terrorists who were now being blamed for the deaths of two of their own.

Crowded in the briefing room, DS Mayer stood at the front, thick arms crossed and a scowl on his face. The noise was a constant growl, like a disgruntled football crowd, as every officer offered their opinion on the situation and what they would want as an outcome.

They were baying for blood.

Knowing their sense of revenge was as malleable as soft putty, Mayer's face soon relaxed into a sympathetic smile, as if he were hearing each and every one of them. He knew that with the increased focus on this case, his profile was about to shoot through the roof. Word had reached him that the PM's office had been in contact, wanting a direct update on their investigation.

If he played this correctly, Mayer would be looking at a hell of a career ladder.

He waited for a few more moments before rallying the troops. After luring them in with his own grief, he began a series of slightly antagonistic questions, each one designed to provoke a revenge-thirsty reaction. After only five minutes, he had split the room into three new teams, each one working on a different thread, each group hoping to bring justice to a sickening threat and ensure their colleagues' lives were not lost in vain.

As they slowly filtered out of the room, Mayer stood, hands on hips, with a sense of pride and purpose. Each officer cast a suspicious eye over DI Adrian Pearce, who stood at the back of the room, his hands stuffed in his pockets. The seasoned detective flashed them his best grin, ignoring any hint of distrust in their whispers. As the final officer stepped back into the office, Mayer looked agitated as Pearce gently closed the door behind them, leaving just the two of them alone in the briefing room.

'Can I help you, Pearce'?

Mayer's words were filled with venom, a usual tone for an internal affairs officer. Also ignoring the lack of respect for rank, Pearce slowly walked towards the detective, passing the rows of empty chairs.

'I just wanted to listen in, you know? An officer has been killed and I just need to cover the bases.'

'Killed?' Mayer scoffed.

'Yeah. Why, what did you hear?'

'Come on, Pearce. What's really going on here? Are you under pressure to get your numbers up?' Mayer shook his head in disgust. 'There are terrorists out there, killing our own officers, and instead you are in here looking for the killer? You are a disgrace to the badge.'

Mayer stomped past Pearce, who reached out and grabbed his arm, stopping him in his tracks. Mayer's eyes bulged with anger as he turned and faced Pearce, whose smile quickly evaporated.

'Listen here, son. First off, respect your goddamn seniors.'

Mayer shuffled uncomfortably.

'Secondly, I am doing my goddamn job. When an officer is killed, I need to make sure we look at every side of the coin.'

'The man committed suicide,' Mayer interjected, his face a mere inch or two from Pearce, who could smell the coffee on his breath. 'Even you can see that.'

'You have witnesses? People who saw PC Harding throw himself off?'

'No, but it doesn't take a genius to see what happened,' Mayer protested, snatching his arm from Pearce's grip. 'He was cut up about Howell, knowing he should have been there. Took himself up to the top of that car park and threw himself off. Very sad.'

Pearce nodded. 'And you have CCTV of him throwing himself off?'

'What the hell is your problem, Pearce?'

'Just because it seems to be clear cut doesn't mean it is,

Mayer. That's what being a detective is. Maybe if you took your tongue out every senior officer's arsehole and actually did some work once in a while, you'd know that too.'

'Fuck you.' Mayer stepped forward, his frame considerably larger than Pearce's, as well as being a decade younger. 'We found enough vodka in his blood to knock a horse unconscious. The guy was grieving, and we couldn't help him. But I will, by not letting you pin this on one of the people out there who are trying to find the *real* bad guys. Got that?'

Mayer jabbed a firm finger into Pearce's shoulder.

'Absolutely.' Pearce stepped to the side, allowing Mayer to step past. 'However, strangely, I spoke to the onsite therapist, Mrs Devereux. Apparently, Harding was given mandated sessions to help him deal with his grief. Understandable, given what happened.'

'Get to the point, Pearce.'

'It's just, I didn't get a feel from her that Harding was in any pain at all. In fact, I didn't get much on him, to be honest.'

'Has she filed her report yet?' Mayer asked in a frustrated tone.

'Not yet. I'll check in with her tomorrow. But like you said…it's probably nothing.'

It was now Pearce's turn to walk towards the door, gently patting Mayer on the shoulder as he did. As Pearce grabbed the door handle, Mayer spoke up.

'How do you do it, Pearce?'

'Do what?' Pearce responded, peering through the gaps in the blind at the busy office.

'Look at yourself in the mirror knowing you're nothing more than an arsehole,'

Pearce offered him a smile as he pulled the door open. 'It's easy being an arsehole, son. It means you can tell when something is full of shit or not.'

Pearce disappeared into the open office, leaving Mayer to stew in the briefing room. With Inspector Howell signed off for the next few weeks on compassionate leave, Mayer knew he had a chance to really make a name for himself. He would bring this horrible terrorist incident to a successful conclusion. As he watched Pearce walk through the office and out into the stairwell, Mayer silently promised that he would get there before Pearce did.

———

Sam had woken that morning with his head pounding, like someone was using his brain as a ping-pong ball. The previous night had almost been pleasurable, Theo being a link to a previous life that was once filled with happiness. As the alcohol had flowed, so had their conversation, and after they had spoken about the pain of his family's absence, and his propensity to violently assault criminals, they had reminisced about their times on tour together.

As his head felt like it was squeezing around his brain, Sam drank two glasses of orange juice and decided to sweat away the hangover.

The following hour was spent in the spare room, his bare knuckles slamming mercilessly against the solid punch bag, the chain swinging gently with each blow. Over and over, he hammered the bag with precision, the coarse leather ripping the skin from his knuckles. Sweat rained down from every pore, causing him to remove his T-shirt after fifteen minutes. By the end of the hour, Sam stood by the window, catching his breath and willing the fresh air into his lungs. Blood dripped from his knuckles as several beads of sweat raced each other down his spine.

It wasn't until he sat down for breakfast that he saw the headline pertaining to Harding. Quickly flicking through the news report on his phone, Sam read in disbelief as a fractured account of Harding's suicide was written, with every report linking it back to the marathon bombing.

After he had read every major UK news report on the situation, he sat in disbelief for a few moments, trying to desperately piece together what was going on.

Just like before, something wasn't sitting right.

Harding had never been anything other than appalling towards him, but Sam would never have wished any harm to come his way. Now the man was dead, apparently drunk and grief-stricken to the point of taking his own life.

Sam spent the rest of the afternoon and evening retracing the same thought again and again. He had spoken of his suspicions the previous night with Theo, the inaccuracies in the eyewitness reports regarding Harding's presence on the day of the bombing.

The therapy sessions.

It just didn't seem to make sense.

As the sun set on another cool spring evening, Sam threw on a pair of jeans and a black T-shirt before sliding his arms into his black bomber jacket.

It had taken him five minutes to log into his work database and find Amy Devereux's address. He needed to speak to her, and with his suspicions rising, he wanted to do it on neutral ground.

He set off into the night looking for answers.

———

As the darkness of the evening grew, Amy Devereux pulled up outside her block of flats in Richmond. Having been on hand to speak to a number of officers throughout the day, many of whom showing various stages of grief at the loss of their colleague, she was shattered. It was hardly her ideal way of spending a Sunday. Whatever happened to it being a day of rest? As she eventually found a parking spot on the road, she collected a few folders off of the passenger seat before disembarking.

She slowly walked up the street towards the large black gate that required a fob to get through. Once inside, she waited patiently for an elevator, not fancying the three flights of stairs after her long day. Her heels were causing her calves to scream in pain and she was hoping for one of Andy's calf massages.

Andy, an accountant, would be home, and she was hoping he had dinner on the go. Her stomach rumbled just to underline the point.

As she shot up to the third floor, her mind raced through all of the meetings she had had that day, the cries of anger or the tears of sadness, all of her colleagues struggling to deal with the death of one of their own. She had her own thoughts after her meeting with Harding the previous day, but they were now clouding the notion of suicide.

He just didn't seem that broken by it all.

The lift doors pinged open and she shook her head, furious with herself for questioning someone's grief, and she ventured down the hallway towards the door to her flat. She and Andy had bought it two years ago, the value skyrocketing to eye-watering levels every year. Two bedrooms, overlooking Richmond Park. The only thing missing was a third member of their family, which Amy had been giving more and more thought to.

Especially after her weekly meetings with Sam Pope.

The love he had for his son was something she craved for her and Andy's marriage.

Suddenly, a jolt of excitement travelled through her like a lightning rod and she wondered if she was too tired to start tonight. Maybe they could wolf down their dinner and get straight to burning it off?

With a coy smile, Amy opened the door to her flat and

stepped into the front room. The smell of Andy's chicken korma fluttered through the living room and she carefully placed her files and keys on the hallway table. It was only then, as she turned, that she saw her husband on his knees, masking tape clasping a cloth into his mouth and the masked man stood beside him with a pistol aimed at his head.

Before she could scream, Amy felt a gloved hand reach from behind and clamp down over her mouth as the other masked man grabbed her tightly before slamming the door shut behind her.

CHAPTER ELEVEN

DI Pearce sat at his desk, the lamp spreading an orange glow across the paperwork. His screen was locked, an image of a classic car filling the page. The rest of the office was cloaked in darkness, the night sky peering in through the window like a nosy neighbour. Across the corridor, the graveyard shift were turning up in dribs and drabs, a few officers arriving together whom Pearce suspected were having an affair.

He scolded himself, constantly piecing together little snippets to come to conclusions he didn't have evidence for. It was almost the reverse of what he had been taught as a detective, but he had something that they couldn't teach: instinct.

It won him few friends, especially within the Met, but Pearce knew his reputation was begrudgingly respected. The man was a dog with a bone, who would dig and dig until he found what he suspected. The results had spoken for themselves, with seventeen cases all closed with guilty verdicts in the last year. Pearce sat, elbows on the desk, his forehead resting in his right hand. The sleeves of his shirt had been pulled up for hours. Small damp patches had begun to form under his arms as his body cried out for a shower and some rest.

The low hum of the floor polisher echoed down the corridor, the janitor trying his best to scrub away the boot marks on the well-worn floor.

Pearce casually tossed the folder closed and leant back in his chair, interlocking his fingers and pushing his arms up. The full stretch did him a world of good, the feeling of a muscle popping out of a knot giving him a small satisfaction.

Something just didn't sit right.

He pushed himself out of the chair and stretched his back once more before sliding his arms into his blazer. He then placed the files into his briefcase—the session notes from Amy Devereux which he had acquired when he had gone to speak to her. He found her very engaging and incredibly professional. She gave him some of her notes on Sam Pope, but after scanning through, there wasn't much beyond what he already knew.

Ex-military. Possibly special forces.

Ex-wife.

Missed his son.

A loner.

Whilst she failed to paint a new picture regarding Pope, he had been fascinated by her comments on Harding. That he seemed completely numb to the notion of grief and at no point did she detect even a modicum of sadness. Which, after speaking with DS Mayer, was the opposite of the tale he was being spun.

He sighed, leaning forward and clicking off the lamp.

Something didn't sit right.

As he headed to the exit, he remembered that it was arriving home on Sunday at eleven that had eventually caused his wife to leave him. He was so tired he felt it all the way through to his bone marrow. As he crossed the tarmac to his car, Pearce hoped that a good night's sleep would help him to steer his investigation in the right direction.

Amy's hand trembled as she gripped the pen. Tears had stained her cheeks, leaving thin, black streaks from her mascara. Sat at the table in their neatly decorated front room, she shook with fear as she felt the gun press against the back of her head.

The masked men had told her that if she made a sound, they would execute her husband in front of her and leave her to take the fall for it. She battled her panic attack and had eventually calmed to the point of being able to breathe properly again, allowing oxygen to fill into her body and let her think clearly.

She begged for his life, which only resulted in the man holding her husband at gunpoint to lash out, striking her husband on the eyebrow with the handle of his pistol. His muffled cries of pain were quickly followed by a steady flow of blood from the blow. She began to cry, telling them she would do whatever they wanted, and soon it became clear. The man who had snared her as she walked through the door demanded that she write an official report to be submitted the following morning, which recounted how PC Harding had spoken at length of his guilt regarding the death of Jake Howell and that she had genuine concerns for his well-being.

She knew what it was.

A cover-up.

Someone had murdered PC Harding, for that she had no doubt. And if they were willing to murder a police officer, what would they do to her?

'Chop-chop, darling,' the brutish man said, pushing the

gun a little harder into the back of her skull. He had a cockney accent, and she could see from his lips and eyelids that he was Caucasian. The man who held her husband's life in his hands had black skin.

Neither of them had given her anything else to identify them.

Whoever had organised this would never have to face the consequences of their actions. But as Amy sat, the pen firmly in her hand, she could feel her heart flipping like an acrobat. If she refused, then Andy would surely die. She probably would too. But what would it do to whoever was behind it all?

'Perhaps you need some persuasion.' The man yanked her by the hair, turning her head so she caught a glimpse of the other man screwing a silencer attachment onto the end of his gun. Andy, hands and feet bound, looked at her for help, his eyes wide with fear. Tears fell down his cheeks and across the duct tape that had been wrapped around his face. As the masked man finished attaching the silencer, he casually aimed the gun at her husband and pulled the trigger.

The bullet ripped through Andy's thigh, exiting out the back and splattering the floor with blood. Andy fell to the side, his anguish held in by the gag as he wept in agony.

Amy instantly screamed and launched out of the chair to his aid, only for a strong hand to clamp onto her shoulder and slam her back into her seat.

'Sit the fuck down.' The masked man spoke with quiet intimidation.

Amy looked to her husband, who was gently rocking on his side, tears streaming down his face as he begged for help. Blood slowly pumped from the wound, a scarlet puddle slowly pooling around him.

He needed medical attention.

And quick.

Suddenly, a measure of calm came over Amy as she turned to the desk, picking up the pen, and started filling in the usual details at the top of the page. Her mind was racing, her heart was breaking for her husband who had just been shot.

The thought of it rocked her and she wobbled slightly, the pen dropping from her hand and clattering off the table.

'For fuck's sake.' The gun was pressed against her head once more and she gasped in terror.

Knock knock.

A shocked silence filled the room at the unexpected *thud* on the front door. Amy turned, the masked man keeping the gun pointed at her as he lifted a finger to her lips.

The message was clear.

She sat silently as he ushered the shooter to the door. The man who had shot her husband obliged, shuffling around Andy's prone body and carefully approaching the peephole.

Knock knock.

The shooter stepped back in shock and then, with an angry scowl, looked again. The next knock was accompanied by a voice.

'Amy. Is everything okay? I thought I heard you scream.'

Amy's mouth fell open in shock as the masked man behind her pushed her with his gun.

'Who the hell is that?'

Amy knew the voice belonged to Sam Pope; she had spent enough sessions with him to know his calm voice. Why he had shown up at her doorstep, she couldn't say, but she was suddenly counting her blessings. Hopefully he would go for help.

Those hopes were soon dashed.

'Deal with him,' the masked man stated coldly, clearly the brains of the operation.

The shooter nodded, pulling his gun up to chest level before quickly pulling the door open. He instantly aimed at the broad chest of Sam, who held his hands up in shocked surrender.

'In. Now.'

The shooter stepped back, keeping the gun firmly on Sam as he stepped in, before closing the door and pressing the gun to the back of his head. Sam shot a glance to Amy, his eyes asking if she was okay. She wiped away a tear and nodded; her terror was clear. Sam followed her gaze to the man on the floor, who he assumed was her husband.

The ever-growing puddle of blood around him told Sam the situation immediately.

Behind Amy, the masked man had a crooked smile, his jagged teeth poking through the balaclava like a rusty zipper.

'Well, well. Looks like you picked a fucking bad night to play the concerned neighbour.'

'I don't know what this is about, but just let them go. We haven't seen your faces and we won't go to the police. But that man needs to go to a hospital.' Sam spoke calmly, both hands still in the air.

'Can you believe this guy?' the masked man asked before chuckling. 'How about you keep your mouth shut, this stupid bitch finishes what we started, and maybe then I'll let you live.'

'Let. Them. Go.' Sam spoke, his words carrying a threat that caused a chill to run down Amy's spine. The man before her wasn't the same broken man who sat on her sofa once a week. This Sam Pope carried himself with purpose, with an air of menace to his every move.

This was the Sam Pope she had read about in the military reports.

The masked man didn't seem as impressed.

'You know what, blow his fucking brains out,' he demanded, and Sam felt the silencer press against the back of his head.

He took one deep breath.

Now.

In an instant, Sam whipped his head to the side, dropping his shoulder and pushing his body weight back. The shooter, caught by surprise, panicked and squeezed the trigger, sending a stray bullet into the mirror across the room, causing the glass to shatter and cascade to the floor. With his shoulder beneath the man's elbow, Sam locked both hands on the shooter's wrist before shooting upwards, his shoulder shoving the man's elbow upwards and shattering his arm. The bone ripped through the skin, with more blood bursting out onto the floor, accompanied by a roar of pain.

It had happened in the blink of an eye and the other masked man panicked, stepping back from Amy and, with a shaking hand, aimed at Sam and fired.

Sam spun the shooter round by his broken, limp arm just in time for the bullet to burrow into his spine. The second one caught him in the right shoulder blade, causing him to fall forward. Sam dove out of the way, falling behind the sofa as another bullet sailed past and hammered into the wall behind him.

The blasts from the non-silenced gun shook the entire room, undoubtedly alerting a terrified neighbour who would already be calling the police.

Amy dove from her chair towards Andy, the loss of blood now leading to a loss of consciousness. In a panic, the masked man yanked her up by the hair, looping an arm around her neck and using her as a layer of protection.

Sam slowly pushed himself onto all fours, reaching

back towards the prone body of the other attacker and wrapping his fingers around the silenced pistol.

'Whoever you are, you're a dead man.' The shakiness of the masked man's voice betrayed his threat. 'You hear me.'

'Just let her go.'

Sam sat with his back pressed against the sofa, ready to move. On the other side of the room, the man held an innocent woman hostage as her husband was slowly dying from blood loss.

This situation need to be concluded.

He waited for the response calmly.

'Fuck you,' the masked man defiantly spat. 'Once I kill you, I might just comfort this poor lady on account of her husband being a dead man.'

That was enough.

Sam spun as he stood, whipping round in a fluid motion that saw him lift both hands up to shoulder height, the fingers expertly gripping the gun in his hand. Without so much as batting an eyelid, he gently squeezed the trigger, the bullet zipping across the room. It shot past Amy and planted squarely between the eyes of her captor, sending a spray of blood and brain matter up the wall behind them.

He slumped to the floor.

Sam slowly lowered the gun.

A moment of silence filled the room, as if mourning the two men who had been killed within it. After a few seconds Amy dropped to her knees, her face paling as she went into shock. Sam quickly engaged the safety on the pistol before tucking it into the inside of his bomber jacket and racing to her. He squatted down, placing both hands on her shoulders.

'Amy, we have to go.'

She stared straight ahead. Seeing her front room turn

into a gunfight was not something she had ever been prepared for.

Sam gently shook her. 'Look at me, Amy.'

She eventually did.

He gave her a smile. 'We need to go. Now.'

'Andy…' she feebly muttered, pointing to her wounded spouse.

'We're taking him too.'

Her eyes vacant, Amy gently nodded and allowed Sam to pull her slowly to her feet. She looked at the bullet holes in the wall, the blood that had stretched across half the room like a shadow, and the dead bodies of the masked men who had held her at gunpoint.

All of it became very real.

She allowed herself to cry, the tears streaming down the mascara stained path left by the previous ones. Sam left her to it, knowing it was part of her acceptance of the situation. He squatted down next to Andy, who was barely awake. The blood loss was taking its toll, draining the colour from his face and pulling him in and out of consciousness. Sam hovered his hand above Andy's face and clicked a few times.

'Andy, buddy. I need to get you up.'

Sam roughly tugged the sleeve of Andy's shirt, tearing the fabric before tightly wrapping it around his leg. The wound was clean and the bullet hadn't seemed to have nicked anything major. It was a crude tourniquet, but it would do for now. Digging into his pocket, he pulled the Swiss Army knife from his keys, flicking open the blade and hacking through the binds around Andy's ankles and wrists.

Amy had snapped back into the room and gently knelt into the puddle of blood, cradling her husband's head lovingly. She kissed him once on the forehead before unwinding the duct tape from around his face, trying her best not to wrench the hairs from his skin.

Andy spat out the balled-up sock and took in a deep breath, his eyes bloodshot.

'What...what...' He couldn't manage anything further before a cocktail of shock and blood loss caused him to drop to his side.

Sam caught him, draping Andy's arm across his shoulders before using all of his strength to stand up. The man was dead weight and Sam gave a small yell of anguish as he pushed up before walking towards the door, which Amy held open.

They had to be quick.

Amy took one last look at the carnage of the evening that would undoubtedly change her life forever. Her husband had been shot and she had nearly been killed.

The room was a warzone.

Luckily, she had the one person with her who flourished in such an environment.

Taking a deep breath to calm her nerves, she closed the door and scurried after her husband and their saviour as the night sky began to echo with the wail of sirens.

CHAPTER TWELVE

It had taken the first car less than four minutes to respond to the scene; the street outside the block of flats was littered with its inhabitants. The fear had stormed through the building like a flood, with each gunshot that echoed from the apartment sending them all scurrying out into the safety of the street.

As with all gun-related calls, the first officers on scene set up a cordon, determining a safe perimeter and securing the area with a roll of heavily labelled police tape. Once the public were taken to a reasonable distance, they monitored the building until the armed response unit arrived.

They were on the scene within three minutes of the police arrival, the van accelerating dangerously close to the building before screeching to a stop, with ten men, heavily armoured, debarking in regimented fashion. Their commanding officer, a burly man named Hyde, bellowed his instructions to his team, who all raced towards the front door in formation, their automatic weapons directed to the floor. The watching civilians lit up the street with their camera phones, the terror of the shooting now replaced with the need to capture the action on social media.

The gunshots had echoed from the third floor, which the response team raced towards, taking the stairs two at a time with the front pair covering the first floor door as the rest carried on. Eventually they made their way to the third-floor corridor, with Hyde giving the gesture to breach. They slid into the walkway with minimal sound, their boots suppressing their steps as they moved with fluidity.

They eventually came to an open door.

Instantly, Hyde could see the pool of blood creeping under the door like an escaping prisoner.

With a flick of his fingers, two of his men burst in, one dropping to his knee and scanning the room through his scope whilst the other swung his gun above, covering the kitchen.

The faint remnants of a curry hung in the air.

Eventually Hyde stepped in, flanked by two more men, their helmets drawn down, their bodies encased in bullet-proof armour. They held their automatic rifles in gloved hands and stepped around the blood, which had now conquered half of the room. They cleared the three other rooms of the apartment before Hyde told his men to stand down. Whilst his second in command radioed outside to confirm no shooters, Hyde began to inspect the two bodies.

Within seconds, he realised what a clusterfuck the night was about to turn into.

DI Pearce felt the same way as soon as he arrived. He had been walking across the station car park to his black Ford Focus when the sudden rush of officers to the panda cars snared his attention. With his ex-wife no longer waiting for him at home, he had slid into the passenger seat and flicked on his radio, tuning into the distressed 999 call regarding the shooting.

It was the address that caught his attention.

It was Amy Devereux's.

His attention to details made him a hell of a detective, especially when it came to interrogating police officers who thought they could outsmart the law, but that gave him little solace as he raced after the police cars, weaving in and out of the spaces their wailing sirens cleared through the London nightlife. When he arrived, Pearce parked further down the street, slowly taking in the scene as crowds of civilians all hung around excitedly, like flies buzzing around an open bin. As he watched the AR team breach the building, he slowly walked up and down the street, failing to find the license plate that matched Amy's.

Thinking about her, Pearce suddenly felt a twinge of guilt in his stomach. They had had a decent conversation regarding Pope and Harding, and he had found her as charming as he had professional. She was good at her job and a respected member of staff.

Now, if the reports coming over the radio were correct, there had been several shots fired in her apartment.

As he stormed back across the street towards her flat, he felt that feeling in his gut once again.

Something didn't sit right.

As he approached the building, he flashed his credentials to the officer guarding the door, who grunted and stepped aside. Pearce was used to it. When you spend your entire career putting away dirty cops, small talk isn't on the menu. He stopped at the bottom of the stairwell, allowing the last couple of armed officers to pass, both of them giving him a curt nod.

Last through the door was Hyde.

'Chief.' Pearce nodded.

'Pearce.' Hyde eyed him in frustration, his fingers eagerly gripping a packet of cigarettes.

Pearce realised then that he was terrified to ask the next question. 'Is Amy Devereux okay?'

Hyde shrugged. 'Don't know who that is.'

'She's the therapist down at HQ.'

'Ah, the shrink. Nice bit of skirt, that.' A seedy grin spread across Hyde's face, revealing his coffee- and tobacco-stained teeth. 'Well, unless she's put on fifty pounds and a beard, then I haven't the foggiest.'

'Excuse me?' Pearce stepped in front of Hyde as he tried to head for the door. A scowl and a sigh greeted him.

'Look, we have two bodies up there. Both male. Both dead.'

'Two men?'

'Yup. One of them looked like he had been through the wringer. Arm shattered, two bullet wounds in his back. The other one, single shot.' He tapped his own forehead, right between the eyes. 'Like a pro.'

Pearce stood, hands on hips, and absorbed the information like a sponge.

'Why the hell are there two dead men in Amy Devereux's apartment?' He shook his head. 'Who the hell killed them?'

Hyde flashed his horrible grin once more before heading towards the door. 'You're the detective, Pearce. Figure it out.'

―――

Sam pulled the steering wheel firmly to the left, the car taking the corner quickly, causing Amy to shunt uncomfortably in the back. She made little complaint, too busy holding her hands firmly on her husband's leg, the blood from the bullet wound turning his jeans an entirely darker shade. Sam had helped Andy Devereux to their car, which Amy had led them to. The Audi was small, enough for a family of two, but Sam was adamant that they squeeze into the back. The struggle from the flat to the car had taken everything from Andy and he almost collapsed on the pavement, but Sam had caught him.

They drove quickly through the busy streets of London, with Sam confidently swerving between two cars and roaring the car into life, shifting through the gears with minimal fuss and hurtling at speed through the bright lights of the city.

The city never slept.

Sam had been amazed when, on a few of his self-assigned missions, he had found people still drinking at four in the morning in the middle of the week. Tourists over-indulging or the rich just enjoying the city when others couldn't afford to. Either way, as Sam sped up towards a sign directing him to Bethnal Green, he clocked how many people were on the streets and shook his head at the state of modern society. The light ahead instantly switched to amber and he slammed his foot down, the car bursting forward and shooting across the junction just as it flickered to red.

'How's he doing?' Sam asked, flicking his eyes to the rear-view.

Amy was watching, her concern in full control of her face. 'He's okay. I think he's still awake.'

'Good. Keep him that way.'

A few moments of silence passed. Amy, gently squeezing her husband's hand, turned her attention to her driver. 'What the hell is going on?'

'I was going to ask you the same thing.'

Sam navigated another corner, turning onto a quiet residential street. The change was startling. Just a few yards from the festival-like streets, the city morphed into a labyrinth of set-back houses, hidden by the branches of trees that lined the roads. A strip of cars lined both sides of the road, each owner undoubtedly charged a fortune by the council just to secure a parking space. As Sam slowed the car, he glanced back into the mirror. Amy was staring at him.

'What were you doing at my flat?'

'Saving your life, by the looks of things.' Sam tried to sound playful. He quickly glanced in the mirror again and saw that Amy had raised both hands to her eyes and was crying.

'Oh my god. We were nearly killed.'

'It's okay. You're safe now.'

'Those men. They had guns.' Amy ignored him; the delayed panic had finally leapt out on her. 'They shot Andy. They had a gun to my head.'

'Amy.'

'They were going to shoot me. They were going to shoot me.'

'Amy!' Sam's voice rose, even causing Andy to stir slightly. She snapped back, her eyes locking on his in the mirror. 'You killed them?' she offered, as if the fragments of the evening's events were slowly being pieced back together.

'I killed one of them. To protect you.'

They drove in silence a little while longer, each road merging into the next like the background of an old school cartoon. After a few more moments, Amy let out a deep sigh. She had wrestled the calm back and looked at her husband lovingly.

'Where are we going?'

'To someone who can help,' Sam said sternly, the car turning to the right.

'Andy needs a hospital.'

'No hospitals.'

'My husband needs to go to a fucking hospital,' Amy barked, leaning forward in anger.

'Amy, listen to me. Whoever those men were, they

weren't there by accident. That didn't look like a break-in to me.'

'They wanted me to forge a report.' She spoke thoughtfully, trying to weave her way through the shock to the memory.

'A report?'

'Yeah. They told me if I didn't forge it, they would kill Andy.' She felt the sadness erupt through her body again and her eyes watered.

'What was the report on?' Sam asked as he slowly pulled the car to a stop on the side of the road. The building they had parked in front of was a small community hall. A notice board was erected just outside the drab whitewashed bricks, a few pieces of paper pinned sloppily and flapping in the calm spring breeze.

'It was to do with Harding.'

'Harding?'

'Yeah.' Amy looked at Sam with confidence. 'They wanted me to write a report to say that I had concerns about his mental well-being. That he was suicidal.'

'And was he?'

Amy shook her head.

Sam let out a deep breath and turned back to the building. The community hall was a dingy building, built many years ago and neglected ever since. A few social clubs used it for meetings of various descriptions, but Sam hadn't taken the time to memorise them.

It wasn't important.

What was important was that the light in the main hall was still on. He pushed open the door and went to step out when Amy reached forward and grabbed his arm, her grip tight and her face full of worry.

'Why were you at my flat?'

Sam ran a hand through his brown hair. 'Because I don't think Harding committed suicide.'

Amy sat back in the chair, the weight of the situation beginning to crush down on top of her. She watched as Sam closed the door behind him and then walked purposefully towards the community centre. She had no idea what was going on or what she was going to do. Her husband was lying next to her, barely conscious and with a bullet wound tunnelled through his leg. Masked men had broken into her house and had threatened her with death. She had looked down the barrel of a gun.

She had come so close to dying.

As she contemplated it all, expecting the fear to take control once more, she realised that she in fact felt safe.

Because of Sam Pope.

She watched as he made his way to the door, rapping a fist on the hard wood and waiting impatiently for the door to open. Eventually it did, and Amy watched with interest as a black man, roughly the same height as Sam, stepped out onto the step, a look of surprise on his face.

Sam Pope shook his best friend's hand before greeting him.

'Theo. I need your help.'

CHAPTER THIRTEEN

The community centre was a small rectangle room with faded floorboards and drab white walls. A few of the walls were covered by notice boards, with A4 fliers promoting local clubs and social events, all scrambling over each other like eager puppies. The roof was stained from years of smoking, and the evidence of some serious leaks caused some of it to sag and bruise. Despite it all, Sam knew that this was a positive place—a place where his friend Theo had turned around the lives of many kids destined for a life on the street.

A life of crime with no way back.

Theo had been approached a few times, as had Sam, by private contracting firms wanting men of their particular skillsets out in the field once more. However, this time they wouldn't be fighting for a flag.

They would be fighting for cold, hard cash.

Wincing at the painful memories that began to tap dance through his mind, his hand instinctively went to his pectoral muscles, a finger pressing through the shirt to the scars. A painful reminder of the bullets that ripped through his body.

Project Hailstorm.

When he allowed that memory to filter from the darkest reaches of his mind, he chortled. He hadn't exactly been fighting for a flag then, either.

'Hold him still.'

Theo's order cut through Sam's train of thought, bringing him back into the dimly lit room. Theo was stood over the table that took pride and place in the centre of the room. As the clock pushed past midnight and into the early stages of Monday morning, Sam wondered who would be sat around it come noon.

Perhaps the local pensioners for a game of bingo? A young mums' club? Right now, the table was occupied by Andy Devereux, his body tense and intermittently jerking, as Theo poured an antibacterial liquid over the bullet wound. They had ripped his other shirt sleeve, rolled it tight, and told him to bite down on it.

As the burning liquid flowed through the corridor that had been ripped through his muscles, he was thankful for that small mercy as he roared in anguish. At the head of the table, gently stroking his dark, neatly cut hair, was his wife. Amy was whispering empty comfort, telling him that he had to be strong.

Sam sighed, feeling the man's pain, having been through the same. However, he had been trained. Conditioned.

Andy Devereux was an accountant. The only thing he was trained for was sorting out the finances for major banking firms. Sensing the agony of the man as Theo began to thread the needle through the skin, Sam reached out his hand and allowed Andy to clamp onto it.

He squeezed until his knuckles turned white and Sam's cracked.

Amy shot Sam a teary, thankful smile.

'Nearly done.'

Sam admired how calm Theo was under pressure. The man had treated bullet wounds and explosion wounds in the heat of battle. Sam himself had covered him whilst he tried to save the life of Private Simon Mulligan, who lost both his legs to a car bomb. Sam remembered firing on two approaching assailants as Theo had tried his best to stop the bleeding.

It had been in vain.

Yet Theo laid down his own life until Mulligan's had ended.

Now here he was, disturbed in the middle of the night by an old friend, a damsel in distress, and her recently shot husband. And without batting an eyelid he had gone straight to work, stopping the bleeding, cleaning the wound, and now patching Andy up.

The patient had calmed down; the few shots of scotch that Theo had made him knock back had done well to numb some of the pain. With his hands, shirt, and jeans covered in blood, Theo flashed a white, reassuring grin as he pulled the final stitch, snipping the thread and then tossing the needle into the rubbish bag which was overflowing with bloodstained towels.

'Good as new. Well, almost.'

Amy thanked him before he nodded to Sam and headed to the bathroom to clean up. Amy stroked her husband's hair lovingly as Sam watched. Without turning to face him, she spoke.

'Thank you.'

'For what?' Sam asked, grabbing the nearby mop and slapping the wet cloth into the blood that had stained the cheap floorboards.

'For saving our lives.'

Sam stopped mopping and turned to face Amy. Her eyes were red, a combination of tiredness and fear that had bled them dry. She offered him a grateful smile. He could see how terrified she was.

All he could offer was a smile back.

'Don't mention it.'

Silence filled the room again. In the rooms beyond, the running water of the taps echoed from the bathroom. Sam slopped some more water, pushing the mop through the blood and trying his best to scrub the evidence of their being there away. Whoever it was that he had stopped back at Amy's, he was sure that they would be back. Different henchmen, but whatever it was they originally wanted, they would now want to tie up the loose ends.

That included him.

Sam placed the mop back into the blood-soaked bucket and slid it to the corner of the room. As he walked back, he could see Amy shaking slightly; the events of the night were replaying in her mind. The gunshot that sliced through her husband's leg. The barrel that was pointed at her. The bullet Sam had placed between her captor's eyes. It was all replaying, causing another wave of shock to course through her.

Sam approached cautiously. 'It's going to be okay, Amy.'

Even he struggled to believe it. She nodded in appreciation and wiped her eyes with the backs of her sleeves, silently cursing herself for her fear.

'Back at my flat. Those things you did. You do that a lot?'

Sam didn't let the question hang for too long. 'What— kill people?'

'Yes.' Amy nodded, a hint of fear in her voice.

'I was trained extensively over a number of years and served this country for over ten of them. In that time, I acquired skills that made me one of the deadliest weapons we had at our disposal. Hand to hand, long distance, extraction, recon… you name it, I've done it. And yes, killing people was just part of the job.'

'How many?'

Amy instantly regretted the question as she saw Sam's face twitch uncomfortably.

'Enough.'

'If more people come after us, will you kill them? Do you feel you need to?'

Sam chuckled, looking up at the ceiling in disbelief. He understood she was grieving and obviously searching for a strain of normality. But she was analysing him, even after he had saved her life. Amy looked at Sam apologetically.

'No, I don't need to.' Sam dipped a hand into his pocket and pulled out his mobile phone. 'I need to make a call.'

———

DS Mayer popped the two paracetamol onto his desk and then reached for the glass of water. Knocking them back, he placed the glass back down before massaging his temples in frustration.

What the hell was going on?

Two men had been found dead in the flat of Amy Devereux, the neighbours calling as soon as they heard the blast of the gun thunder through the building. Upon arrival, the officers had found no sign of Amy or her husband, yet two masked men, described by his officers as intruders, had been gunned down. Annoyingly, DI Pearce had found his way onto the scene and had pitched in with his own opinion that someone had come to their aid.

The CCTV of the hallway confirmed everything. It showed the two masked men knocking on the door, surprising Andrew Devereux with a sharp blow to the head before storming into the flat. It showed Amy returning home, her arms wrapped around a number of folders. Then the most surprising part of the video.

Sam Pope.

When it was first reported to him, by DI Pearce of all people, he didn't believe it. The quiet loner from the archive room. Mayer was aware of a military background, but Pope wouldn't have been the first or last member of staff to have served.

What the hell had he been doing there?

Even more worrying was a few minutes later, the door opened and Pope ventured into the hallway with Andy Devereux's arm slung over his shoulder as the man woozily hobbled alongside. His entire trouser leg was a thick red and they were closely followed by a panicked-looking Amy Devereux.

Then they were gone.

Now, sat at his desk with his head in hands, he ran his palm across his balding skull. With Inspector Howell signed off through compassionate leave, Mayer knew this was his chance to make a play for the role, to lead the Metropolitan Police with distinction and slip seamlessly into a more senior role.

But how could this have happened?

It was such a mess.

Two men dead. Amy and her husband missing, possibly kidnapped.

Sam Pope apparently killing two men.

With a deep sigh, he turned towards the phone on his desk, reaching out with his meaty hand, when suddenly it burst into a shrill ring. Slightly caught off guard, Mayer snatched the receiver and pulled it to his ear.

'Mayer.'

'Sir.' Mayer recognised the voice. 'It's Sam Pope.'

Mayer sat up straight, his hand slamming against the table. Whatever was happening, the biggest piece of the puzzle may have just dropped into his lap. He knew the pressure would be building for him to get a handle on things, and now having Pope call him was the first piece of good news he had had all evening.

'Pope.' He tried to maintain his calm. 'Are you okay? What happened?'

'Sir, Amy Devereux was under attack. Two men had her and her husband at gunpoint in her flat. I intervened and now I need your help. Her husband has been shot.'

'Jesus,' Mayer muttered. 'What were you doing there?'

'I'll tell you everything, sir. But right now I'm not sure it's safe for us to go to a hospital. The men who attacked Amy, they were professionals.'

'And you killed them?'

'I had to, sir. To save Amy and her husband.' Sam spoke with complete conviction. If he was apologetic for his actions, Mayer detected nothing.

'Where are Amy and her husband now?'

'I have a friend of mine who has treated the wound, but like I said. I need your help.'

'Of course. Is Mrs Devereux okay?'

'A bit shaken. Scared for her husband. But she is unharmed.'

Mayer sat forward on his chair, carefully picking his words, knowing he would be able to extinguish this fire earlier than anticipated. 'Yes, it must be quite a shocking evening for her. But of course we can help.'

'Thank you, sir.'

'Where are you? I'll have an unmarked car come and collect you all swiftly.'

'We are currently at Bethnal Green Community Centre.'

Mayer balled his fist in celebration. 'I'll dispatch to you immediately. They'll be with you in a few minutes.' Mayer keyed in the location to his mobile phone before sending it to an unassigned number. 'You just keep them both safe. You've done a hell of a job, Pope. We'll find out why the hell those men wanted Mrs Devereux to forge that report on Harding and we will ensure her husband is safely delivered to a hospital. You have my word.'

Mayer stood up, a smug expression filtering across his face as he looked out the window at the dark, cool evening that had engulfed the city.

The entire situation had been calmed.

'Sir?' Pope spoke, his voice cold and calculating.

'What is it?'

'I never told you that they were trying to forge a report.'

The silence sat uncomfortably between them, with Mayer's fist once again balling, this time with frustration. He could feel his unkempt nails digging into his palm. He turned from the window, took a quick glance at the corridor to ensure he was alone, and lowered his voice.

'Look, Pope. Just don't do anything rash, okay? We can sort this out and...'

The line went dead.

Furiously, he slammed the receiver down, cursing himself for letting it slip. What was becoming clear was that Sam Pope was not who Mayer had thought he was and could potentially become a problem. His fears were soon quelled when he glanced at the response on his phone.

'Two minutes.'

Mayer sighed, knowing that the men he was sending round would make sure Pope was silenced and that Mrs Devereux would cooperate. It was getting messier than he had promised, but he would ensure that the job was done.

With a newfound sense of calm, Mayer closed the door to his office and picked up his phone, his hand nervously shaking as he found the contact number for Frank 'the Gent' Jackson and clicked call.

CHAPTER FOURTEEN

It always rained back then.

When Frank Jackson was ten years old, he used to sit by the window of his bedroom and stare at the downpour. From the thirteenth floor of the council estate, which shot up through Canning Town's skyline like a jagged grey tooth, he could see the poverty-stricken streets below. Bags of rubbish lined the streets like ghastly bushes. An ever-changing roster of homeless people lay in shop doorways or rummaging in the alleyways, all of them willing to do whatever for their next fix.

The world ignored them all, allowing those below the breadline to do as they pleased as long as they never tried to climb out.

Frank knew his family were poor.

Their flat was a modest two-bedroom cell in a building designed to keep the 'have-nots' locked away. His dad had never had much of an education, working tirelessly from one underpaid job to the next, doing his level best to put food on the table. His mother, despite her honest upbringing, demanded the finer things in life, conducting herself with an etiquette that the Canning Estate had never known before.

She expected them to say their 'pleases' and 'thank yous', to wear their Sunday best every week, and to speak in full sentences.

When your entire world was enveloped by cockney rhyming slang, it was difficult. Frank himself had received many a clip round the ear for dropping a well-known phrase at the dinner table.

Manners didn't cost a penny.

Back then, with money as tight as it was, he wondered if maybe his mother was so strict on the manners for that very reason.

After six years working as a street sweep, his dad finally got a job bouncing at a local bar. Not the biggest man, but pretty nifty with his fists, his dad took to the job well. Pretty soon the money improved along with his hours, and it was only then that Frank's mum realised he wasn't bouncing anymore.

He was pushing.

Working the doors at certain nightclubs that were owned by the a few local gangsters, Frank's dad provided drugs to those wanting more than just a drink.

In the bleak, depressing times of the 1970s, many wanted to disappear for a night. To lose themselves in a binge that would pull them from any type of sensible thought.

It was all going so well, and after two years they finally left the high-rise, the dark corridors and the depressing life that those below the line were forced to toe.

They moved to a small two-bedroom house on a neighbouring street, with enough of a garden for his mum to grow flowers with exotic names and to show them off in beautiful displays on the table.

The money continued to flow.

Eventually he welcomed a sister into the world, who—sadly —would not see beyond six months due to health complications.

Her name was Annabelle.

His dad took it hardest, working longer hours and coming home a wreck, dishevelled and wiry, his eyes darkened and his mouth dry. Even as a kid, Frank could tell that his dad was using the drugs he was supposed to be selling.

It led to arguments.

To violence.

His dad struck his mum one evening when she questioned him regarding their rent money. She told him he was a waste of space and that Annabelle had been lucky she died, so she wouldn't have to live in a world with him as her dad.

That night, after what witnesses described as a careless drug binge, Frank's father committed suicide by hurling himself off the Hammersmith flyover.

The fall had broken his spine, and the twenty-tonne lorry that he fell in front of had done the rest. There had hardly been any of him left to cremate.

After that, it was just Frank and his mother.

She tried to make ends meet, but after so many years of demanding to be a kept lady, she couldn't find enough work to cover the bills. The poverty began to spill back into the house like an overflowing bathtub, and soon they were spending their winter evenings huddled together under as many blankets as possible, the house falling below zero but with no way of heating it.

Eventually his mum found a new man. At first it was the same man for a few times, but then more men began to frequent the house. His mother seemed to have more money too, and with it she brought him a brand new Walkman, to the envy of his friends. Her only demand was that when her gentleman friends came to call, he would go to his room and listen to his tapes until they left.

She didn't want him to hear.

One day, he came downstairs after a night of listening to his new Bon Jovi tape to find his mum sat at the table, a cigarette in her hand and a thick purple bruise swelling around her right eye.

Her lips were split and bleeding too.

She told him she had walked into the door.

At thirteen years old, he knew better. The kids at school all snickered behind his back about his mother being a whore. About how if he needed money for lunch, they could pay for it by getting his mum to blow them.

He ignored them. He allowed himself to be swept away with his music.

But he knew the truth. His mother had done what she had had to to make ends meet. To put food in his stomach and a roof over his *head. He would forever love her and knew that when he grew up and made something of himself, he would pay her back.*

He would never get that chance.

The beatings became semi-regular, usually occurring when a man named Malcolm Breaker visited. One evening he put her in hospital with a broken arm and three broken ribs.

Throughout it all, as the world of drugs and prostitution began to slither into their world like a shadow, his mum retained that same etiquette.

They never used rhyming slang. They always dressed their best.

Manners didn't cost a penny.

Frank had been brought up to say his 'pleases' and 'thank yous'.

He never got to thank his mum for doing the best she could, as a few days after she was discharged from hospital, Malcolm Breaker beat her to death.

Frank had found her the next morning. She had been punched repeatedly, and by the blood dripping from the nearby lamp and the deep, jagged dent in her skull, had been bludgeoned to death.

Thirteen years old and orphaned.

As he called for the police and ambulance, he held his mum's body and wept, knowing that he was about to be swept away into the system with little to no chance of escaping.

He promised her he would make something of himself.

He promised he would never forget what she had taught him.

He thanked her one last time.

Manners didn't cost a penny.

————

Sat in an expensive leather chair with his legs tucked under the broad mahogany desk, Frank Jackson shook his head with disappointment as he hung up the phone. DS Mayer had promised him that everything would be in hand, that he would be the man for the job.

He had failed.

What should have been a slam dunk was now turning into a car crash of errors. It was meant to be a simple explosion they could pin on ISIS, and the world would thank them for their efforts in protecting the UK.

Now he had a dead policeman, another one they had had to silence, and now a rogue office worker killing two of his men.

Such disappointment.

With a deep sigh, Frank lifted himself from his chair and walked across his well-lit office. His expensive leather shoes clicked across the wood panels as he reached across and buttoned the top button of his blazer. The tailor-made suit was worth over a thousand pounds and fit nicely around his long, toned frame. At just over six foot three, he knew he was imposing, if a little on the light side. Now, rapidly approaching his half century, he knew that his days of being 'the muscle' had long since passed. They had passed six years previously, when he took control of the sordid nightlife of London.

He didn't control the drugs and women who passed through his building. They were part of the wider network.

He provided the safe haven. The place where the law was forbidden. His rapid expansion led to the hostile takeover of three large buildings, all of them gutted and turned into his luxury offerings.

The High-Rises.

Frank knew he had pushed it as far as he could, but with the hierarchy existing within the criminal underworld, there was only so far he could go unchecked. He knew that, but he also knew there would come a time where money wasn't the prize anymore.

It would be power.

His office sat on the top floor of the High-Rise, one of the four penthouse suites he offered to the higher-paying customer. It still had the familiar layout of the others, but the four-post bed was replaced with a thick desk. Frank walked through the door and took the lift down to the lobby area, where a few gentleman sat on the sofas. One of them was reading a book. The other was engrossed in his phone, pointlessly trying to line up confectionery for points.

Frank Jackson shook his head, that feeling of disappointment refusing to leave.

To the left was the large desk, where a couple of attractive women would usually greet guests. Where the two men were stationed was the waiting area—a couple of comfortable leather sofas, and a glass table littered with magazines and financial material about the local companies' seemingly booming business.

To the right was a taller table with a few stools dotted around it. One of them was occupied by Mark Connor.

He was the one who was known as 'Grant Mitchell'.

Frank had always found their Mitchell Brothers nickname pointless, but it carried weight with it. He had witnessed first-hand Mark and Brian's loyalty to him, the number of kneecaps that had been shattered or fingers removed due to disrespect.

Frank was under no illusion. He was feared because of his power. The Mitchell Brothers were feared because of their violence. Mark pushed himself off the stool; the fluorescent lights above bounced off his shiny bald head and his massive frame bathed the floor in a mighty shadow.

'Evening, sir,' he offered, his thick cockney accent bursting from behind his jagged teeth.

'Mark.' He approached confidently. 'Is he here?'

'Of course. Shall we?'

'Let's.'

Mark told the two other thugs to stay where they were and then led his boss towards the stairwell. He held the door open for his boss, an act of chivalry which was much appreciated, and then he followed through. Frank let him go first as they headed down the brightly lit staircase towards the basement, the white walls displaying the usual fire safety signs most buildings demanded.

Frank was adamant it all had to look legitimate.

He watched his burly companion, appreciating the smart appearance. He didn't command that they wear suits in his presence, but they all knew he appreciated it. He thought about their loyalty once more and smiled, knowing that once this whole issue with the Marathon was wrapped up, he would ensure they were treated to a night in the High-Rise with no expense spared.

It worked for everyone else. It was how he kept most of the city in his pocket.

'Mark. I just heard from Mayer.'

'What does that wanker want?' Mark instantly held up an apologetic hand. He knew Frank would let him get away with the odd curse word.

'To apologise and reassure me that everything is in hand.'

'Is it?' Mark asked with a smirk as they reached two levels below the ground and he held a large metal door open for his boss.

Frank stopped at the threshold. The room before them was shrouded in darkness.

'What do you think?' Frank asked.

'I think Mayer couldn't organise a piss-up in a brewery. But we should be able to clear up his mess pretty easily. Brian is already watching the police station.'

'Do we know who this man is? This Pope chap?'

'Not much. Mayer says he's ex-army gone doo-lally. But from what Brian has seen on the CCTV, the man isn't playing around.'

'We've seen the CCTV?' Frank asked, readjusting his cufflinks. He always looked immaculate.

'Yup. Brian's headed over to the police station now. Mayer is going to get him a pass and whatnot, set him up with some access so we can help with the manhunt.'

'It's hardly a manhunt,' Frank dismissed and then turned his attention to the dark room. 'Just don't let it get out of hand. Right, shall we?'

Mark entered the darkness and switched on the lights. Four long beams burst into light in succession, each one buzzing enthusiastically. The walls were a bright white, with see-through plastic sheets taped up, covering every inch. To the right was a small trolley; atop it a number of sharp, perfectly arranged tools as well as a few power tools which were plugged into an extension cable and raring to go.

Hanging from the middle of the ceiling, completely nude but for the masking tape that kept him quiet, was Nathaniel Burridge, a local cocaine dealer who had decided to step on Frank's toes and put one of his pushers in hospital with a broken nose.

He had stolen over thirteen thousand pounds' worth of cocaine, as well as four grand in cash.

Frank could see from the gash across the man's terrified face, the bruising which was beginning to show on his dark skin, and the missing index finger, that Mark had already had a warmup.

Right on cue, Mark wheeled a plastic chair towards the naked man, whose stomach was wet with urine.

Nathaniel was terrified.

Frank walked with extra purpose, exaggerating his grandeur as he took the seat beside the man, draping one leg over the other and regarding him with a polite smile.

The man responded with a muffled cry for mercy and tears streaming from his face.

'Nathaniel. What you did was very silly. Now, I am going to give you one chance to apologise to me. Otherwise my good friend Mark is going to take you apart, starting with your testicles. Do you understand?'

The man, with his bloodshot eyes wide, nodded frantically, the blood sitting heavy in his skull.

'Mark, I don't bluff, do I?'

'Absolutely not, guv.'

'Take off his gag.'

Mark leant forward with meaty, scarred fingers and ripped the masking tape from Nathaniel's face, tearing the stubble clean from his jaw.

'Mr Jackson, I'm so fucking sorry. I swear, I'll never do it again. Just please don't kill me.'

Mark stepped forward, and with a force that made Frank wince, he rattled Nathaniel's body with a hard right hook before spitting an intimidating warning.

'Language.'

Nathaniel rocked from the punch, trying his best to catch his breath.

Frank regarded him once more. The street hoodlum was possibly part of a street gang—one which believed in bright clothing and post code division. Frank found it all rather pathetic, wondering why, if they wanted to 'run the streets', they didn't pool their resources and find a way to work together.

'Thank you, Nathaniel. I accept your apology. However, Mark is going to cut you to pieces now and send it back to your little gang so they know to stay the fuck off my streets.'

'No, please, I beg you, bruv, please don't…'

'Apologies.' Frank held up a hand. 'Please excuse my French. Mark, kill him.'

'Yes, guv. My pleasure.'

Nathaniel screamed once more for help, as Mark ran his hand suggestively over the torture trolley before lifting a set of stainless steel pliers. He snipped them a couple of times, allowing Nathaniel to see what his near future held. As Mark slid his arms into a plastic apron, Frank headed towards the exit. He turned back one final time, at the twitching, naked body and the butcher ready to maim it.

'Once you have finished here, find that Pope chap. And kill him.'

Mark gave the thumbs-up before turning back to Nathaniel and reaching for his genitals.

Frank headed back up the stairs with the bloodcurdling screams echoing around him like a choir.

CHAPTER FIFTEEN

'Fuck.'

Theo and Amy both looked up as Sam marched back into the room, sliding his phone into his back pocket. His muscular arms stretched the sleeves of his T-shirt, the vein running down the centre like a river. Andy was unconscious; the emergency surgery, despite draining his energy, had been a success. Amy sat vigil next to her husband, holding his hand lovingly. Her eyes were sore, the tears long since dried up and replaced by a harsh redness.

Theo stood, a fresh T-shirt replacing the bloodstains from earlier.

'Sam, what is it?'

'That fucker Mayer.'

'What's going on?' Theo asked bluntly, causing Amy to turn.

'This was an inside job. The Detective Sergeant, acting in charge, he set this whole thing up.' Sam picked up his black bomber jacket and slid his arms into the sleeves.

'Wait, what?' Theo held his arms up in confusion.

'I don't know how or why, but I just called in what happened and Mayer knew about the men in Amy's flat, the men that were going to kill her—he knew what they were after.'

Amy watched the conversation in shock.

'And he knows where we are and I don't think he's sending people here to give me a medal.'

Theo ran a hand over his head, exhaling deeply as he tried to process the information.

Amy joined them. 'You think Mayer did this?'

'He did. Harding. Howell. The bombing. Something didn't add up.' Sam patted his jacket and jeans down until he found Amy's car keys.

'But why?'

'Look, right now, we need to move.' Sam turned to Theo. 'Theo, I need you to take these two and get them somewhere safe until I get back.'

Theo nodded in agreement, the look of reluctance etched across his war-weary face. 'You got it, Sam.'

He extended his hand and Sam took it, drawing his old war buddy in for a quick hug. The danger of their situation buzzed around them like a beehive. Sam clapped his friend on the shoulder before turning to Amy.

'Wake up Andy and help Theo get him somewhere safe.'

Sam picked up the gun he had taken from Amy's flat, cocking back the chamber to check the live round. He then slipped the cartridge from the handle, the bronze bullets neatly stacked atop each other.

Amy, amidst the panic, reached out and grabbed his forearm, fear in her eyes. 'Where are you going?'

Sam slammed the cartridge back, the metal clunking loudly with completion. 'I'm going to buy us some time.'

Stuffing the gun into the waistband of his jeans, Sam marched across the wood floor before hauling open the door and leaving. Amy watched in silence, shaking slightly as the fear gripped her and treated her like a child's rattle.

Theo gently reached out a calming hand and rested it on her shoulder. 'Amy, we need to go.'

They turned and headed to her husband.

———

Outside, the warm evening greeted Sam eagerly. A gentle breeze danced through the street, sliding through Sam's hair and tickling his scalp. He marched to the Audi, silently thanking Amy for her indulgence in the unnecessary sports model. The TT Roadster Sport was equipped with an even beefier engine, and as Sam opened the door he looked forward to testing it. Suddenly two figures approached him.

'Hold it there.'

Sam stopped, slowly closing the door as the two police officers approached. One of them he recognised as Murphy, an overweight Irish lout who knew more about racially abusing kids than he did about reading someone their rights. The other man, also in uniform, Sam had never seen before. He was tall, with the build of a fighter. His skin was a deep caramel colour and his hair was shaved to the scalp. The man extended his hand out with caution.

'Easy does it,' Murphy joined in, his hand nervously twitching to his hip, which was covered by his jacket.

Sam's eyes flicked back to the other man, whose hand was creeping to the base of his back.

Both men were armed.

'Where is she?' the mystery man demanded, taking another step closer.

'Who?' Sam asked, slowly closing the door to the car. In the distance, he could hear the wail of sirens. Suddenly it was all clicking into the place. These two were here to clean up the mess.

The sirens in the distance would be there to clean up theirs.

'Don't be a fool,' Murphy spat, his thick Irish drawl almost as heavy as the gut that hung over his belt buckle. 'The woman. What's-her-face? Where is she?'

'Oh, are you here about my call?' Sam asked, his eyes not leaving the nameless man, who was expertly taking a few steps to his left, increasing the distance between the two officers.

'That's right, son.' Murphy spoke with ill-judged confidence. He looked at the apparent hitman and smirked. 'We're here to help.'

'Funny.' Sam shrugged. 'How come you didn't come in a police car?'

As the two men turned to cast an eye on their vehicle, the penny dropped. Murphy cursed loudly as they turned back, the hired gun's arm whipping to the base of his spine, his fingers sliding around the base of the gun like a hungry snake.

A bullet cut through the cool evening air and shattered his shin.

The man went down straight away, screaming in agony, as Pope turned the gun towards Murphy, a small trail of smoke rising from the end of the silencer. Murphy, in a blind panic, struggled to unhook the gun from his waistband, wrenching at the handle and causing his rotund stomach to jiggle.

'Leave it,' Sam commanded, the gun pointed squarely at the police officer's forehead.

Murphy obliged instantly, the cocky attitude replaced by paralysing fear. On the ground, the man grasped his destroyed patella in anguish, blood pumping through the shattered bone and pooling around him. He began to drag himself across the pavement in desperation, his gloved hand reaching for the Glock 19 that had fallen to the ground.

Sam marched forward before planting a skull-shaking kick to the man's jaw.

The man rolled over motionless.

Keeping the gun pointed at the terrified officer, Sam reached down and picked up the rogue pistol, admiring the matte black finish. The gun was weighty, fully loaded with the standard 15-round cartridge. He slid the gun into band of his jeans and approached Murphy, who held up both hands in surrender.

'Come on now,' Murphy tried to bargain, sweat oozing down his pasty, balding skull. 'This isn't your fight. So why fight it?'

Sam stopped a few steps from the man, his body odour clinging onto the wind. Sam shook his head. 'Because someone has to.'

With that, Sam lifted the gun and brought the base of the handle crashing down into Murphy's temple. The man was unconscious before he hit the pavement, just as three police cars and a van—which Sam assumed was an armed response unit—burst around the corner, their tyres squealing as they straightened up. Sam raced to the TT once more, throwing open the door and jumping in.

Moments later the engine roared to life, the lights illuminated the street ahead, and Sam slammed his foot down, the car lunging forward into the street. He spun the wheel, leaving his own skid marks on the pavement as he shot down the street.

One of the police cars turned off to the entrance of the Community Centre to check on the two motionless bodies on the ground and to search the premises. Sam knew that Theo would have the Devereuxs far from there already.

They had been trained to always have their escape

route ready, to be prepared for every outcome, and when that training helped you through a series of life-or-death situations, it becomes more than just lessons learnt.

It becomes memory.

Glaring into the wing mirror at the flashing lights chasing him, Sam realised he was ignoring his training. There was no plan. As he spun the car down another residential street, he pressed his foot down, the car roaring like a wild animal as it burst forward, topping seventy within seconds. A few pedestrians watched with excitement as he raced past, followed by two panda cars and a truck. Within minutes he turned onto the A12, the road wriggling through the Queen Elizabeth Olympic Park like a concrete worm. The greenery surrounded the mighty London Stadium, home of West Ham Football Club. Originally erected for the Olympics in 2012, the stadium had controversially been rented to the Premier League club much to the dismay of the UK taxpayer. Despite the calmness of the evening and no fixture, the stadium was brightly lit, commanding everyone's attention.

Sam sped on, the car turning through the park and then hammering through Stratford. Behind him, the blue lights flicked on and off. They sped past Epping Forest, with Sam deep in the knowledge that Amy and her husband were safe and that he was now likely to be one of the most wanted men in London.

As he approached the turnoff for the M11, Sam shot through a red light, narrowly avoiding a lorry, who blasted a loud foghorn through the air with anger.

One of the police cars swerved, careening off the side of the road into the nearby shrubbery. The car and van stayed right behind, following closely as he rounded the roundabout, heading for the exit to the motorway. Taking a deep breath, Sam suddenly jerked the wheel to the left, lifted the handbrake, and allowed the car to take the corner with a loud shriek of burning rubber on pavement. Narrowly missing an oncoming Mercedes, Sam straightened up and floored the car down the descending road, shocking the passers-by as he sped onto the opposite side of the motorway.

Directly into oncoming traffic.

With the clock pushing past eleven o'clock, the Sunday night traffic was minimal, but Sam carefully manoeuvred between three oncoming cars, each one blasting their horn and watching with astonishment as he shot past at over a hundred miles an hour. He flicked his eyes to the rear-view mirror, noticing that the other police car had joined him in the pursuit but the van was no longer following.

He knew the radio waves would be going crazy and it wouldn't be long until the motorway was closed off and he would be greeted by a barrier of flashing blue lights and loaded weapons.

As the police car struggled to keep pace with him, he dodged between two cars, missing them both by a fraction before gunning the engine once more, the impressive machine roaring proudly as it guzzled fuel. As he rounded the corner he spun the wheel again, diverting off the motorway and onto the slipway, narrowly avoiding a car that was merging on at speed. As he dashed past, he heard the screeching of tyres and the air-piercing shrill of a car horn as the police car weaved around the car, which clipped it slightly, causing it to spin out.

The police car spun frantically before colliding with the metal barrier, the sirens whimpering to silence. The officer would be okay, but would have a serious case of whiplash.

Unperturbed, Sam raced onto the roundabout, flicking the handbrake expertly once more to slide back into the right direction before bringing the car to a quick stop under a tunnel. He flicked the hazard lights on to warn any oncoming traffic before exiting the car quickly. The tunnel was half a mile long, leading back in towards London via Woodford. The shrieking call of the sirens echoed loudly throughout the dark passageway as more police cars were approaching.

With a quick pace, Sam exited the car and out the other end of the tunnel, heading towards Woodford Station.

By the time he got to the station, the night sky was silent, the police unable to locate him and undoubtedly blocking off the tunnel and going through everything with a fine-tooth comb.

The streets had been empty the entire brisk walk to the station, with everyone tucked up in bed, ready for the start of the working week. Sam knew he wouldn't be able to go back to what he had called his 'normal' life—not now that DS Mayer and whatever was going on knew about him. Whatever was happening, Sam had a feeling it was big. It sat in his well-toned gut like a heavy meal and his mind raced back to when he last had that feeling.

Project Hailstorm.

That ended with two bullet holes in his back and a golden handshake.

This time, he was going to find out what the hell was going on and keep Amy and her husband safe.

With both pistols tucked into the back of his jeans, Sam calmly paid for a train ticket and waited the few minutes for the next train back into city centre, where he knew he was now their most wanted man.

CHAPTER SIXTEEN

DS Mayer sat at his desk, his head resting in his hands.

It had just passed eight in the morning, and he watched from Inspectors Howell's office window as the morning shift were arriving, full of excitement at the rumours that were inevitably fluttering around the office like pesky wasps. In Howell's grief he had vacated the office, allowing Mayer to firmly stake his claim to power. Mayer was the one calling the shots, and had it all gone smoothly, he would have been looking at a swift climb up the ladder.

Frank 'the Gent' had more than his fair share of police officers bought and paid for. His High-Rises were an urban myth, an Atlantis that most cops dared not dream of wanting. A slice of the other side, a haven to go and be or do whatever you wanted. Drugs. Women. Men.

But it came at a price.

A lifetime membership to the High-Rise also included a lifetime membership in the Gent's back pocket.

Mayer had sampled it. Once. It had been over six months before, when Mark Connor, aka Grant Mitchell, had propositioned him. They needed a potential witness to be intimidated and Mayer was only too happy to oblige.

His reward? A penthouse suite, five grams of cocaine, and three very accommodating Eastern European women.

It had been the greatest night of his life.

Now, with the Gent's expansion project resting on Mayer's plan, he knew he couldn't let this draw out.

The bomb had killed Jake Howell, which was only one of the birds that the stone was intended for.

The other two were still breathing, which meant the longer that went on, the likelihood was that Mayer wouldn't be.

Frank Jackson was a gentleman.

But he didn't accept failure.

Harding was an unfortunate piece of collateral damage, but Mayer felt little remorse. The man was a buffoon, who Mayer knew was on the take anyway. Mayer himself had had to quash a complaint from a young couple about Harding harassing them on a stop-and-search, patting down the female in a questionable way. The Metropolitan Police was a better place without him.

The Mitchell Brothers had seen to that, sending him over the edge of the car park to a twenty-foot concrete collision that had turned his skull to paste.

That should have been it. All they needed was the report from Amy Devereux, who would have been threatened to silence. Civilians are easy to control when you shove a gun in their face.

Even more so when it was shoved in the face of a loved one.

Now the forged report was sitting in an evidence bag along with a fired weapon and several bullet casings. The well-maintained flat that Amy Devereux shared with her husband was now a crime scene, closed off to the world by a zigzag of police tape and a watchful police car. Two bodies were in the morgue—one with a shattered arm and two gunshot wounds (one which ripped through his lung), and the other with a deliberate bullet placed squarely between the eyes. Brian, aka 'Phil Mitchell', would be arriving at some point during the day under the guise of a temporary Archive Administrator, to keep an eye on things and, Mayer assumed, him. What should have been his grand welcoming to the High-Rise was now a complete clusterfuck.

And what angered Mayer the most as he sat in his superior's chair, was that he knew why.

Samuel Pope.

Mayer's knuckles whitened at the thought of the man who had ruined everything. For years he had dismissed the man as a nonentity, a former soldier who had struggled to adapt on returning home from all he knew, pushed his family away, and ended up in a job that kept him hidden from the real world.

Never late. Never spoke. Never a problem.

Sam Pope. Nobody saw him coming.

The mystery that was sweeping through the Metropolitan Police office was just who he was, with his army records pulled apart, a fine-tooth comb looking for anything and everything. But Mayer knew almost instantly when he saw the mediocre records that the British Army kept on him.

They were only half the story.

Medals. Confirmed kills. Tours in Afghanistan and Iraq.

It felt like breadcrumbs to Mayer. There were also years of service not accounted for.

Which told Mayer that Pope was involved in teams that are not even on a 'need-to-know' basis. Which meant the man was a lot more dangerous than anyone suspected. Whilst every available officer was scouring every available source for information, only a few tidbits filtered through that Mayer assumed were true.

Over sixty confirmed kills.

Highly trained in covert and recon.

Expert in hand-to-hand combat.

Trained to survive.

Mayer leant forward in his chair and massaged his temples, the grey just dusting the tips of his thinning hair. He felt older than his forty-three years, and his body wasn't the powerful fighting machine it had been in his heyday.

He needed to fix this.

He needed to find Sam Pope.

A knock on the door snapped him back to reality, his bloodshot eyes landing on the young, petite officer in the doorway. He was so tired he couldn't even remember her name.

'Yes?' he demanded curtly.

'Sir, we are all waiting for you?' The young officer nodded to the briefing room, humming with activity like a sold-out cinema.

Mayer quickly turned his wrist over to glance at his expensive watch.

Ten past nine.

He pushed himself out of the chair, his joints creaking with fatigue as he cursed himself for wasting an entire hour worrying about how to fix a situation he was allowing to spiral out of control.

The young officer speedily walked back to briefing room, undoubtedly to find her seat missing. Mayer composed himself, straightening his tie and quickly checking his body odour.

He knew he needed some sleep and a shower.

But some things were slightly more important. With the very real threat of one of London's most dangerous criminals losing patience with him, as well as a highly decorated war veteran seemingly intent on getting in the way, Mayer marched towards the briefing room, hoping that the full fury of the Metropolitan Police would be able to save him. As he approached the door, he stumbled back as DI Pearce stepped round the corner, catching him off guard.

'Jesus, Adrian.' He scowled. 'You scared the shit out of me.'

'Sorry about that.' Pearce peered through the blinds at the rows of eager officers. 'Big crowd.'

'Well, we have something big going on. You know, real police work.'

Mayer went to step by but Pearce stepped into his path, the corners of his lips threatening to break into a smile. Mayer's eyes bulged with fury at the intrusion.

'That's funny—"Real police work." Almost insinuating that what I do isn't similar to yours.'

'It's not,' Mayer said bluntly, folding his meaty arms so the forearms squashed against each other.

'See, I disagree. Because in that room there, you have forty or so officers chomping at the bit to find out just what the hell is going on.' Pearce stepped close, reducing his voice to a slight whisper. 'So am I.'

'Well, you're welcome to join us,' Mayer retorted smugly.

'Hmm, I think I'll give it a miss. I'm more interested in looking in the right direction.'

Mayer chuckled, stepping forward so he was a few inches from Pearce's face. A few of the officers in the room had turned, watching the confrontation with silent excitement.

'Listen to me, Pearce. You might have a few people higher up who think your shit don't stink, but this is now my team. And as far as I'm concerned, I have two police officers dead within the last week, a terrorist attack, and now an ex-soldier has attacked his therapist and taken her and her husband hostage. So you're either here to help or you can get the fuck out of my way.'

Pearce raised an eyebrow, showing no signs of intimidation at all. Having worked in the Metropolitan Police for nearly thirty years, he had come across a lot worse than Mayer. 'You think Pope has abducted her?'

'Absolutely.' Mayer nodded to emphasise the point.

'See, I saw the footage. Two masked guys break in, Amy returns home. Sam Pope then arrives. Then we receive three phone calls reporting gunshots and then we see Sam Pope helping a clearly injured Andy Devereux from the flat, followed by Amy. I actually responded to the call and we found the two masked men dead. Two hours later, Sam Pope is seen in Bethnal Green before embarking on a car chase through London before going dark.' Pearce stepped in even closer, the bristles on his grey beard close to tickling Mayer's own unshaven face. 'Tell me, at what point are we actually going to investigate this properly?'

'Fuck you,' Mayer muttered. 'You're a snake, Pearce. You try to finger good, honest men who give their lives for this badge. Whilst real police officers are out on the streets, giving their lives like Howell did, you're in here sniping at those who are trying to help this fucking country. All so you can keep your goddamn numbers up.'

'Is that right?' Pearce said, maintaining his calm.

'Yeah, it is. So instead of coming in here and scrutinising what we are doing, why don't you try and help us? Either that or get the fuck out of my way.'

Pearce let the tension strain just a few seconds longer before holding up his hands in surrender and slowly stepping to the side. Mayer sent him a victorious sneer before stepping to the door. Pearce shot out his hand and placed it around Mayer's solid bicep, stopping him. Pearce leant in.

'The officer found at Bethnal Green Community Centre, Officer Alex Murphy, was off duty when the call came in. Yet he, and the blood of an unidentified man, were found out the front of the community centre.' Pearce felt Mayer's muscles tighten. 'Do you think that *that* is worth investigating?'

Mayer turned, his eyes boring a hole through Pearce. 'I think you need to let go of my arm, Pearce.'

Pearce leant in closer. 'I think, until you are actually the inspector and not just playing dress-up, you should refer to me as 'sir'.'

Mayer shrugged Pearce's grip and pushed past him into the briefing room. All eyes were on their confrontation and Pearce was suddenly in the gaze of over forty people who either disliked or distrusted him.

But it was that nagging feeling once more.

That horrible, gnawing sensation at the bottom of his stomach.

Mistakes were being made; he just couldn't see them yet. That was always how it happened. Someone thought they could get away with it, bend the law that they had vowed to uphold to their own needs but then forgot one minor detail. That was how he was looking at it. An officer was killed in an explosion that everyone was too quick to label as terrorism. Another officer, mandated to see a therapist, apparently committed suicide—and then a day later an attempt was made on the life of said therapist.

The wild card was Pope.

The fascinating man who Pearce had originally come to look into was now his most valuable lead. Pope was highly skilled and highly trained and had seemingly slipped under the radar. But not to him. Pearce was sure that Pope was the person exacting a vigilante justice on those that beat the system. He just couldn't prove it yet. As much as he wanted to, he knew that what was happening was far bigger than an ex-soldier gone rogue.

Pope was the key.

The man had visited Mrs Devereux at just the right moment, and judging by the expertly executed men, he had saved her life. Had he stumbled upon something himself? The man's past was littered with redacted files, with allusions to dangerous, off-the-books missions and a wayward family life.

He needed to find Pope, and was certain that when he did, he would start piecing things together. As he approached his office, the inner pocket of his blazer violently shook and he reached in and pulled out his mobile phone.

Unknown number.

Pearce sighed, closed the door, and clicked the green button.

'Pearce,' he stated bluntly, rubbing the bridge of his nose. He instantly perked up.

'Sir, it's Sam Pope. We need to talk.'

CHAPTER SEVENTEEN

Sam stood on the patio that separated Theo's house from the neatly trimmed grass of his garden. The high fences, clean and well painted, lined a long rectangle garden that was lined with freshly dug flower beds. The spring season had encouraged a plethora of colour to burst from the soil, with neat arrangements of flowers standing proudly in their designated rows. Sam knew Theo had taken to gardening as a means to relax after he left the military, a way to keep his mind active and away from the harrowing memories.

Sam had his own harrowing memories.

Memories that had brought him to this moment.

As the call connected, his eyes scanned the morning sky —another clear sky as Britain threatened an unlikely heat-wave. His eyes were heavy, the lack of sleep hanging from his eyelids like weights.

The ringing stopped, replaced by a gruff voice.

'Pearce.'

'Sir, it's Sam Pope. We need to talk.'

Sam could feel the urgency in Pearce's voice as he told him to hold on before the muffled noise of someone eagerly making their way to seclusion filtered through. Eventually he returned to the receiver.

'Pope. What the hell is going on? Is Mrs Devereux okay?'

'She is fine. So is her husband.' Sam glanced back over his shoulder to the house. Andy had finally fallen asleep after Theo's charitable painkilling concoction. Amy had allowed the worry to nurse her to sleep.

'Where are you?' Pearce spoke, his tone low but his words full of purpose.

'I can't tell you that. Not right now.' Sam knew that Pearce would likely track his phone. 'I need your help.'

'Sam, do you know how much trouble you are in? There is a briefing going on right now, led by Mayer, where you are the main event. The line here is, is that you are an ex-soldier who finally reached the end of his rope and has assaulted and kidnapped your therapist and her family.'

Sam shook his head. 'That's a nice story.' He smirked. 'Did Mayer come up with it?'

'Let me help you. Tell me what is going on?'

'I don't know. All I can tell you, Pearce, is that something is happening and it's from your end. Mayer knew what those men were doing at Amy's flat, and then moments after I told him where I was, an unmarked car turned up with one of our own and a guy with a gun.' Sam shook his head, disgusted by it all. 'So whatever the hell it is I've stumbled on, Mayer acted pretty quickly to try and cover it up.'

Sam waited patiently as he let the information play through Pearce's head. The man may have been annoying and antagonistic when he had interviewed him, but Sam knew the man was smart. Eventually Pearce responded, and Sam could hear the strain in his voice.

'That's a hell of an accusation, Pope.'

'It's not an accusation, sir.'

Silence.

'Before we take this any further, I need you to be completely honest with me.' Pearce spoke with a sense of urgency. 'What were you doing at Mrs Devereux's flat? And what happened?'

Sam cast another glance back to the house, knowing the innocent couple were sleeping soundly. Had he not been there, they may well have been taking a permanent nap.

'I saw the news regarding Officer Harding and I didn't believe it. It felt too convenient that he was racked with guilt, especially as the guy didn't have a grieving bone in his body. I saw him leaving a session with Amy, so I wanted to speak to her about it.'

'But why? Pearce probed. 'What does it matter to you?'

'Look, sir. I know what you think of me and what you suspect me of doing. And you know what, when this is all said and done, we can have another discussion.' Sam could feel his grip tightening on the phone. 'But right now, I'm not what's important here.'

Sam could picture Pearce on the other end of the phone, the world-weary eyes holding up a furrowed brow, the wrinkles that cracked at the edges.

'Okay, Pope. You are not the focus. For now.'

'Thank you, sir.'

'So what happened at Mrs Devereux's?'

'I knocked on the door and had a gun shoved in my face. They led me in. Another man, who I assume was in charge, had a gun pointed to the back of Amy's head. Her husband was on the floor, bleeding out. They were both terrified.'

'And you weren't?' Pearce's tone was almost accusing.

'Sir, I have spent the last twenty years of my life in combat, so having some amateur point a gun at me is like a child with a water pistol. Eventually the guy in charge made a threat to Amy, so I acted.'

'You killed them?'

'I did what I had to do.' Sam had never spoken with such conviction. As he said the words, knowing that he had ended another life, just another notch on his legendary tally of pinpoint deaths, he felt his heart ache.

He had broken his promise to his son.

He felt a tremor of guilt shudder through him like a sudden chill. Reading the books, something Sam had never done, had been surprisingly enjoyable. He had promised Jamie he would read through the long list of classics. Some of them had been a hard slog, but he had made a promise to his son that he would read more.

The other promise, to never kill again, Sam was sure he would keep.

He had failed.

'Sam?'

Pearce's voice echoed in his ear and brought him back into focus.

'Sorry.'

'So why did you run? Why not go to a hospital?'

'Sir, I am trained to disappear and to survive. If someone had broken into their house, with a motive based on confidential police information, I made a snap decision that putting them on show in a hospital may not be the smartest move. They are fine. Andy has had some treatment, but he needs to see a proper doctor. I need you to arrange that.'

'Okay, I will see what I can do.'

'Thank you.' Sam waited a few moments, allowing the awkward tension to sit. 'Sir, do you believe me?'

'I don't know. What you are saying is a hell of an accusation to make.' Pearce sounded like he was struggling to process it all. 'However, I think you may be onto something. I can feel it in my gut. Something isn't right. I confronted Mayer before you called, about the unmarked car, and he brushed it off. He brushed everything about Harding and Howell off, swept it under the rug for everyone to forget about. You are the focus now.'

'I'm touched.' Sam smiled.

'Well don't be. I'd say in about five minutes' time, you're going to have a whole fucking division hunting for you.'

'Wish them luck for me.'

'This isn't a game, son.'

'No it's not.' Sam felt the cooling breeze slither around him. The fatigue of the night before was beckoning him. 'Right now, all I know is that Mayer has gone through some extreme lengths to make it seem like Harding was grieving over Howell.'

'But why?' Pearce wondered out loud, and Pope could almost hear the cogs of his brain clicking over the phone. Suddenly, Sam's revelation sliced through the intense silence.

'Howell.'

'I beg your pardon?'

'Think about it: whilst the world has been spun a story of another terrorist attack, where is the evidence that there even was one?'

'That's a bit of a stretch.'

'Really? Who is in charge of the Counterterrorism Squad?'

'Mayer.' Pearce's lightbulb pinged.

'Mayer,' Sam confirmed, nodding to himself. 'Sir, I think Howell was targeted and I think Mayer is now covering this up. First he tried to show the city under attack and paint the boy out as a hero. Then stage Harding's suicide to scare the country into fighting terrorism.'

'Make everyone look left as you move right,' Pearce

agreed, his desperate sigh confirming his agreement. 'But why? Howell was a good kid.'

'Maybe to get at Inspector Howell?' Sam offered, looking back to the house. Theo was stood by the kitchen window holding two mugs of tea. He lifted one to Sam, beckoning him inside, and Sam held up his hand in thanks. 'He's running things in his absence, right?'

'But that wouldn't be permanent. Inspector Howell is distraught with grief, but he will come back, all guns blazing, to find out what happened to his nephew.'

'And he'll be spun the same story as the rest of the world.'

'Maybe Howell found out something he shouldn't.' Pearce said, a hint of excitement as he found a potential thread to pull. 'Maybe he stumbled across something that Mayer needed kept quiet.'

'Perhaps. We should pull the files of the last case he was working before Sunday. See what he was up to.'

Pearce cursed under his breath. 'All the files were archived after his funeral. Apparently Inspector Howell wanted them frozen until he returned so he could honour his nephew by finishing his work for him. He treated that boy like a son.' Pearce took a respectful moment. 'Can you imagine what it would be like to lose someone that close to you?'

Sam took a deep breath, the agony of missing his son intensified by Howell's loss. He wanted to pick up the phone, hit the speed dial, and hear Jamie's voice.

Explain to him that he had broken his promise. But that he had to.

He wanted to tell him how much he missed him and how much he loved him and his mother.

But he couldn't.

'Pope?'

'I'm here.' He took another deep breath, putting his

training into use. Sam had been trained to control his breathing and relax under heavy fire, or when a high-risk target was looking into his scope from over a mile away.

He knew how to stay calm. How to stay in control.

Pearce drew him back to their theory. 'Whatever Howell was working on, I can't access them. I don't have clearance for the archive room.'

'I do.'

Pearce laughed off the suggestion.

'Wait, you're serious?'

'We need to see those case files.'

'You're insane. You're currently prime suspect *numero uno*. You can't just walk in here like another day at work.'

'No. But you could.'

'What?' Pearce hushed his voice.

'Walk me in as your prisoner. Slap the cuffs on, drag me to an interview room, and then let me loose. I'll need five minutes, max.'

'This is insane.'

'No disrespect, sir, but we don't really have much else.'

Pearce let out an exasperated sigh.

A few birds zipped across the sun-filled sky, the cool morning bringing to light the immaculate state of Theo's garden. Sam stared at the spot that he had helped Theo re-lay.

'I guess you're right,' Pearce reluctantly agreed. 'But say I did bring you in and you did get out—what the hell are you going to do if Mayer finds out? You'll have the world and its mother after you then'

Sam smiled. 'I'll do what I always do. Survive.'

Pearce gave Sam a time and a place to meet later that evening, warning him not to go home. Although Sam already knew Mayer would have had his flat turned inside out, he thanked Pearce for the heads-up, doing his best to try and gain his trust. Despite the fact that he wanted to expose Sam for his after work activities, Sam liked Pearce. The man was not only a great detective, but he actually had a moral compass. In a world where the justice system was treated like a game of chicken by two overpaid lawyers, it was a relief to see someone willing to fight the good fight.

Pearce was loathed by the majority of the police. Because the majority of them had something to hide.

Sam was under no illusion that he would be exposed by Pearce eventually, but for now, he was the only option for getting to bottom of just what the hell was going on.

The patio door slid open and Theo ambled up beside him, passing a now-lukewarm tea into his hand.

'Morning.'

Sam smiled back, sipping his tea and looking over the garden. In the house behind the two ex-soldiers, innocence slept.

Innocence that Sam was breaking his promise for.

Theo finished his tea with a satisfied sigh and then motioned to the plot of land Sam had been looking at. 'Need me to get my shovel?'

'No. Not yet.' Sam turned to his friend and patted him on the shoulder. 'Hopefully not at all.'

He began to head back into the house, his body dragging him towards the sofa and the promise of a few hours of rest. Just as he reached the door, Theo called after him.

'Just be careful, Sam. There are somethings you can't come back from.'

Sam offered him a tired smile before heading inside. As he hit the sofa and felt himself begin to drift into unconsciousness, he realised that this time he was unlikely to come back at all.

CHAPTER EIGHTEEN

The gun chamber pressed against the back of her head and Amy felt a sudden burst of heat, accompanied with a loud *bang* as everything went black.

Amy sat bolt upright in bed, sweat clinging to her body. She took sharp, quick breaths as the sheer terror of the nightmare resonated in the back of her mind like an echo.

She knew she was suffering from post-traumatic stress disorder, a common outcome of a particularly haunting experience. Many soldiers suffered from it on return to the 'real world', finding that the horrors always clung to the corners of their minds like a deep shadow.

She was treating Sam Pope for the very same thing—although his PTSD wasn't a side effect of war.

Swinging her legs over the side of the bed, she took a moment to collect her thoughts, the terror and panic of the night landing in different parts, like waves crashing on a beach.

She was in Theo Walker's house, a medic who had served with Sam. The spare room was modest and painted in a basic white. The bed, of moderate comfort, was pressed against the wall, with a cheap wooden wardrobe opposite. Next to her, Andy's breath calmly filtered from beneath the covers. With concern on her face, she lifted the covers to check the bandages that were strapped around his leg, the faintest hint of blood seeping through.

Theo had stopped the bleeding and saved Andy's leg. For that, they would be eternally grateful.

But Sam Pope had saved both their lives.

A tear built in the corner of her eye and then gently glided down her cheek as she remembered how close she had been to death. The dream was a painful reminder. A gun was rested against her skull. She had been a finger-pull away from redecorating her flat with her brain. Then she recalled the brain matter that had splattered her walls as Sam had sent a bullet shooting through the forehead of her captor.

The blood. The brain. The bits of skull.

The death.

The contents of Amy's stomach suddenly launched upwards and she shot out of bed, her bare feet hammering the wooden floor as she scarpered to the bathroom, dropped to her knees, and unloaded into the toilet. An entire night's worth of fear and disgust shot from her body in an odorous waterfall of vomit. After a few moments she fell back onto her bottom and rested against the cold tiles behind her.

Her throat burnt.

Her head pounded.

Her entire life had been turned upside down.

And for what?

'Rough night, huh?'

Amy jumped slightly as she turned, only composing herself when she recognised the warm smile of Theo greeting her from the doorway. He held up an apologetic hand and then reached forward with his other, his fingers clutching a glass of cold water.

'You could say that,' Amy responded dryly, gratefully accepting the drink and sipping it, the liquid soothing the fire in her throat. She took another deep breath before tipping her head back till it tapped the tiling.

'I'm going to check on Andy.' Theo stepped across the landing and poked his head into the room.

Andy was still sleeping, the sheet beside him drenched in sweat.

Theo returned to the bathroom, where Amy sheepishly smiled. Her face was pale and she pulled down the shirt to cover her bare legs.

'There are some tracksuit bottoms in the wardrobe in your room. Grab yourself some and come downstairs. I'm about to cook some breakfast. You must be starved.'

Amy hadn't realised just how empty her stomach was until he mentioned food and it growled in acceptance. She shot him an embarrassed grin and he headed back to the stairs. She took his advice, and moments later she reached the bottom of the stairs, her hand clutching the banister for balance. In the sheer panic of the night before, she hadn't noticed the cleanliness of the house. She imagined Theo was as regimented as Sam, taught in an army base to have the beds made and the shoes shiny.

A small oak table sat proudly in the hallway, with medals and photos adorning it—a shrine to a career that Theo was obviously proud of. As she scanned them, she found herself smiling at a photo of Theo and Sam stood together. A military helicopter loomed behind them, the dust of the sand sweeping around them. The photo must have been a decade old, but the friendship was genuine, the two of them with their bare arms around each other's shoulders, their dog tags twinkling around their necks.

'That was from our first tour.' Again, Amy jumped as Theo silently entered the hallway. 'Sorry, I didn't mean to startle you.'

'It's okay. I'm just a little on edge, I guess.'

Theo responded with a smile and handed her a porcelain mug; the steam drifting from the top told her the coffee was freshly made.

'Understandable,' Theo mused. 'I guess it's not every day you see that kind of thing.'

Amy followed Theo back into the back room of the house, which was surprisingly big. The large, open-plan kitchen was a classy mixture of grey wood and black marble top. In the centre a breakfast counter stood, with plates of buttered toast waiting. The room opened onto a small dining room which had a weights bench and treadmill.

Regimented, Amy thought.

Theo turned to the stove. The smell of eggs and the familiar sound of crackling was most welcome to Amy as she took her seat. As Theo began to dish the eggs up onto the plate in front of her, she scanned the room, a look of worry on her face.

'Sam's fine.' Theo read the signs. 'He's asleep in the front room.'

'I don't know how I will ever thank him. And you.'

'You don't have to.' Theo wolfed down some eggs before continuing. 'I spent my life saving lives and healing battle wounds. Usually it's soldiers, but hey, beggars can't be choosers, right?'

Amy cracked a smile and tasted the eggs. With her body craving food, they tasted sublime. She shovelled two more bites in before turning to Theo.

'You're not like Sam.' She motioned with her fork. 'You're not as cold.'

'Sam isn't cold.'

'Apologies,' Amy corrected. 'What I mean is, he is kind of a closed book. You're welcoming, talkative and—'

'Normal?' Theo interrupted.

'Well, yeah.'

'Believe me, we all bring stuff back with us. The things you have to do out there, the things you see, they change you. To your marrow. Those memories, you can box them away or talk them through, but sometimes when you're alone, you have to confront them. I've done as much as I can to get through, but I still see the flashes of gunfire, the bullet-ridden bodies. Hell, I panicked so much when I came back, I built a safety bunker under this kitchen.'

'Really?' Amy raised her eyebrows.

'Maybe,' Theo playfully offered before the smile faded. 'But Sam, he was beyond anything we had ever seen. The Taliban even named him 'Silent Death'. Then he got the call, moved on up, went dark, and then came home two years later with bullet holes in his chest.'

'Project Hailstorm?' Amy asked cheekily, knowing the stern look she received put an end to that line of questioning. 'He is in pain though, isn't he?'

'Look, like I said, we all have things we are dealing with. You're his therapist, so you know his situation.' Theo glanced to the doorway, ensuring they were alone before lowering his voice. 'When we were out there, surrounded by desert and death, the only thing that got him through was coming back to Lucy and Jamie. So not seeing them every day, it's broken him more than any war could.'

Theo finished off his coffee and pushed himself from his seat. Amy stared at her empty plate, impressed that her appetite hadn't deserted her. Her mind, however, was analysing the sheer pain that Sam Pope must have been going through.

The one thing that got him through over ten years of service.

Gone.

Her finger instinctively rubbed her wedding ring and she felt more thankful than ever for Sam's arrival the night before, saving her and her husband's life.

The man may have been broken.

But he was a hero.

She turned to Theo. 'Well, it's my job to help him through it.'

Theo offered her a forced smile. 'There are some people you can't piece back together.'

As Theo turned the tap on, allowing water to wash over the dirty breakfast plates, Amy finished her coffee before warmly smiling at a man she had just met, but whom she trusted completely. She broke the silence.

'You don't really have a bunker under this kitchen do you?'

Theo turned, a smirk on his face, and stamped his foot once, the echo off the panel flooring giving little away.

———

Later that evening, the spring sky had cracked slightly, allowing a sprinkling of rain to accompany the bright moonlit sky. Pearce slowly pulled his Focus into the Metropolitan Police car park, slipping it between two panda cars. With a shake of the head, he turned to the backseat and locked eyes with Sam Pope.

'Are you sure about this? Because if you are right, then walking into that building is a very bad idea.'

Sam offered a confident smile.

'We need those files,' Sam reiterated. 'Unless you want to go looking for a needle in a haystack, this is our best shot.'

Through gritted teeth, Pearce agreed. He flashed a glance to the entrance to the building, the famous emblem slowly turning on its display pole. That badge stood for justice and enforcing the law. Pearce had spent his entire career living those morals, chasing down the officers who bent those laws to their own whim. The sheer thought that two of their own had been murdered filled him with rage and underlined the need to seek the truth.

'A heads-up—as soon as they see that I have you, word will reach Mayer,' Pearce warned. 'And I don't have any idea just how desperate this situation has gotten.'

Sam shrugged his shoulders. 'Let's go.'

Pearce pushed open the door and slid out before pulling open the rear door. Sam stepped out, his muscular arms pinned to his sides, his hands fastened behind his back in a pair of metal cuffs. They had to make it look like an arrest, and Sam willingly shuffled in front of Pearce, who allowed himself a few rough shoves to keep up the façade. A few officers passed them on the steps on the way in, both of their faces filling with awe as the man they had been told to hunt was being brought in by the detective most of them despised.

Sam instantly felt the severity of the situation. All eyes locked onto him as he was led through the office, into the interview room nearest the archive office. The expressions lurched from shock to confusion, and even a few glances held more sinister intentions. The volume of the office rose, everyone excitedly discussing Pearce's arrest, whilst undoubtedly a few secretive phone calls were made to Mayer. For a man who was trained to scout and scope out the locations of his mission, Sam felt unprepared beyond getting into the archive room and going from there.

He had no clue as to how much time he had, or where the viable threats came from.

All he had was his work pass and his faith in Pearce who, less than a week previous, had been looking for a way to bring him down.

The chances that they were entering shit creek were increasing with every step into the building. And by the look on Pearce's face, he knew they didn't have a paddle.

Eventually, they stepped out of the office and into the brightly lit corridor, with Pearce, keeping up the illusion, shoving Sam in the direction of the door. Sam glanced over his shoulder, only for Pearce to flash a quick grin.

Despite the fact that Sam was sure Pearce wanted to see him behind bars, Sam was starting to like him. A man who had dedicated his life to ensuring the police did their job was worthy of his respect.

And at this moment, handcuffed and walking into the lion's den, he was certainly worthy of his trust.

Sam saw the familiar sign for the archive office as they stopped out the front of the interview room. The sign said it was vacant, and just as Pearce reached for the handle, a burly officer stepped towards the door.

'Evening, sir.' The Officer was Darshan Khambay, a large Indian man with a portly stomach and thick beard. Younger than he looked, his dark eyes locked onto Sam. 'Sarge is looking for this guy.'

'I am aware.' Pearce noticed a few other officers loitering behind Officer Khambay, like a high school gang. 'I will let him know when I am done with him.'

Officer Khambay took another step forward, his eyes never leaving Sam. 'Sarge has made it clear how important he is—'

'And as his superior, I will let him know when he can have access to him. So remember your rank, Officer.'

Sam watched on, impressed, as Pearce took a step closer to Khambay, who held up his hands in apology.

'Yes, sir,' he spat. He trudged off, followed by the other officers, and Pearce stood, hands on hips, until they had disappeared back into the office.

'Impressive.' Sam smirked.

'Yeah, well, like I said. We haven't got long.' Pearce pushed open the door and ushered Sam inside. He slammed it shut and turned the lock. 'Apparently they have hired a temp to cover you in the office, so you shouldn't have any problems. Now, hit me.'

'Excuse me?' Sam said, shocked.

The interview room was similar to the very one they had shared the previous week—except this time the tension was outside the room. Pearce leant forward and unlocked the cuffs. He then tipped over one of the chairs.

'I need it to look like you overpowered me,' Pearce said, shoving the table at an angle, knocking over the other chair in the process. 'Trained soldier versus a man in his fifties. Piece of cake.'

'I'm not hitting you,' Sam stated, rubbing his wrists after their freedom.

'We don't have time to discuss this. Just hit—'

Sam swung a right, catching Pearce directly on the cheekbone. Although not his most powerful strike, he landed the punch cleanly and spun Pearce around, who splayed out onto the table. The shock and pain sent him dizzy, and Sam uttered an apology as he slipped out the door and into the corridor, not hearing the slew of curse words that Pearce sent his way.

Eager to not attract tension, Sam hurried back down the corridor, past the door to the office, and followed the sign towards the archive room. Luckily, the screen for the counter had been pulled closed and there were no agitated officers harrying a panicked temp. Knowing the police wouldn't have had the foresight to shut down his access, Sam swiped his ID badge, the light pinged green, and he slipped inside. As he entered, he sent a quick glance to the admin office; the temp was shuffling around, oblivious to his intrusion. Sam quietly stepped into the rows of boxes and folders and set out to find Howell's last case.

Little did he know that in the admin office, Brian Stack was watching him on the CCTV monitor. With a fiendish grin and an order to kill, 'Phil Mitchell' removed a knife from his coat pocket, switched off the security cameras, and set off into the labyrinth to find his target.

CHAPTER NINETEEN

Sergeant Mayer adjusted himself in the leather seat, taking deep, concentrated breaths. A bead of sweat began to dribble down the back of his neck. He knew he had taken a risk coming here, but now, as he sat opposite Frank Jackson on the top floor of one of his infamous High-Rises, he wished he hadn't. When Mark Connor had arrived at the Costa coffee shop to meet him, he had felt the tension. The usual manners, which Frank was well known for, had been replaced with curt orders.

Mayer had lost control of the situation.

Sitting in front of one of the most notorious gangsters in London, he began to wonder if he had ever had it to begin with.

'Relax, Colin,' Frank demanded, sitting with one leg draped over the other, a glass of expensive scotch in his hand. 'You look nervous.'

'Sorry.'

'You told me this was all under control.' He took a slow, measured sip. 'It is right?'

Mayer nodded, clearing his throat anxiously and feeling every bit the worm on the hook. His mind flashed back to the night he had spent in the High-Rise, his face covered in cocaine as the two women went to town on him.

It was pleasure beyond pleasure.

He had wanted more and he had promised it would all be taken care of. The original targets. Howell.

All wrapped in a bow.

Now, the very real scenario of everything caving in was getting ever closer. Earlier that morning, after a sleepless night, he had sent the whole of the Metropolitan Police on a manhunt.

Samuel Pope.

'Tell me, Colin,' Frank mused through a smile. 'What do you plan to do, should your people find this Pope chap?'

'My men are the best in the country, sir.'

'Ah, yes. The thin blue line. It actually is very commendable and, believe it or not, I do believe in the law. I believe in the work you do, keeping the people safe.' Frank placed his glass firmly on the oak desk between the two of them, his eyes resting on the TV screen mounted on the wall. 'However, so far, your operation hasn't filled me with confidence.'

Frank nodded to the screen, diverting Mayer's attention. A news reel was running, the day's events scrolling across the bottom as a heavily made-up women spoke. Though the volume was muted, Mayer knew what she was presenting.

Video footage of Amy's flat was shown, with scene of crime officers patrolling the area. The headline read

"Double Murder in London".

Frank tutted before clicking the screen off with the control.

'I assure you, this will be fixed. We'll find him, and when we do, we'll bring him to you.'

'Because you need me to handle it for you?' Frank raised an eyebrow.

'No, not at all,' Mayer stammered. 'I just thought, well, with all the problems he has caused, you would—'

'First off, he hasn't caused any problems for me. Those problems are your problems—because you assured me that this would all be taken care of. That I would get what I wanted and have those people who stood in my way removed. Now that hasn't happened, because of *your* problem. Which means you are becoming *my* problem. And I already have people who handle those for me.' Frank leant forward, his forearms resting on the desk. 'And secondly, if you ever interrupt me again I'll take your tongue out of your mouth.'

Mayer apologised nervously before startling as the door swung open. The guard watching the room, a broad man in a black suit and a concealed firearm, went to stand, but refrained as Mark Connor marched in. The expensive lightbulbs reflected from his shiny bald head as he strode towards the two men.

'Sir.' He nodded to Frank, ignoring Mayer. 'Grant Mitchell's' disdain for the police was well known. 'Your guy came through. We have a name.'

Mayer searched Frank's face with confusion. 'Oh do we?'

'Yep.' He checked his phone. 'Theo Walker. He works at Bethnal Green Community Centre with underprivileged kids.'

'Well, he sounds like an upstanding gentleman.' Frank smiled, sipping his scotch. Mayer was stunned by how much danger emanated from him.

'He is. He also served his country as a medic. Guess who he was stationed with?' Mark leant down toward Mayer with a smug look. 'It's amazing what you can do with a little detective work, eh?'

Mayer sat still, refusing to make eye contact and regretting every decision he had made to that point.

Connor smirked again, pushing himself up and turning to his boss.

'Go. See what he knows,' Frank ordered. 'Reasonable force if necessary.'

'Of course.' Mark threw a thumb in Mayer's direction. 'Should I take useless with me—show him how it's done?'

Mayer turned back to Frank in a panic.

Frank sat back in his chair, patting a wrinkle from his immaculate waistcoat. The blazer hung from the door of the office, a designer suit that cost half of Mayer's wage.

'No. Leave him here.' He stared him dead in the eye. 'I want him here in case this doesn't get sorted.'

'Fair enough, guv.'

'Guv?' Frank asked in disgust.

'Sorry, sir,' Mark offered politely before turning and stomping back across the office and into the hallway.

Mayer finally relaxed, realising his entire body had been tensed. Mark and Brian had a reputation for their extreme brutality. Loyal as two guard dogs, but there were whispers of Frank having to step in when they got too out of hand.

Especially Mark.

Mayer didn't even want to think about the potential future. Should they not catch Pope and remove Devereux from the equation, he knew Frank would give the order.

Mark would likely kill him. Painfully.

Suddenly his phone buzzed, and he flicked open the message. For the first time in nearly two weeks, he felt a degree of positivity.

It was Officer Khambay.

Sam Pope had been brought in. Excitedly, he told Frank that they had him. When Frank demanded more, Mayer relayed the question. Khambay explained that Pearce had locked Pope in an interview room, but he had just seen Pope leave and head to the archive room. Before

Mayer could try and wrest control of the situation once more, Frank ended their communication. He then called Brian Stack, who was in the very office that Sam was headed to. As Mayer sat, emasculated and praying for it all to be over, he felt his heart jump with panic at the order that followed. Without a hint of remorse in his voice, Frank 'the Gent' Jackson said two terrifying words.

'Kill him.'

———

Under the glare of the halogen lights, Sam quickly ran his finger across the document separators, each one tagged to a set of boxes pertaining to certain cases. Before all of this had started, and after his family had left him, this had been his life. Countless hours spent in these darkened corridors, lined by dusty shelves packed to the brim with old boxes. Inside was a myriad of paperwork, all of them pertaining to different cases, all diligently filed away by himself.

The quiet of the archive room was what had attracted him to the job. After what had happened all those years ago, when he lost his drive to serve the country once more, he welcomed the solitude of the darkness. No one else had access to the room, and the walkways between the shelves were so narrow he could only just stand straight.

It was the loneliest place in the station.

As his hand began to run along the tags marked *H*, he heard a shuffle behind him.

Instantly he turned, fists clenched and his defence up.

The temp shuffled by, holding up an apologetic hand as he pushed the metal cart, the wheels squeaking under the weight of the two boxes. The temp was middle-aged, stocky, and bald. He looked more like an ex-convict than an administrator, but Sam had seen worse. Harding was hardly a saint. He scolded himself for thinking ill of the dead, a state that his previous job had made him accustomed to.

He found the box.

Eagerly lifting it from the shelf to the floor, Sam squatted down and began to rummage through. The files had all been labelled and he found the manila folder that had all the case notes for Howell's final case.

Sam snatched the paper from the folder and stuffed it into his jacket pocket, hoping it would hold a clue.

At that second he realised he had seen the temp before —driving the four-by-four that Chris Morton had left the court in a few weeks previously.

He heard the footstep behind him just in time.

Brian reached around Sam's head, his gloved hand eagerly grasping a jagged blade with the intent to slice his throat. Sam managed to raise his arm just in time, wedging it between the vicious weapon and his throat. The rough, coarse metal sliced into his forearm and the burly man applied as much pressure as he could, intent to push Sam to the floor and murder him in cold blood.

Sam's fists clenched.

Survive.

With all his might, Sam launched backwards, dropping the attacker onto his back and driving the air out of both of them. With a hard shunt of his arm, Brian loosened his grip from his throat and Sam sprang forward, the blade wildly slashing behind him and running across his calf.

It split the skin, a roar of pain shooting to his brain, but Sam instantly shut it down. Brian got to his feet, blood dripping from the blade and a murderous glee shimmering in his eyes.

Sam faced him, and in that moment the silence sat between them in the narrow confines of the archive.

They stared at each other, silently agreeing that this was to the death.

Brian lunged forward, slicing the air with the blade as Sam took a few steps back, the pressure causing more blood to pump from his calf. Brian took one step too far and lunged too close, allowing Sam to turn in and throw a forearm up to block the attempted stab before rocking him with a hard right to the ribs. Brian stepped back before swiping once more for the throat. Sam dodged, ducking under and nailing another few hits before kicking out and catching Brian on the shin. Brian stumbled, the knife flailing wildly through the confined space, and Sam grabbed his wrist, trying to snap it and disarm him. Brian, considerably heavier, threw himself into the shelving unit, crushing Sam against the metal.

Sam refused to let go, digging his thumbs into the pressure points and relenting as the knife clattered to the ground. Brian responded by head-butting him, crashing his forehead into Sam's jaw before slamming his head off of the shelving unit. Sam fell backwards and Brian swung a vicious right. Sam, gathering his thoughts, threw up an elbow, catching Brian in the centre of the forearm. His arm jolted back and Sam followed with two left jabs before catching his attacker with a hard hook. The skin above Brian's eye split, blood trickling down like war paint.

The bald gangster yelled in anger before hauling a box of files from the shelving unit and hurling it at Sam. Despite Sam deflecting the heavy box with his shoulder, it still knocked him off balance, the next box catching him hard in the chest.

He stumbled back, the air driven from his lungs before Brian charged, slamming his shoulder into Sam's midriff and lifting him from the ground. A few more steps and Brian dropped him onto the hard tiled floor below.

The air shot from Sam's body.

His vision blurred as his skull cracked against the floor.

As his brain rattled in his skull, Sam knew he had to get

up, turning onto his front and hauling himself towards the end of the aisle. Behind him, he heard the blade scrape against the floor as his attacker retrieved it. The footsteps echoed behind him as he pulled himself up, turning just in time for the knife to be driven into his shoulder.

Sam shot both arms up to hold off the attack, the bald attacker pressing forward with both hands and his entire body weight. The blade split the jacket and his skin, the top inch slicing through his muscle and into his shoulder as the two men stumbled backwards.

Sam let out a groan of pain and they stumbled back through the shelving units and into the small admin area, slamming into an old metal filing cabinet. Sam felt the strength in his shoulder giving out as the blade slowly burrowed into his body.

His eyes dashed around his surrounding area, looking at anything he could use.

He needed to get free.

With a roar of pain and adrenaline, Sam pushed the blade out of his shoulder and lifted the man's arms above his head. Then, as quick as he could, he drew him forward and spun to the side, slamming the man's face into the edge of the filing cabinet, his nose exploding as blood and cartilage splattered the metal.

Three striking blows—one to the neck, one to the ribs, and another to the base of the spine—sent the man crashing into the cabinet once more. From the bloodcurdling wheezing, Sam knew the man was beaten.

He picked up the knife, shaking his head as the pain from his shoulder began to intensify.

Sam needed to leave.

With a limp, he slowly made his way back through the shelving units towards the door, hoping to God that Pearce was waiting for him. Whatever the hell he had stumbled onto, they had tried to murder him in the Metropolitan Police Office.

They wanted him silenced.

As he shuffled through, the sudden sound of footsteps thundered behind him, the shelves shaking in terror.

Brian raced at him, his face a broken and bloodied mess.

Sam instinctively threw the knife, the blade spinning through the air and embedding itself right in Brian's meaty neck.

The blood sprayed like a Las Vegas fountain as the man hit the ground, twitching feebly as his life quickly escaped through the gushing pool of blood that quickly filled the aisle.

Sam sighed, knowing he had broken his promise to his son yet again.

Brian was dead.

With the file notes in his pocket, blood pouring from three knife wounds, and a dead body to explain, Sam slowly made his way to the door and back into the police office.

CHAPTER TWENTY

As Sam opened the door, he was immediately slammed against the wall. Officer Khambay snarled as he tried to cuff Sam, latching one of the metal clasps around his wrist. The other officers, who were previously lurking behind their apparent leader, were cheering him on.

He was going to be the one to catch Sam Pope.

The glory was his.

'You are under arrest for...' Sam cut Khambay off by slipping his grasp and tugging the stab-proof vest that rested on his broad torso. The momentum pulled Khambay face-first into the wall, the hard surface breaking his nose.

'Enough!'

Pearce burst through the crowd, stepping between a clearly injured Sam and a furious Khambay.

'He broke my fucking nose!' Khambay roared, provoked further by the lack of fear on Sam's face.

'Just back off,' Pearce ordered.

A few of Khambay's colleagues moved forward, pulling Khambay away from the senior officer. Pearce turned back to Sam, whose face was grimacing as he clasped his shoulder. The stab wound was clear and Pearce was terrified at what he would find in the archive office. As the officers led Khambay to get medical attention, Pearce knew it was only a matter of time before the order came down from higher to hand Pope over.

'Thanks,' Sam offered as Pearce hauled him away from the wall. Blood dripped between the fingers of the hand pressed against his arm.

'Well, don't thank me yet.' Pearce smiled, guiding Sam towards the corridor.

They moved quickly, with Pearce pushing open the door to the office. Through the gap in the door, he could see Khambay and his crew talking to a few other officers.

They were baying for blood.

'We need to go out the back,' Pearce decided, turning back to Sam, who nodded his agreement. Just then, the alarm squealed from the ceiling above and the building instantly went into lockdown mode. The shrill alarm echoed down the corridors, ricocheting off every surface like a ping-pong ball. As the noise tore its way through their ears, Sam tried his best to yell over it.

'I don't think that's the bell for lunch.'

Pearce shook his head, then nodded to the stairwell, which they headed to, taking them two at a time. They almost collided with a few panicked admin workers, who were stunned at the sight of Pearce and a bloodied man bounding up the stairs. They burst out into the corridor of the third floor with Sam groaning gently with pain, the blood seeping through the back of his jeans. Pearce stopped at a green first-aid box attached to the wall, ignored all regulations, and ripped it from its plastic bracket.

Suddenly the drumming of regimented boots hurtling up the staircase they had just taken caused them to turn.

Pearce ducked back through the door, only to see eight armed response officers racing up the stairs.

Whatever it was that Sam had stumbled upon, Mayer was determined to keep him quiet.

'This way,' Pearce yelled, jogging down the corridor and pushing open the door to a small conference room. The walls were a bland white, faded with age. A few posters adorned the walls, offering membership to the police pension and encouraging officers to trust each other. Sam could have laughed at the irony. He shuffled in behind Pearce, who closed the door before quickly turning the latch. The armed response unit would march to the top floor before systematically working their way down, floor by floor, sweeping the building before they found them. With the exits blocked, Pearce knew it was only a matter of time before the door crashed open and a number of laser dots befell both men. Whether or not they would be followed by bullets, Pearce couldn't be sure.

Judging by the look on Sam's face, neither could he. Sam eased his arm out of his bloodied jacket, the sleeve looking like it had been dipped in water. His T-shirt had a small tear in it, revealing the stab wound. Pearce instantly placed the first-aid box on the table, wrenching it open before pulling out some antiseptic.

'This is going to hurt,' he warned, but Sam reached up, snatched the bottle, and tipped it over the tear in his skin. He gritted his teeth, his fist clenching with pain causing his bicep to stretch his T-shirt. Pearce, impressed, took a cotton pad and pressed it against the wound before taping it down with the surgical tape. It was crude, but it would be enough until they could get to Theo.

Or, more likely, they were both arrested at gunpoint.

'What the hell happened in there?' Pearce demanded, slamming the box shut and pushing it to the side.

'Someone attacked me. Not police. He's a henchman for The Gent.'

'The Gent'? Pearce questioned, his grey eyebrow arching. 'How the hell do you know about him?'

Sam sighed. 'Really, Pearce? You want to do this now?' Sam said angrily, lifting his ruined jacket from the conference table and rummaging in the pockets.

'I was right, wasn't I?' Pearce stated confidently. 'You were my guy. You've been working those night shifts.'

'You know what, yes. I have been. And you can arrest me for it or you can help me figure out what the fuck is going on. Because right now, whatever is happening is bigger than you and me.'

Pearce smiled, happy with his own suspicions being confirmed but also knowing that despite having been correct about Pope being a dangerous vigilante, he was also a soldier. A man who had risked his life for his country. And a man who, at that moment, was going against the Metropolitan Police to get the truth.

'Okay. We'll park it for now,' Pearce confirmed, turning to the paperwork that Sam was laying out on the table. 'What's this?'

'It's Howell's final case before he was murdered,' Sam said, not looking up as he sifted through the files. 'Nothing too interesting. A complaint by some government man about being intimidated. Nothing new.'

'Who?' Pearce asked, lifting one of the pages.

'Hold on.' Sam lifted the paper. 'The head of city planning.'

'Earnshaw?' Pearce said. The look on his face told Sam that a puzzle piece had just fallen into place.

'Yeah. Why?'

'Derek Earnshaw was one of the injured people at the bombing that killed Howell,' Pearce stated. 'He was passing the corner when the damn thing went off. Took his leg.'

'Jesus,' Sam said, remembering the injuries he saw during his tours, watching Theo treat an amputee in the heat of battle. They continued reading through, with Sam slapping a piece of paper down.

'Here.' He pressed his finger on the paragraph. 'Earnshaw made a complaint that two bald men tried to break into his office after he denied an application for a takeover of three derelict buildings in the city.'

Pearce scooped up the sheet of paper, his eyes scanning back and forth like a typewriter. 'How do you know it's that?'

'Because two bald men work for The Gent and he just happens to have a few buildings like that in the city.'

'Yeah, the High-Rises. Where the police don't go and the law doesn't exist.'

'You know about these places?' Sam asked with interest.

'Of course I do. Son, I've been investigating corrupt cops since back when you popping spots. I know all about the perks that man offers.' He shook his head in disgust. 'I'm guessing I don't want to know how you happen to know about them.'

'Morton,' Sam confessed, getting a reserved nod in return. 'And those bald men, one of them just tried to kill me.'

'Is he—?' Pearce didn't need to finish the question. The stairwell door burst open, the sound echoing up the corridor. Their boots clapped against the tiled floor, their guns rattled as they burst into the first office, the commanding officer confirming it vacant as they moved on.

Time was fast running out.

'Earnshaw was released from hospital a few days ago.'

'Then we need to speak to him,' Sam said, walking

towards the window of the office, and with his one good arm, shunting it open. 'We need to know what exactly what is going on.'

'Why?' Pearce asked, stopping him in his tracks. 'Why are you doing all this?'

Sam stopped, staring out at the Thames over twenty feet below. Across the river, the London Southbank burst to life in an array of lights, the London Eye towering over everything.

That question had run through his mind a few times; when he was ducked behind the sofa at Amy's whilst bullets flew past him. As he drove down the wrong side of the motorway, confirming his stance as a fugitive. Or as he faced down a brutal killer with a knife in his hand.

Every time he arrived at the same answer.

The same one he replied with.

'Because it's the right thing to do.'

The door to the office next door slammed against the wall as the armed officers filtered in, their combined movements causing the table to shake. Sam nodded his gratitude to Pearce, knowing he had confessed to his own crimes before he slowly draped one leg through the window.

'What the hell are you doing?' a worried Pearce said, throwing down the paperwork and rushing towards the window.

'I'll be in touch.'

At that moment, the door to the office flew off its hinges, and black-clad men burst in, assault rifles pressed to their shoulders, their trigger fingers itchy. Pearce threw up his hands in surrender, blocking their view of the window and their line of sight to Sam.

'Get down!' the first through the door ordered, his gun aimed squarely at Pearce's chest.

Sam leapt.

Pushing his feet off the wall, he launched himself away

from the building, watching as the bright city whipped past him. The spring breeze rushed into his lungs as he plummeted, the Thames rushing towards him as he crashed into the water. Behind him, he could hear the muffled cries of the angry officers that had burst into the room. He swam, his shoulder creaking with every stroke, his breath held tight as he waded through the polluted water.

After a few minutes he pushed himself above water, scanning the area to ensure a rogue party boat wasn't about to decapitate him.

Sirens blared through the night sky, undoubtedly for him. He took another grateful breath of fresh air before disappearing under again, his mind flashing back to the muddy ravines he had crossed during his time in service, the way he could block out the horrors of his surroundings.

The river, as iconic as it was, was filthy, and after a few more minutes, as his lungs threatened to open in the water, he shot out once more, finding himself a few metres from the South Bank. The wailing of the sirens was everywhere, their shrill screams cutting through the night sky. A party boat was docked a short distance away, a stream of drunken patrons clambering aboard and indulging in the expensive alcohol and awful music. With his shoulder burning with agony, Sam swam towards it, reached up with his good arm, and grabbed a life support ring that was attached to the side.

With gritted teeth and extreme anguish, he pulled himself up to the side of the boat, hooking his foot onto the ring before reaching up and grabbing one of the decorative ropes that hung down in symmetrical loops beneath the railing.

With the adrenaline of knowing that he had figured out what was happening, and the net tightening, he hooked his arm over the railing and pulled himself upwards.

With the last of his strength, he rolled over the barrier

and collapsed on the decking, breathing in as much air as he could. A few drunken lads cheered him, offering him a shot of tequila as he slowly got to his feet.

He took one, knocking it back to hopefully stave off the pain for a little longer before marching through the ship, ignoring a few other patrons before entering the gents'.

It was empty, and he sat in the cubicle with the door locked and allowed himself a moment of peace.

The boat departed, taking him away from the manhunt and inevitable capture. He needed to get back to Theo, collect his 'rainy day fund', and then go to see Derek Earnshaw.

He needed to get the facts right before he brought it all crashing down.

As he sat, drenched through and stinking like a burst sewer pipe, he waited patiently for the next full bladder. It only took a few moments before an inebriated man stumbled in, dressed in a shirt and sweater, jeans and shoes. He leant against the wall, eyes closed, making little effort to aim as he urinated around the urinal.

'Good evening,' Sam offered, causing the man to turn, cock still out and shock on his face.

A hard right hook and few minutes later, and Sam stepped from the bathroom wearing an ill-fitting shirt and jeans and waited patiently for the next pick-up point.

CHAPTER TWENTY-ONE

It had been a long day and Theo felt every moment of it as he stretched his back. His leather reclining chair was the most extravagant purchase in his modest living room, wedged into the corner of the room next to the bay window. To his side, a leather sofa stretched across the back wall, adjacent to the large HD TV that sat atop an oak cabinet. A WIFI router sat on one of the shelves, along with a few potted plants. On the wall above was a shelving unit fixed to the wall, lined with medals and photos of his distinguished career in the armed forces. Theo leant forward, allowing his vertebrae to creak loudly as he twisted out the ache.

'You okay?' Amy asked, sat on the end of the sofa. Her eyes pulled away from the documentary on the TV.

'Yeah.' Theo smiled. 'I'm just old.'

Amy chuckled before quickly flashing a look to her lap. Andy lay, asleep, his head resting on her lap. She ran her fingers through his ruffled hair, thankful for the colour that was slowly returning to his cheeks. He had slept for most of the day, with Theo assuring her it was his body dealing with the shock and the blood loss. By the early evening he was awake, with Amy sat beside him, helping him to eat an entire bowl of soup. Theo then helped him down the stairs, surprising Amy with his strength as he carried her husband down to the living room.

Now, as he snoozed in the warmth of the front room, she once again took stock of what had happened. The guns pointed at her head. The bullet that had ripped through her husband.

Sam Pope, who had killed two men to save her life.

'Are you okay?'

Theo's concerned voice brought her back into the room, and only then did she realise a tear had trickled down her face. The PTSD was alive and kicking.

'Yes,' she uttered quietly, her eyes glancing to the folded duvet and pillow stacked in the corner of the room, which Sam had used earlier. 'I'm just worried about Sam.'

'Sam's a big boy,' Theo reassured, sitting forward and stretching once more. 'He can take care of himself.'

Amy shook her head. 'It's not his problem. None of this. Or yours.' She had begun to panic, the horrors of the last few days threatening to overspill. Suddenly, breathing became difficult.

'Hey, hey.' Theo pushed himself off the chair, leaning forward. 'You're fine, okay? You didn't come knocking on our doors, did you? Sam knocked on yours, remember?'

'But why?' Amy shook her head. 'Why is he doing this?'

'Because he is a good man.' Theo smiled warmly. 'We were soldiers and damn good at it. We swore to protect, and that is what we are doing.'

After a few moments, Amy found her breath. She took it in deeply, letting her diaphragm rise and fall, feeling the oxygen whip around her body like a rollercoaster.

After a few more deep breaths, she looked at Theo.

'Thank you.'

'You're welcome.' Theo smiled again, pushing himself up so he was standing. 'I fancy a drink. A proper drink.'

'Wine if you have it,' Amy said, allowing herself to smile. On her lap, her husband, though injured, was alive and safe.

They were safe.

'Coming right up,' Theo said, when suddenly the shrill *ding* of the doorbell cut through the house. Theo tutted. 'That's probably Sam right now. As soon as you mention wine, eh?'

Amy chuckled again as Theo headed towards the front door, feeling a true friendship blossoming. She gently stroked her husband's hair and returned to the soothing voice of David Attenborough as he narrated a dolphin swimming through the ocean.

Theo approached the door, shaking his head joyfully as he yanked it open.

'You weren't gone too long, were you…?'

Theo stopped talking as he came face to face with a man he had never met before. The man was bald, a rugged face that looked like it had taken a fair few whacks in its time, with dark eyes that begged for more. He was broad, maybe carrying a few extra pounds that pressed against the leather jacket he had zipped to the collar, and stood with his feet planted, knowing he was unmovable. He gently rubbed his hands together, with Theo noticing the worn knuckles, clearly from a lifetime of fighting. Beyond, Theo noticed the two men sat in the Range Rover that was parked across the road, their eyes fixed on the house.

The bald man's face broke into a terrifying smile.

'Evening, Mr Walker.' The man's East-End accent shone through. 'I'm looking for Sam Pope.'

'Sorry, who are you?' Theo asked calmly, pressing one foot slowly against the bottom of the door, ensuring it couldn't be shoved open. However, by the size of the visitor, Theo wondered if it would even matter.

'That doesn't really matter, son.'

'It does to me.'

'My name is Mark. Mark Connor.'

'You have a badge?'

'Let's just say I'm a concerned citizen.'

'Me too,' Theo said, his voice firm. 'I'm pretty concerned right now, because I've got a strange man knocking on my door asking for someone I don't know.'

Mark smiled again, the streetlights above reflecting off his shiny skull. The sky had darkened, giving way to a cool spring evening. The breeze jostled through the leaves on the nearby tree.

'Come on now.' Mark shook his head. 'Samuel Pope, who you served with for a number of years. The very same Samuel Pope who murdered two men and abducted a woman named Amy Devereux and her husband, and whose last known location was Bethnal Green Community Hall, your place of work. Now, please don't insult my intelligence, Mr Walker. That wouldn't be a good idea.'

'Are you threatening me?' Theo said purposefully, knowing it had zero effect.

'I'm strongly suggesting,' Mark warned, trying to look beyond Theo into the house. 'So where is he?'

'I don't know, I haven't seen him.'

'Who were you expecting?' Mark's voice was starting to turn colder, his brow beginning to furrow.

'How did you find my address?'

'Oh, you know.'

'No, I don't know. You're not the police, and most detectives don't have two thugs sat in a car watching their back.' Theo leant forward. 'So why don't you leave, before I call the police?'

'Is she in there?' Mark asked, ignoring the threat. 'It would be a wise idea for her to come with me.'

'It would be a wise idea for you to leave.'

Theo refused to break Mark's stare, feeling anger boil inside him as the bald intruder smirked once more in his face. For a moment, the only sound was the buzzing of the TV, the hallway bursting with intermittent colour as the image changed. Mark held the stare for a little while longer before raising both hands up in surrender and taking a step backwards up the garden path. Theo stood in the gap of the doorway, making himself as big as possible.

'Fair enough, fella.' Mark spoke as he headed to the gate. 'Just remember, I tried to do this the polite way.'

With the barely disguised threat lingering between them, Theo watched as the burly man straightened the lapels of his leather jacket before striding through the gate and across the street. A few youths, dressed in their baggy hoods and tracksuit bottoms, watched from a nearby wall, all of them looking away as the man stared at them, daring them to say anything.

None of them did.

The man was dangerous.

He threw open the car door and turned once more, meeting Theo's stare with a silent promise that this wasn't over before the car roared to life and sped off up the road. Theo waited until it had rounded the corner and disappeared into the night before slamming the door shut and taking a deep breath. Within minutes, the entire situation had changed and the safe haven he had offered the Devereuxs was gone. He needed to speak to Sam, but more importantly, Amy and Andy needed to be moved somewhere safe. He pulled his phone from his pocket and found Sam in the contacts and pressed ring.

He heard the generic tone in the living room and as he

walked back, and Amy met him in the doorway, the phone in her hand.

'Shit,' Theo uttered under his breath, pocketing both phones and running his hands over his shaved head.

'We need to go, don't we?' she asked, fear spreading across her face like wildfire.

Theo offered a warm smile before following her back into the front room, where Andy was sitting up, his eyes glazed over as he tried to remember his surroundings.

Amy rushed to him, her fingers wrapping around his hand and gently stroking his wedding ring. 'Andy, honey. Are you okay to get up?'

Andy slowly stirred and mumbled, with Amy stood in front of him, trying to guide him up.

Theo watched carefully.

Then he heard the sound of a car door slamming shut.

His eyes widened with terror.

'Get down!' he yelled, lurching forward and shoving Amy and Andy onto the couch as a stream of bullets, followed by the street-shaking roar of an automatic rifle, burst through the window. One of them sliced straight through Theo's right shoulder, a burst of red spraying up the white wall and spinning him on the spot.

Another passed through his hip as he tumbled, both of them ripping out the other side of him and burying themselves in the blood-splattered wall.

He roared in agony as he hit the floor, blood oozing out and across the wooden slats. Amy screamed in terror as another avalanche of bullets pelted the house, embedding in the wall in a horrifying line. Amy pulled Andy off of the sofa and ducked down, frantically trying to attend to Theo, who was gritting his teeth and trying to apply pressure to two bullet wounds.

'Kitchen,' Theo yelled through quick breaths. 'Now.'

Amy nodded, her cheeks shiny with tears as she began

to drag Andy, who was sloppily trying to help, towards the kitchen. Outside the house, Theo could already hear the wailing of sirens, but he could also hear the unmistakable sound of a gun being reloaded.

He wished Sam was there, who would be more than a match for the onslaught, especially if he had access to his 'rainy-day fund'.

With the pain becoming unbearable and the blood loss beginning to slow him down, Theo slowly dragged himself across the floor, leaving a smear of scarlet on the wood as he followed the terrified couple. In the kitchen, Amy, breathing heavily after dragging her husband through the house, was overturning the kitchen table and chairs. Theo, straining to pull himself forward, nodded to the panel beside the breakfast bar.

Amy ran her fingers across it, finding the ridge at the end of the panel and pulling with all her strength. Three slats lifted, disguised as kitchen tiles, revealing a few stairs and a small security bunker beneath the floor. Never, in all her years as a therapist, had she been so grateful for some-one's war-related paranoia. Theo, who was taking controlled breaths and wincing with pain, nodded for her to get in, and she guided her husband to the stairs. He navigated them woozily before collapsing underneath the breakfast bar in the dark room. Another spray of bullets littered the house, causing Amy to jump as she scurried down the few steps to check on her husband and Theo slowly dragged himself towards the opening.

Then he heard the sound of the metal bouncing into the hallway, the pin having already been pulled from the grenade. With Amy and her husband safely inside the bunker, Theo pushed himself forward and pushed the lid closed, drowning out Amy's screams of horror at his action. He could imagine Mark stood outside, hands on hips, as his two thugs unleashed round after round of bullets on his house, the one that had been his home since he had left the army, and had required a woman's touch ever since his divorce.

He thought about Denise and how they could have had a happy marriage had he left the army sooner, but his constant nights away had deprived her of the baby she had wanted and she had packed her bags before he had returned.

Theo thought of her face, her smile, and knew it was better served as a mother, which she was to three girls.

He thought of all the lives he had saved during his service, knowing full well the pain those men were going through as he pressed his hands against the bullet holes that plagued his body.

He thought of Amy and Andy, safely secured underneath his house.

Lastly, he thought of Sam, and the hell that would be unleashed when he found out what happened.

Theo then closed his eyes and moments later there was a giant flash of light and heat and everything went black.

CHAPTER TWENTY-TWO

It was on a dusty side street in Baghdad that Sam had learnt how to hotwire a car, the unrelenting sun beating down on the Iraqi capital. He was being covered by Corporal Murray and Private Jensen, the latter fresh out of the academy, with more spots than facial hairs. But he was a good kid with an incredible brain, and it was he who showed Sam how to hotwire the vehicle. Sam had assumed Jensen learnt from a tough life on the streets, a past littered with petty crimes and needless gang culture.

He later found out, when Jensen was heading up the data analysis centre back in GCHQ, the large 'donut' building that housed the government's military information and secrets, that Jensen knew how to hotwire the vehicle due to his incredible intellect.

He was a fine soldier, but his main weapon was his mind.

As Murray scanned the derelict alleyway, brushing his assault rifle left and right like a pendulum, Jensen had walked Sam through the process. Once he had jimmied the plastic panel beneath the steering wheel, Jensen had pointed out the bundles of wires, how they connected to separate parts of the car, and how to differentiate between them. It was simple science, but Sam was more comfortable pulling a trigger than pulling wires.

They segregated the battery and ignition bundle and Sam stripped some of the plastic casing of the battery wires with his pocket knife, which he returned to the pocket of his camo trousers. He twisted the exposed metal together before doing the same to the ignition wire. Jensen badgered him about being careful, the ignition wire holding a live current that could kill him.

Sam knew a life-and-death situation—he had been holed up in an abandoned factory with six Russian operatives hunting him less than two years before—but said nothing. With his confidence growing, he pressed the exposed wiring together, a spark leaping between them both and the engine letting out a guttering roar. Laughing with triumph, he pressed his foot on the accelerator, revving the engine as the car jolted to life.

The timing was impeccable, as a stream of bullets rocked the side of the car, with Murray diving into the back seat, returning fire through the shattered glass. Sam flipped the car into gear and accelerated, the car leaping forward and leaving nothing but the thundering of the enemies' weapons and a large cloud of sandy dust behind.

———

Six years later and those skills had come in handy once more, as Sam drove the stolen car out towards New Malden. It hadn't been too hard to locate Earnshaw—a quick stop at a twenty-four-hour internet café on Lambeth High Street had proven fruitful. Hunting down those criminals—or working the 'night shift', as Pearce had an annoying way of saying—had led Sam to a number of websites that weren't strictly by the book. It allowed people to search for data that people had unwillingly or, more likely, obliviously allowed companies to take and sell on.

Sam was aware of a public uproar when a popular social media site was found to have allowed a vast amount of data to be sold. Not one for social media, Sam wasn't too bothered, but it had made him chuckle at the fear it struck into the people who really didn't understand just how deep those websites had their claws in their lives. The world existed online. People ordered food online, read books on tablets, and posted every intimate detail of their lives in a bizarre quest for social acceptance.

It came at a cost.

And that cost worked to Sam's benefit as he found Derek Earnshaw's home address within five minutes before wandering onto a nearby estate and selecting the oldest-looking car he could find. Under the flickering light of the estate, he found himself a lot calmer than under the incoming fire all those years ago. The newer cars had fail-safes that would prevent a hotwiring, but the door to the Renault Clio popped easily, and within moments the engine was illegally purring.

Now, as he passed through the quiet residential streets of Balham, he thought about Pearce. Sam was confident that the armed team that swarmed the room moments before he plunged into the Thames wouldn't hurt Pearce. He was a high-ranking officer, after all. But there was no way Mayer or anyone else on the take would stand for his intervention. Now, with a city-wide manhunt underway for him, Sam knew he wouldn't be able to return to his old life.

There would be no more trips to the archive office—especially as his last visit had resulted in a dead body.

No more 'night shifts'.

As he passed Wimbledon train station, slowing to allow the drunken arrivals to stumble across the road, he realised that none of his old life mattered. An empty flat, a soulless room where he pined for his wife and son. A job he had taken to 'serve' after he had quit his police training.

None of it mattered. Not anymore.

Now he had a purpose, a reason to protect, and knew he was on the verge of bringing down a major gangster and the crooked cops he had in his pocket.

He just had to connect the dots.

Fifteen minutes later, he slowed the car to a stop across the road from Earnshaw's impressive five-bedroom, three-storey house. As head of city planning, Earnshaw was not only a highly regarded member of the government, but was also well remunerated. As Sam exited the stolen car, he scanned the street quickly; the middle class were all tucked up in their pristine homes, and the silence of suburbia hung over the street like a cloud. With no one in sight, Sam approached the steel gates that split the stone wall, reaching up and pulling himself over with discomfort, the pain of the stab wound in his shoulder rocketing through his body like a space shuttle.

He dropped down on the other side, half expecting a pack of wild dogs to be released to chase him away, but all he was greeted with was silence. There were no lights on at all, and as Sam approached the front of the house, he noticed that they hadn't installed a ramp yet.

Earnshaw had lost a leg during the blast, but from the quick search Sam had done to find his address, he had read an article about how it might propel Earnshaw to be the next mayor of London.

Quietly pressing himself against the side of the house, he followed the brickwork through a side gate and to the back door. The patio before him was covered with expensive-looking garden furniture, a two-tier barbecue, and a swinging hammock chair.

All the ingredients for a garden party.

Sam then noticed the broken glass on the back door, the shards piled carelessly on the inside of the door. Sliding his hand into the ill-fitting shirt he had stolen on the party boat, he pulled the handle down and the door opened.

Someone had been there.

Carefully, Sam pushed the door open, stepping over the glass and into the plush kitchen. The marble counters were clear of any clutter, with top-of-the-range appliances placed strategically around the open room. In the centre, a breakfast bar stood proudly, the stools on one side moved for Earnshaw's recent disability. With slow, measured steps, Sam moved into the hallway, the wooden floor creaking slightly under each step. He checked the living room and the dining room; both were empty, both furnished with high-quality furniture. The TV in the front room was almost the size of the wall.

With the downstairs clear, Sam made his way up the stairs, the only light from the moon filtering in through the windows in sharp strokes. The wall of the staircase was lined with photos of Earnshaw and his wife at various stages of their life. Their wedding. His first day on the job. A few holidays.

No kids, Sam noted, a twinge of pain hitting him as he wished to see his son.

As soon as he got to the landing, he tensed up. A faint, ominous smell was creeping under the door at the far end of the hallway. It was a weak but unmistakable smell.

One that he had smelt a number of times.

A dead body.

Cautiously, Sam approached the door, nudging it open with his shoulder and immediately looking away.

Hanging from the doorframe to the en suite bathroom was Derek Earnshaw. The belt, strapped to his neck, was attached to a chin-up bar that was fixed to the inner frame. The leather strap was already ripping into the skin of his neck, dried blood crisping over the side like a burnt pie. His eyes were open, completely bloodshot from the strain of choking to death, his body doing everything to fight the apparent suicide.

His one leg hung loosely; the other, missing, was covered by the folded leg of his trousers. His skin had faded, almost to a translucent shade, and the aroma was pungent, a warm, bitter smell of finality.

It was the tiny river of blood in the doorway to the en suite that caught Sam's eye, and as he moved into the room and peered past the swinging body of his intended visit, he saw his wife.

She was slumped in the bath, back against the white tiles. The bath was filled with blood, almost to her waist. The deep vertical gashes that ran vertically from her wrists to her elbow joints had long since emptied and her vacant eyes felt like they were locked on him.

Another apparent suicide.

A proud man, handicapped by a senseless act of terrorism, couldn't stand to live his new life. His wife, heartbroken, helped him to commit suicide and then, with the guilt and loss too much to bear, she took her own life.

A tragedy.

That was how they would spin it.

Sam knew, after what they had attempted with Amy, that this was the work of The Gent and was designed to close the case early. Undoubtedly the responsibility would fall to someone like Mayer, a police officer who had long since stepped away from the thin blue line. They would make the mess go away and The Gent would make their dreams come true.

A note was placed on the closed lid of the porcelain toilet, but Sam didn't bother to read it. It would have been a crudely written suicide note, just to underline it all. Careful not to touch anything, Sam backed out of the room, retracing his steps to the hallway. With the two dead bodies slowly decomposing, the house had taken on a more haunted quality. This spaciousness had turned to emptiness.

The darkness permanent.

Sam ducked his head through the other doors, finding

the grandiose main bathroom, with a walk-in shower and two sinks. A white Caitlyn bath sat in the centre of the room. Two of the other doors led to guest bedrooms, with Sam guessing another two were up on the third floor. Each room had a double bed, immaculately made, with an assortment of desks, cupboards, and decorations that put his empty flat to shame. Despite the effort and expense put into each room, Sam still preferred the simplicity of nothing.

Perhaps it was the years in the army, where trivial things like the colour of bedsheets or the assortment of photo frames didn't play a part.

All it was about was the mission. About following the orders and protecting the innocent.

That's what he was doing there, the fundamental reason he had saved Amy's life, breaking his promise to his son and putting three men in the ground. That was why he was now the most wanted man in London.

Because innocent people had been killed or threatened and someone had to protect them.

As his mind wandered, he opened the final door, the moon bathing the neat office in a pale glow. The desk was a thick oak, with a Macbook placed on top. A stack of files were neatly placed to the side and a photo of Earnshaw's wife gazed longingly out of its frame. There was a card on the desk, interspersed with a few others and recent pamphlets for dealing with disabilities.

It was Inspector Michael Howell's card.

Sam picked it up straight away, scanning his eyes over the name and the accompanying mobile phone number. Howell had been signed off with grief after the death of his nephew, but it was known that he had made it a priority to visit every family that had been damaged by the bombing.

A bombing that Sam was sure had been carried out by

Howell's subordinates, all in the vile act of lining their own pockets and those of the very people they were supposed to stop.

He took a deep breath, feeling the rage building inside him. He had risked his life for years to ensure the protection of not just his own country, but for all people who were subjected to the horrors of the world. He had fought the Russians, the Taliban, Isis.

But this one hurt the most.

The Metropolitan Police.

Howell deserved to know the truth about what was happening in his absence and why his young nephew wouldn't get to follow in his footsteps anymore.

Sam pulled up the phone that sat on the edge of the desk and punched in the number.

After a few rings, a tired voice echoed through the receiver.

'Howell.'

'Sir, it's Sam Pope.'

'Pope?' Howell questioned, the sleep still clinging to his brain like a sloth. A moment later, clarity sprang into his voice. 'Pope. Jesus, what the hell has been going on?'

Howell had obviously been kept in the loop, and if Sam was right about what was going on, that loop would have him pegged as public enemy number one.

'Sir, I need to speak with you.'

'You need to come in.'

'Sir, it's about your nephew.'

'Jake?' Howell suddenly sounded vulnerable.

Sam felt his pain. Grief was a horrible companion. 'Yes sir. I know who killed him,' Sam said firmly. 'And, I know why.'

CHAPTER TWENTY-THREE

The crystal glass shattered against the white wall of the penthouse, the remnants of the expensive whisky spraying across the paint work in chase of the glass fragments. Frank Jackson knew this would be the reaction and had lightened his usual almost tyrannical insistence on manners as he broke the news to Mark Connor.

His best friend, Brian Stack, had been found dead.

There was no denying what had happened. Brian had confronted Sam Pope in the archive room and, judging by the bruising to the face, body, and his own knuckles, had engaged him in a hand-to-hand fight to the death. A fight he had lost. The knife embedded in his throat had been the exclamation point and had brought an end to the Mitchell Brothers.

Now, as a triumphant Mark had returned to the High-Rise with a smug look on his face, pleased with the destruction of Theo Walker's house, Frank had told him of his friend's demise.

That Sam Pope, the man who had shot to the top of every wanted list in the city, had executed him.

Mark had taken the news in a stoic anger, calmly

pouring himself an expensive drink from the drink table that sat atop an old, rustic trolley in the corner of the room. Floor-to-ceiling windows on the sixth floor of the High-Rise gave a breathtaking panoramic view of the city, even in the midst of a storm. After calmly downing the entire drink in one swig, Mark had furiously hurled the glass at the wall, screaming profanities as the news began to sink in. Although Mark was as cold and as ruthless as anyone The Gent had ever met, he was a human being who had just been informed of his friend's murder.

A fist followed soon after, Mark's worn knuckles colliding with the solid concrete, the anger pummelling the wall like a jackhammer.

After a few more thunderous right hands, he withdrew his hand, the knuckles cracked and his blood dripping over the spotless wooden floor panels. On any other occasion, Frank would have insisted on a punishment for such disregard for the cleanliness of his luxury suite, but he allowed Mark to grieve.

He knew what was coming next.

'I want his head,' Mark eventually spat, his teeth gritted and his eyes burning with fury.

'I know.' Frank nodded, resting a reassuring hand on Mark's shoulder. 'And like I say to all my clients, your wish is my command.'

'This isn't some bent copper looking for a pound of Charlie and a hooker, boss. I want him alive and I want to take him apart.'

Frank smiled, allowing the backtalk to slide due to the situation. He prided himself on being able to provide whatever his customers wanted. Right now, despite Mark always having been an employee, he knew he needed to provide something for Mark. His most loyal man, an attack dog who had maimed and killed without question for over a decade. Frank Jackson might have been one of the most terrifying criminals in London, but he was also a friend. He watched as Mark stood, staring into nothingness and letting his anger convulse through him like an electric current. The man's black jacket was tight to his stocky frame. His knuckles were smeared with blood.

Frank thought he could see the hint of a tear forming in Mark's eye.

'Follow me,' Frank said with authority, turning on the heel of his expensive shoes and marching across the living room to the door, pulling it open and stepping into the hallway.

Mark took a deep breath before following, pulling a handkerchief from his pocket and wrapping it around his broken knuckles. They passed a few doors to the other suites, one of them currently occupied by a high-ranking politician and the underage boy he had paid thousands for. The Gent never judged what the requirements were.

The High-Rise was a place for every fulfilment.

Eventually they came to the door to the stairwell. Frank opened the door, living up to his nickname as he offered Mark to pass first. He did, and they soon found themselves descending the staircase, their footsteps echoing up through building. Eventually they came to a stop and Frank marched to the door, unlocking it and pushing it open. The previous day it had been the final room Nathaniel Burridge had entered before he was strung up and hacked apart by the furious man by Frank's side. As Frank pushed the door open, they were greeted by nothing but darkness.

'Mark, I know how close you and Brian were, and I am truly sorry for your loss. I promise you, we will do everything we can to kill Samuel Pope.'

'Okay,' Mark grunted, his fists clenching at the very mention of the name.

'But whilst I can't give you him right now, I do have

something to maybe take the edge off.'

Frank reached into the door and flicked the light switch, the halogen lights bursting into life with a continuous hum. The room was once again covered in clear plastic sheets from corner to corner. To the side was the usual table, rows of tools and blades laid out like a display cabinet.

The wheeled seat sat next to it, which Mark had sat on and watched as Nathaniel had bled to death. All of that had been cleared away; the remnants of his body had been dropped off at the docks, where it would be placed in an acidic vat, melted to nothing, and dropped into the ocean within the next week.

The room was squeaky clean.

Except for the mixture of sweat and piss that had pooled beneath the man that hung, nude and upside down, from a meat hook in the centre of the room. His ankles and wrists were chained and a strip of tape had been slapped across his mouth.

His eyes, red from crying, were wide with fear.

DS Mayer.

'He's all yours,' Frank said, patting his friend on the back before heading back to the stairs, the muffled cries for mercy blocked out as the door slammed shut. And just as Frank approached the top of the staircase, he could hear the brutal impact of a right hook.

———

Pearce took a deep breath and recomposed his thoughts, the tiredness reaching up to him like a needy child. The bags under his eyes were heavy and he looked at the clock on the dashboard of his car. It was just after three in the morning and it had been a hell of an evening. He had marched Sam Pope into the station and had helped him steal a file and escape, incurring the wrath of the captain of the armed response unit, who had burst into the room just as Sam had leapt to the Thames.

It was a hell of a jump and Pearce found himself admiring the man. He had been right, of course: Sam was the vigilante who had been assaulting the 'innocent' men, even admitting to the brutal maiming of Chris Morton a few weeks before.

The man was a dangerous criminal.

Yet, as he sped through the downpour that had decided to invade the night sky, Pearce couldn't help but feel they were on the same side. He had spent the majority of his career hunting down corrupt policemen, which had alienated him from the usual lifestyle of a police officer. When he had first joined the force, his aptitude and calmness had led him to be fast-tracked to the armed response unit, which he had served on with distinction for over four years. After that he had moved to CID, where he became known for his diligence and his integrity.

He soon found himself opposing his colleagues, who weren't adverse to the odd bribe to look the other way. Yet when he had finally reported it, he was ostracized and pushed to a desk job.

Swept under the rug.

When he finally joined the Department of Professional Standards, he was chomping at the bit to bring down the parts of the thin blue line that had become discoloured. It hadn't been easy. The Met, despite being one of the finest police services in the world, were happy to let him off the leash but never to see it through. Those who he eventually brought to justice never saw jail time.

The majority were given a slap on the wrist.

The worst were given a golden handshake.

But Sam Pope wasn't playing by the same rules. The man had served his country for a decade, with a personal cost that had been huge. His wife had left and he never got to see his child. That loneliness, mixed with a lifetime of killing, had resulted in his 'night shifts'. But the man was a soldier and Pearce had seen, as Sam had turned back from the window before he leapt to the cold waters below, that he would see this through to the end.

He had killed to protect Amy Devereux.

He had become London's most wanted man to get to the truth.

Now, as Pearce shot through another red light, he felt himself feeling the same way. Something was rotten about the whole bombing, right to the core. Mayer was involved, that was obvious, and the fact that he had officers and armed squads at his beck and call didn't bode well. In fact, they had held Pearce for over an hour, questioning how Sam had overpowered him—the bruise that was forming on his face was testament to the right hook. They asked about the dead body and if Pearce had been in on it.

It was easy enough to deflect, with Pearce using his seniority to pull rank and let himself go, but he would undoubtedly be pulled in by his own boss.

Adrian Pearce. Just as corrupt as the rest of them.

He would have chuckled had he not have been so horrified by what had come over the radio just before he left the building. A house had been subjected to a barrage of gunfire and an explosion had levelled it.

It was the address that Sam had shared with him for his friend.

As he sped through the London night, his windscreen wipers swung in repetition, clearing his view through the downpour. As he entered Bethnal Green, another voice crackled across the radio, discussing the man and woman they had found under the devastated kitchen.

Amy and Andrew were alive.

Theo Walker was being rushed to hospital with

multiple burns and severe blood loss. There were mutterings over the radio of the loss of a leg, but Pearce couldn't hear through the commotion. What had scared him most was that Officer Khambay's voice had filtered through the airwaves and had taken responsibility for taking Amy and Andrew to safety.

Which was where he was heading.

Turning onto the road, he was immediately met with the blurred sight of flashing lights and an array of emergency vehicles. Rows of drenched, terrified neighbours watched in dismay as the fire service checked the building for the structural damage of the grenade whilst an ambulance passed him, its sirens wailing cries of help into the night sky as it raced Theo to hospital.

Pearce uttered a silent prayer for him.

He then saw a police car begin to move and swung his car in front of it, quickly stepping out into the rain and squinting into the bright headlights. He held up his badge as he approached.

'Detective Inspector Pearce,' he yelled above the furore of the crime scene.

The door to the car flung open and two officers stepped out. The large man with a bandage wrapped across his face was Khambay, who glared with anger through his bruised eyes. The other officer, a stocky woman with short-cropped hair, accompanied it with her own sneer.

'What the fuck are you doing?' Khambay snarled, wincing at the pain that shot through his broken nose.

'How dare you speak to a superior officer like that?' Pearce barked, stepping forward to assert his authority.

Khambay shot a glance to his partner, who stepped to the side, slightly circling him. He squinted through and saw Amy Devereux in the back seat, her arms protectively around her husband.

As Pearce was about to square off with the two officers, a voice dripping with authority cut through the wet night sky.

'What the hell is going on here?'

Superintendent Michelle Bellows stepped forward, her hat covered by the plastic sheet whilst her high-vis raincoat rested over her petite frame. A career woman in her mid-forties, she had always respected Pearce and had been one of the reasons his marriage eventually failed. He still felt she harboured some desire to bed him again, but her professionalism would always trump her attraction.

She was firm but fair.

And at that moment, Pearce couldn't have been happier to see her.

'Ma'am, these officers were about to transport the two survivors of the blast to a medical facility. However, I need to speak to them about an ongoing case,' Pearce said, stepping forward and lowering his voice, much to the agitation of the two officers. 'If it wasn't urgent, I wouldn't intervene.'

'The bombing?' Bellows asked, a perfectly shaped eyebrow arching upwards.

Pearce smiled. She was good.

'Yes, Ma'am. I need to question them somewhere safe and neutral.' Pearce looked over his shoulder. 'I will take them to a medical facility as soon as possible once I have completed it.'

'Can't it wait, Adrian?' she asked, catching him off guard by using his first name.

The rain pelted against his body, the cold filtering through his bones. 'Ma'am, Mrs Devereux is Samuel Pope's therapist. She may have some information on how to find him.'

Bellows looked beyond Pearce at the car, the request processing through her mind like a bank transaction.

'I wouldn't ask if it wasn't important.'

'Okay, Adrian.' She sighed.

'Thank you, ma'am.'

Superintendent Bellows turned to an irate Khambay who stood, arms folded and rainwater dripping from the brim of his helmet. Beyond them all, the firefighters were yelling as they knocked through one of the obliterated walls of the house whilst a few other officers were discussing the events with the local residents. Bellows shook her head at the very thought of a gun and grenade attack in the centre of London. Pearce was glad she wasn't fully up to speed with why that house had been targeted.

'Officers, please transfer your passengers to DI Pearce.'

'Ma'am…' Khambay began, met with a raised hand and a stern look.

'Just do it.'

Khambay shot a glare that could kill at Pearce as he nodded to his colleague to open the back door. She did and Amy stepped out, shivering in the pouring rain as it pelted her small frame. She reached in, helping her husband to drape an arm over her shoulder, and guided him out of the car. A fresh bandage was wrapped around his thigh, a few specks of blood eagerly pushing through. Amy walked slowly, allowing her husband to hobble along until they reached the car. She mouthed a 'hello' to Pearce as she passed and he reached across and pulled open the door. As Andy lowered himself into the back seat, Amy marched to the other side and joined him.

Pearce turned back to Bellows. 'Thank you, ma'am.'

She nodded before turning back to the chaotic scenes behind her. Pearce opened the driver's side door only for Khambay to wrap his meaty fingers around the top of it.

'Watch your back, Pearce,' Khambay muttered through gritted teeth. 'You just made a big mistake.'

Pearce pushed Khambay's hand from the door and

squared up to him. He flashed a glance to the burly side-kick, who was sneering under her soaked cap. The street-lights bounced off the shimmering bonnet of his car and his mouth broke into a smile, two rows of perfect white teeth.

'Don't worry. I've been making them all day.'

Pearce stepped into his car and slammed the door, watching as Khambay marched back to his own vehicle, already reaching for his radio. Undoubtedly he would be followed, so Pearce threw the car into gear and sped off, his tyres screeching loudly into a night already filled with the echoes of agony. As they spun around the far corner and allowed the devastation of the street to disappear, Amy broke down into tears.

'He's dead,' Amy muttered, to herself.

Andy reached over and squeezed her hand as Pearce watched them in the rear-view mirror. The two of them had been through so much, all to hide the truth of what happened.

Sam Pope had killed to protect them.

Theo Walker was willing to die to save them.

As he spun off the side road and onto the motorway, Pearce pressed his foot down as hard as he could, the engine roaring to life as they sped towards safety. He had no idea where he was heading or how many men they would send after him.

All he knew was that he was going to keep them safe.

He was willing to break the law to do it.

'Don't worry,' he assured them, glancing into the mirror once more. A sea of car lights twinkled behind them. 'We're going to be okay.'

He hoped they believed him, as he shot through London as the rain continued its unrelenting downpour, trying it's damn hardest to wash the city clean.

CHAPTER TWENTY-FOUR

Inspector Howell stood in the conservatory of his four-bedroom house, staring out at the immaculate garden that surrounded it. The rain lashed down on the rows of beautiful flowers his wife fawned over, colours bursting forth like fireworks. The spring had been mild, with intermittent storms, and he couldn't help but feel this one was linked to his mood.

It had been twenty minutes since Sam Pope had called him, adamant that his nephew had been murdered.

Jake.

He felt a lump stick in his throat and he lifted the glass in his hand, knocking back a large swig of scotch which quickly vanquished it. The alcohol was warm and comforting and he nervously reached for the decanter, pouring himself another generous helping. His nephew had been dead for almost two weeks and it wasn't getting any easier.

He hadn't been able to focus on anything. His wife, Amanda, had tried to help him grieve. He had pushed her away. His sister, who had argued against a career in the police for her son, had kept silent, but every glare was laced with blame. It was never meant to be this way. He had wanted to watch Jake rise through the ranks, become a highly ranked officer or branch off for a career in a specialist area. He'd win commendations for his bravery and dedication, meet a woman and settle down.

Have the family that Howell himself never had.

The rain patted against the window like chattering teeth, and he took another swig.

How the hell had it all gotten so out of hand?

He had been given daily updates since he had taken his leave of absence; the manhunt for Sam had been the headline. The man's past was being dug into, with various records of one-man missions in faraway lands, dangers that one could only imagine. A long list of deceased, all sent to the afterlife by the squeeze of his index finger.

The man was dangerous—more deadly than they had ever imagined. Sam could have been an asset, but he had dropped out of his police training three years before when his own demons had cost him his family.

Since then, he had hidden in plain sight.

Now he was at the top of the list.

Howell stared at his phone, knowing he should have called for backup the minute Sam had agreed to drive to his luxurious house, but he had resisted.

He needed to hear him out.

Howell needed to know what Pope knew.

As his stomach twisted like a coiling snake, a burst of light washed over the gated entrance to his drive. Howell took a deep breath and pressed the intercom button, watching as the gate slowly slid open, welcoming the truth into his home from the dark, wet night. The car, most likely already reported as stolen, slowly crawled up the driveway, parking just in front of his pristine Range Rover.

Sam stepped out, the rain lashing against him with fury. Howell watched as the most wanted man in London trudged towards the door, a small bloodstain pressing against the shoulder of his ill-fitting shirt. As Sam approached the front door, Howell knocked back the last of his drink, rubbed his lips with the back of his hand, and marched to let him in, ready to hear the truth. He pulled open the door and ushered Sam inside straight away.

'Don't stay out in the cold, son. You'll catch your death.'

'Sir.'

Ever the soldier, Sam respected authority before stepping into the open hallway, the wooden floor leading to a carpeted staircase that disappeared to apparent luxury above. The rain dripped from Sam onto the wooden floor, slithering into the thin lines. The décor was modest, painted by a professional, and an enormous oval mirror took pride and place on the wall. Sam looked beyond the friendly face of the inspector towards the door at the end of the corridor. A large open-plan kitchen peeked through the doorway: fresh tiles and marble worktops.

'First things first: up the stairs, second door on the right. Help yourself to some fresh clothes in the chest of drawers. Some of them belonged to Jake and….'

Howell's voice cracked and a sudden wave of sadness washed over him as he mentioned his nephew.

Sam knew not to pry, and placed a hand on the grieving man's shoulder. 'Your nephew was a good man who died protecting the public. I'm sorry for your loss, sir.'

'Thank you.'

Sam forced a smile and nodded and headed towards the stairs.

Howell took a deep breath before calling after him.

'Sorry, Sam. Shoes.' He pointed at the drenched shoes on Sam's feet. 'Not on the carpet, eh?'

Smiling, Sam slid them off and Howell nodded appreciatively. As he ascended the stairs to change into anything not wringing wet, he heard Howell make his way to the study and drop two ice cubes into a glass.

With each step, he took in the details. It was what he was trained to do. He already knew he was fifteen steps from the front door, that there were three windows within the hallway, one of which would be too high for an escape route. Years of training, drilled into him day after day. He had already spied a knife set, sat proudly on the kitchen unit, which was approximately eleven steps from the bottom of the stairwell.

The study was to the right, and the sound of Howell mixing a drink led him to believe there would be a number of implements and bottles which could be fashioned into a weapon.

He was trained to survive.

To take everything in and use it to stay alive.

As he entered the second door on the right, he peeled off the white ill-fitting shirt he had taken from the man on the party boat.

A deep, ugly wound glared from his shoulder, like a closed eye just waiting to burst open.

Across his chiselled chest, the two bullet scars stared wide-eyed and proud.

Sam Pope. Going through the wars once again.

He swiped a pair of underwear and socks, balling up the wet remains of his clothes and sticking them in the bin under the desk next to the drawers. The room was sparse, a clearly barely used guestroom. Sam, in his quick absorption of details, found little hints of a family life.

Howell was a police man through and through.

Slipping into a pair of jeans which hung slightly and a black T-shirt which wrapped tight around his arms, Sam took a deep breath, ran a hand through his damp, flat hair, and headed downstairs to try to figure a way out of it all.

Forty-five minutes later and Howell stood by the drinks trolley, fixing himself another scotch with shaking hands. The study was warm and relaxing, with three large floor-to-ceiling bookcases proudly lining the walls, each one filled to the edges with books. Sam had noted a random mixture of thought-provoking non-fiction interspersed with thriller novels from the likes of Lee Child and Robert Ludlum. Sam compared it to the list of books he had made in the hopeless promise to his son that he would read more.

He had already broken the promise not to kill.

Shaking the thought of his son from his mind before he became distracted, he held the empty glass in his own hand. Sam had never been a big fan of scotch, but he found the warmth it offered most welcoming, especially after his earlier plummet into the freezing Thames. Howell had sat him down on the leather sofa which sat opposite a large oak desk and had stood rested against the edge whilst Sam relayed everything. Sam spoke, leaving out the details of his attacks on Morton and others, but ran through everything.

How the eyewitness accounts didn't add up. That Harding didn't seem to be grieving at all, but ended up allegedly committing suicide with grief. That Mayer had sent two men to intimidate and potentially kill Amy Devereux, putting a bullet through her husband, and how Sam had just happened to be in the right place at the right time.

He told Howell how he had killed the man with a bullet between the eyes.

Howell finished his drink and fixed another, his kind offer waved off by Sam as he continued, explaining about the dirty cop and the mystery man who had confronted him before Sam had sent Amy and her husband to his friend whilst he had led them on a goose chase.

His dealings with Pearce.

Killing his attacker in the station.

The potentially long list of police officers all on the take, all at Mayer's beck and call.

Then the reason why Jake was killed.

Howell shuffled uncomfortably as Sam explained his theory that Jake was murdered in a planned attack on Derek Earnshaw, who Jake had been assigned to when Frank Jackson's men threatened him after he rejected planning permission.

When Howell questioned how Sam knew of the High-Rises, Sam merely offered that he kept his ear to the ground.

Before Howell could finish his next drink, Sam relived the moment he had leapt from the police station into the crashing, freezing water of the Thames, before heading to Earnshaw's only to find him and his wife dead. Despite all the evidence to the contrary, it was no suicide.

'Who else knows about this?' Howell finally said, his back to Sam as he fixed yet another drink, the horrors of the reality causing him to shake.

'Just Pearce. My friend who is looking after Amy,' Sam confirmed, exhaling deeply as the weight lifted from his shoulders.

'What a mess.' Howell shook his head.

'I'm sorry to bring this all to you, sir,' Sam offered. 'But I didn't know where else to turn. I thought you should know the truth.'

Howell turned, a hurt-filled smile betraying his mood. He took another sip before shaking his head, muttering under his breath. 'Mayer. Fucking hell.'

'I know, sir,' Sam agreed, sitting forward and twirling

the small glass tumbler in his hand. 'It's hard to believe it, but it's true.'

Howell shook his head again, taking a large sip. 'All he had to do was get her to write the goddamn report.'

Sam sat back, turning quickly with raised eyebrows. As he struggled to process what he had just heard, Howell finished the last of his drink and slammed the glass down on the sideboard. The creaking of his gate echoed through the rain and a large beam of light flooded through the window to the study as a black SUV pulled into the drive-way. Howell walked towards the hallway, headed for the front door. Sam shot to his feet, adrenaline already seeping into his veins.

'Sir?' he asked curtly, his fists clenched.

'You don't understand, Pope. This world, it's not what you think. We don't just play cops and robbers, we can't just chase the bad guys down and slap them in cuffs. Not anymore. The world has changed. The only way to police these streets effectively is to co-exist.'

'You son of a bitch,' Sam said through gritted teeth, his knuckles turning white. 'You're not drinking through grief. You're drinking through guilt.'

'You're damn right I am.' Howell turned back, his aged face rife with pain. 'I sanctioned the killing of my own goddamn nephew to keep the fucking peace.'

Sam stepped forward into the doorway of the study as Howell took another two steps backwards, a few feet from the front door. A number of footsteps crunched across the wet gravel outside and Sam counted three figures through the frosted glass.

'You did it to line your pockets,' Sam stated. 'You're just as bad as they are.'

'I don't expect you to go quietly, Pope. Your friend didn't.'

'What?' Sam stuttered, Howell's words catching him off guard.

'Your friend. Theo Walker.' Howell spoke with little regard. The respectable senior figure had long disappeared. 'Jackson had his men fill his house with bullets before blowing it to kingdom come.'

'No,' Sam uttered in disbelief.

'Yup. Mayer has some of his men collecting Amy as we speak. So that clears up one mess. So now, we clean up one more.'

Howell reached for the door as three men, top-to-toe in black, burst in, each one holding his pistol at eye height.

The first one in, with a shaved head and a chubby face littered with acne scars, pulled the trigger as Sam dashed from the hallway to the kitchen, the bullet whipping past him and clattering into the doorframe, wooden splinters spraying out like dust. The man headed straight for the kitchen, quickly followed by another man with brown skin and a thick brown beard. Howell recognised them as two of Jackson's most efficient killers and almost felt a twinge of sympathy for Sam Pope, who would be killed within seconds. The third man placed a gloved hand on Howell's shoulder, reclaiming his focus.

'Sir, the boss has insisted I accompany you to the High-Rise until this passes. He will meet you there.'

'Good,' Howell barked, reaching for his raincoat, which hung lazily from the coatrack by the door. 'I could use something stronger to drink.'

The treacherous inspector stormed out into the rain, swiftly followed by his protector. They leapt into the car and reversed instantly, spinning out onto the quiet, pleasant street and speeding off into the raining night towards safety. In the house, the first man stepped into the kitchen, instantly checking around the door, pistol ready to fire. He walked carefully; the large island sat in the middle of the floor, a few leather stools positioned opposite. A large light hung above it, bathing the sink and chopping area in a bright white glow. The other henchman turned into the study, checking the nooks and crannies of the inspector's office as they hunted their prey.

Neither man noticed the large carving knife missing from the knife set atop the marble.

Neither man noticed Sam slowly etch his way around the island, listening to the wet, squishy footsteps of his assailant. The man, pistol at the ready, slowly reached the edge of the island and then burst forward, leaping out like a jack-in-the-box.

There was no one there.

Sam silently approached behind, crouched down, and in one swift movement, he sliced the blade across the attacker's Achilles, carving the tendon in two. The man buckled forward instantly, but before he could howl in pain or crash to the floor, Sam caught him with a hand across his mouth.

In another swift movement, he drew the blade across the man's throat, the skin opening like a packet of crisps as a spray of blood shot forward, followed swiftly by the man's mortality.

Sam let him slump forward, choking on his own blood as his movements slowed and he finally let go.

Another broken promise.

Footsteps boomed in the hallway and Sam scurried forward, collecting the handgun and ducking behind the large dining table that led out to the conservatory. The other hitman, gun held out front, whispered into the room.

'Mike.' He entered, scanning with his gun. 'Mike. Where are you?'

At that moment, he saw the blood slowly creeping around the side of the island.

That one split-second of distraction.

It was enough. A bullet shot through the kitchen and burrowed into the man's temple, crashing through the other side of his skull and embedding into the fridge. A splatter of blood and brain matter accompanied it as the man fell to the floor to join the recently deceased.

Sam stepped over both men, collecting the other gun and tucking them both into the back of his uncomfortable jeans. He sprinted to the front door, hauling it open, and rushed to his car, hoping beyond hope that Theo was okay.

As he sped away into the night, he made a silent vow that the two dead bodies he had left in the house were not the last.

CHAPTER TWENTY-FIVE

The heat was unbearable, with the sun relentlessly beating down upon the rocky, barren wasteland of Mes Aynak. The mountainous part of the Logar Province was roughly forty kilometres southeast of Kabul, the war-torn capital of Afghanistan. With George W Bush declaring war a few years earlier, the fight against terrorism had become blurred, the political and financial implications weighing down upon every politician, the balancing act of saving the world and lining the pockets of the rich almost impossible.

But as the world discussed and argued over the morality of the war itself, Sam sat on a round boulder, his boots off and his shirt undone. A lukewarm bottle of water rested next to him and he squinted into the distance.

Somewhere out there, amongst the darkness of the caves, was a rogue terrorist cell. The initiation to Project Hailstorm was almost a week old and he, along with the other highly trained operatives selected, were beginning to feel the strain. Endless trekking into the treacherous mountains, the weight of the equipment strapped to him like a carrier mule.

The ferocious heat.

The very real threat that the next step would be into a sniper's scope.

Now, at one of the highest points, he looked out, wondering which direction their targets were and when he would need to retrieve his rifle and pick them off before they even knew what was happening.

He thought of home.

The constant disappointment of the British summer, where a nice day turned to a thunderstorm like the flick of a switch. Wandering around a garden centre with Lucy, watching as she sniffed flowers and pointed at the ones she would buy if they had a bigger garden.

Sat outside in a beer garden, enjoying a cold Moretti as groups of his friends and their partners chatted endlessly about television and future plans.

He longed for home. To start that family he and Lucy had spoken of ever since they got married.

He longed for home. But he lived for war.

The medals that adorned shelves in his study back in London were evidence that he was highly regarded. The list of kills were the basis of his legend.

That was why Project Hailstorm had recruited him. It was why he was sat on a rock in the middle of nowhere, hunting a terrorist cell in the midst of a war he was no longer sure about.

Sam Pope was a killer.

One of the most efficient the United Kingdom had ever produced.

He was there to wipe out the cell and join the most prestigious black ops team the UK and US governments had put together. It was a chance of a lifetime, and as he watched the overbearing sun begin its descent beyond the furthest mountain, he realised his life would always consist of him wishing he were in two places at the same time.

The arms of his wife and looking down the scope of his sniper rifle.

'You working on that tan?'

Theo's voice broke Sam's train of thought and he snapped back into his surroundings, his unshaven face cracking into a smile.

'Very funny. Just because you don't have to.'

'You racist bastard,' Theo joked, plonking himself down on the rock next to Sam. He was shirtless, his black skin tight over his defined muscles. 'Plus, as you well know, black don't crack.'

'Is that right?' Sam chuckled, appreciative that his best friend had joined him. He cast his eye over Theo, whose easy-going aura had been replaced with a worried frown. 'What's up, mate?'

'I think I'm done.' Theo sighed, looking out over the impressive terrain.

'Done?'

'Yeah.'

'With what?'

'This. All of this.' He gestured around with his hands. 'I'm so far from home, Sam. I want to get back, meet a woman, and settle down. Have some kids. Be a good person.'

'You are a good person,' Sam stated with authority. 'Just because we have to deal with the shit doesn't mean we aren't good people.'

'Really?' Theo asked cynically. 'How many good people do you know who have killed as many people as we have?'

'It's our duty.'

'Our orders, you mean.' Theo shook his head once more before running a hand through his short black hair. 'I'm tired of killing, Sam. I know I'm here to put people back together again, but I've got more than just their blood on my hands. For what? A war we never started? To get into this crack team that is so far off the fucking book it's still in the inkpot?'

Theo hunched forward and raised a hand to his face, rubbing his eyes with his fingers.

Sam knew how proud Theo was and he reached out and placed a hand on his shoulder. 'Then you should go.'

Theo wiped away a tear, embarrassed by the sudden break in his psyche. They both knew what war could do to people; they had seen enough of their friends and comrades break at much less.

They were beyond the line now. Project Hailstorm would chew all of them up and spit them out. They all knew that, and only those who could accept it would survive.

Theo wasn't a killer. Which meant, in this environment, he wouldn't be a survivor either.

They sat in silence for a few minutes, both of them watching the impressive emergence of shadows as the sun set, long dark fingers reaching out between the mountains and bathing every stone in a dark shade.

Sam took a swig of his bottle.

Theo eventually broke the natural silence between them. 'Thanks, Sam.'

'No need to, mate. Just promise me, even when you get back home, you never stop fighting.'

Sam held out his hand and Theo took it, shaking it firmly.

'You got it, brother.' Theo flashed a white grin. 'You got it.'

He pushed himself up and headed back to the camp to begin packing and the long process to return home.

Sam turned his attention back to the phenomenal view before him, knowing his own journey into the dark, secretive centre of the war was only just beginning.

———

That had all seemed so long ago.

Now, as Sam stood outside the Intensive Care Unit where Theo was lying, he could feel the tears escaping from his eyes. He had driven through the pouring rain, the bars and restaurants kicking out the stragglers, who were either too drunk to care or too coked up to go quietly. A number of clubs boomed loudly on the roadsides, queues of scantily dressed women and overly groomed men all braving the rain for the chance to listen to terrible music and buy expensive drinks. As soon as he had gotten to the hospital, Sam had screeched to a halt, abandoning the stolen vehicle to be towed away. As he burst through the doors of the hospital, he gazed over the map, locating the ICU and walking briskly to the elevators, each step leaving a wet footprint on the white floor. Two police officers stood by the coffee machine and Sam ducked quickly into the stairwell before taking them two at a time.

The whole situation had escalated. Inspector Howell had given the greenlight to the hit on his own nephew and now his best friend clung to life by the thinnest of threads.

Sam watched through the window, the rainwater dripping from his clothes as he stared at the motionless body of his friend.

His right leg was missing, a thick, white bandage over the stump. His right hand was missing three fingers. The entire right side of his body was charred, the skin glazed as if he had been recently polished. The third-degree burns had scorched his skin, destroying the tissue completely.

His lungs had been devastated by the blast and his breathing was laboured, the plastic tube placed in his throat doing its best to pump oxygen into his lungs.

'Fight it,' Sam whispered angrily, his fists clenched.

A lifetime of war had showcased to him the horrors of man. But seeing his best friend fighting for his life had hit him like a freight train.

He had seen these injuries before.

Had watched Theo himself tend to them.

But he knew the outcome.

'Never stop fighting,' he spat again, through gritted teeth, the tears rolling down his cheeks as his friend took slow, assisted breaths. 'You promised me, Theo.'

Suddenly, the machine next to Theo's bed lit up and a horrifying high-pitched beeping wailed from the room like an air-raid siren. Instantly, two nurses raced into the room. A doctor barged past Sam and he watched, hands pressed to the glass, as the team tried to save his friend's life.

Sam felt sick, watching as the doctor began CPR on Theo, pressing down on the chest with regimented precision as the machine mockingly flatlined. The doctor kept going, counting out each press as the nurses watched on with a resigned look of defeat.

Sam's fists clenched with fury.

The doctor stopped his compressions.

Theo was declared dead a moment later.

Sam looked away, horrified, as they pulled the sheet over Theo's corpse, hiding him away from the living. The doctor walked out, deflated and seemingly moved, and he patted Sam on the shoulder as he passed. The two nurses followed, one of them dabbing at her eyes with a tissue whilst the other, a world-weary Irish woman, stopped and rested a comforting hand on Sam's shoulder.

'I'm sorry, dear,' she offered, looking back over her shoulder. 'Were you close?'

'He was my best friend,' Sam spoke, his words slathered in pain.

'Jesus,' she uttered under her breath. 'Well if you need a moment, go ahead. The police will be up in a minute.'

She squeezed his wet shoulder and walked off down the ward, fighting the good fight for a healthcare provider that was fighting a losing battle.

Sam watched as she went before he turned and slowly entered the room.

An eerie silence had taken over. The machines had been shut down and all that echoed were his footsteps and his breathing. He wiped away the final tear from his face and then looked at the bed. His best friend was underneath it, ripped apart by a fight that wasn't his.

He had died fighting, Sam was sure of that. But doing the right thing scarcely provided anything other than a slap in the face. This time it had wiped a good man from the world.

All for what? The greed of the corrupt.

Suddenly, a surge of rage shot through Sam like a bolt of lightning.

'I'm sorry, Theo.'

Sam turned to leave, eager to disappear before the police arrived, when suddenly he realised Theo's possessions were in the corner of the room. His clothes, blood-stained and bullet-ridden, were balled up next to a leather wallet and two mobile phones.

One of them was Sam's.

Quickly, Sam snatched the mobile phone from the pile and turned to the door just as a large middle-aged police officer walked in with a scowl on his face.

'Stay where you are,' the officer demanded, a hand outstretched whilst his other reached for the pepper spray attached to the belt that sat under his rotund stomach. Instantly Sam grabbed his wrist, pulling him towards him and crashing his forehead into the man's nose. The loud *crack* and subsequent burst of blood told him it was broken, and the man fell to the floor, wailing in agony.

Sam gave one final glance back to his deceased friend, vowing to make those responsible pay for everything they had done.

Sam stepped over the fallen officer and hurried to the exit, willing the torrential downpour to swallow him whole.

———

Pearce stood by the window, looking out at the drenched car park of the Premier Inn. The hotel was in a derelict part of Hertfordshire, beyond the M25, and hopefully, he assumed, the last place they would look for them.

He had booked two rooms, flashing his badge and feeding the young, gullible receptionist a story of espionage and national safety.

The young man had devoured the story with an innocent enthusiasm, handing over two room keys and watching in awe as the detective had ushered in a beautiful woman and a wounded man. Pearce had insisted on the man's secrecy, laying it on thick with a 'can I trust you, son?' Now, as he stood by the window, he watched every car headlight with apprehension. After what had happened at Theo Walker's residence, there was no doubt that they would do whatever necessary to tie off the loose ends.

They would kill him.

They would kill Amy and her husband.

And they would sweep it all under the rug like it never happened.

Slowly, he lifted a cigarette to his lips, taking a hard drag of nicotine before silently cursing himself for slipping back into the habit. It had been six years since he had last tasted a cigarette, and whilst the taste made him want to vomit, the soothing relaxation that the nicotine poured into him was most welcome.

The mini bar had next to nothing to accompany it, and leaving Amy and Andy unattended was not an option.

Two innocent people, holed up in a hotel to preserve their lives.

An innocent man murdered just to get to them.

For the first time, Pearce began to realise that what Sam was doing to these types of people may not have been so bad after all. He had dedicated his entire life to ensuring that the police badge represented the law, a safe haven for people against the evils that lurked on the street.

But now, as he stood a vigil to ensure the safety of two people from the very police service he had served with distinction for years, he began to wonder if maybe the line was too blurred to put right. Such were Pearce's fears that he had signed out an active firearm before he had left the station, using his seniority as well as his previous contacts in the armed response unit. A Glock Seventeen. It sat idly on the small, empty side table of the room, glaring at Pearce with brutal intent.

As he exhaled a large plume of smoke out the window, ignoring the 'no smoking' sign affixed to the frame, his phone began to vibrate in his pocket.

Sam.

He clicked the green icon and lifted it.

'Sam.'

'Theo is dead,' Sam said sternly. His breath told Pearce he was marching somewhere. 'They killed him.'

'I know. I'm sorry,' Pearce said sincerely. 'Amy told me he died protecting them. He was a good man. A hero.'

'Amy? Is she…'

'She's with me,' Pearce assured. 'Khambay got to her first but I intervened. Got her and Andy the hell out of there.'

'Off the grid?'

'Yup.'

'Good,' Sam continued, his breath heavy as his pace quickened. 'Earnshaw is dead. So is his wife. Suicide.'

'Suicide?' Pearce said sceptically.

'It's a cover-up. Same as with Amy. But it gets worse. Inspector Howell gave the green light on the hit.'

Pearce nearly choked on the smoke he had just inhaled, batting a fist against his chest. After spluttering it out, he lifted the phone again, his words alive with shock. 'Inspector Howell?'

'Yep. He confessed to me before trying to have me executed.'

'What the fuck?' Pearce stammered, flicking the cigarette butt out the window, the wind and rain instantly extinguishing it.

'Three guys pulled up, one of them took him to the High-Rise whilst the others came for me.' Sam sounded furious and Pearce knew he was grieving for his friend. 'Howell is in league with Frank Jackson.'

'Jesus.' Pearce sighed, processing the bombshell. 'What

224

happened with the men who…'

'I killed them,' Sam said coldly.

The silence sat between them, a strict man of the law knowing that the man on the other end of the phone was now their best hope of true justice. It hung heavy in Pearce's gut; an entire career devoted to upholding the law was being pulled apart at the seams. The very fabric of what he believed in was not just being questioned, but stomped into the mud.

They both knew where the conversation was going. Pearce decided to take the wheel.

'You know, they will never let her be,' Pearce said, glancing to the door of the room where Amy and her husband slept. 'Both of them. They know too much.'

'Understood,' Sam said, both of them understanding the meaning of what was being said, what Pearce was actually doing.

Giving him permission.

The rain hammered down on the broken country and Pearce once again gazed out into the cold, wet dark. The rain would wash away the bloodshed, just like everything else.

The city would at least be a little cleaner.

He could picture Sam, stood in the downpour, a statue of complete fury and terrifying violence.

A man of war.

With the trail of violence, devastation, and betrayal reaching its crescendo, Pearce rubbed his temples with frustration. Sam Pope was a good man trained to do bad things, and now driven to only one outcome.

'What are you going to do?' Pearce asked, awaiting an answer he already knew.

'What I do,' Sam responded instantly. 'I'm going to bring it down around them.'

With that, the dial tone went dead and Pearce doubted

he would see Sam again. Bullets would be fired and blood would be shed, all in the name of greed and power. He looked at the downpour once more, and couldn't help but feel it was the weight of the world hammering down upon him.

He picked up his cigarettes and lit one more before blowing the smoke out into the elements.

'Good luck, son,' he said solemnly.

'Was that Sam?'

Pearce suddenly shot round to find Amy stood in the doorway. She had her arms crossed, hugging her petite body, and she offered a tired smile.

'It was,' Pearce replied, blowing more smoke out of the window.

'Is he okay?'

'He's having a hell of a night,' Pearce replied. 'Grief does that to people.'

'I can only imagine.' Amy shook her head. 'Especially after everything that has happened.'

'Yeah, it's been a crazy few days.'

'No, I meant before. With his family,' Amy said, confusion across her tired face.

'What do you mean?' Pearce said, stubbing out the cigarette on the frame of the window and tossing it into the downpour.

'Why do you think Sam has mandated sessions with me? Or why his wife left?'

Pearce stepped forward into the room, trying to retrace the files he had read about Sam. About his life.

'He killed a lot of people during his service.' He tapped the side of his head. 'It can mess people up.'

'He comes to therapy to deal with his grief.'

'Grief?' Pearce said, hands on hips. 'Grief for what?'

'His son.' Amy's words were heavy with sadness. 'Jamie died three years ago.'

CHAPTER TWENTY-SIX

Three Years Earlier…

The morning had begun like any other, the sun peeking through the cracks in the blinds and cutting thin stripes across the bed. Sam woke naturally, reaching over to the bedside table and switching off the alarm. Lucy murmured, still half asleep as he pushed himself up from the mattress. He gazed back at her naked body, remembering the passionate love they had made the night before. Even more excitedly, the conversations of expanding their family.

With carefully considered steps, he made his way across the landing and gently reached for the handle on the opposite door. A train was hanging from the wooden panels, the name of his son proudly displayed across it.

Jamie.

Slowly, he pushed the door open, the room bathed in the warm glow from the nightlight. The wallpaper was alive with pictures of cartoon animals, monkeys and elephants giddily chasing each other around the skirting board. The far corner was a mountain of toys, a series of teddy bears all clamouring atop each other for dominance.

Then in the far corner was the 'library', an assortment of cushions laid out, surrounded by rows of books.

The boy was a bookworm.

Sam felt his heart beat with pride, especially as he had never taken reading seriously. He could read, but found no pleasure in it, and after coming through the care home system at seventeen years of age, he had fled to the army for his real education.

His son would be different.

He was smart. Too smart, in fact. It worried Sam, and he and Lucy had laughed at how early on it would be that they wouldn't be able to help him with his homework.

But that was far away.

Now, asleep in his bed, was a five-year-old boy that was everything Sam had ever worked for. Jamie slept soundly, his bright blond hair swept across his forehead, his slim chest rising and falling with soft, delicate breaths.

Sam had never known a love like it, and he watched his son sleep for a whole minute before Lucy slid her hands around his waist and pressed her cheek against his muscular back.

'Let's have another one.'

Sam felt a warmness spread through his chest, covering the two bullet scars that had sent him home a year before. He had nearly died in the battlefield; vague flashes of that night often leapt at him during his sleep.

A gun pressed against his back.

A derelict building.

The realisation he would never see his son grow old.

All that had passed and there he was, watching his perfect son sleeping whilst his perfect wife wanted another.

The perfect life.

He turned to Lucy and nodded. Her smile was uncontrollable as she tiptoed to kiss him.

'Now back to work, Officer.'

He chuckled as she pointed to the bathroom for him to get ready *for work, even going as far as to slap him on the buttocks as he walked past.*

———

Sam sat on one of the few picnic benches dotted around the Hendon Police College in North London. The grounds were huge, the main building welcomed recruits and staff into the complex before expanding onto a large running track. There were derelict buildings for trained exercises, mock-up roads for traffic procedures, and a rigorous driving track, where a young officer was screeching around corners under the watchful eye of an instructor.

The far corner saw two rundown buildings shoot towards the sky like crusty fingers, the housing barracks for many of the recruits. Sam had been offered a place with the other trainee police officers, but with a young child and his adaption back to a normal life, he was granted permission to commute in every day. He did use the rest rooms inside the recruit quarters to iron his shirt before he began his training, regulation dictating he wasn't allowed to travel into work dressed as an officer for his own safety.

Despite his varied training, he humoured them and abided by the rules. He was sure it was that very training that had pushed them to give him a few extra benefits, and they were already discussing him being fast-tracked into the AR.

The day had been strenuous, and he could still feel his eyes burning.

It had been one of the most dreaded days of the police training. Every recruit was to be sprayed with pepper spray, to measure their reaction and to experience the pain and sensation caused by it. It was a truly harrowing experience, as eighteen of them had been lined up on the field and sprayed in order. A few instantly fell to the floor, crying in pain and roaring in agony. A few stood their ground, Sam included, whilst others marched in random directions, trying to breathe their way through the experience.

They all needed to know how debilitating it was, in case they were ever caught in a crossfire.

Sam had been one of only three to remain calm, the burning more of an irritant, and he had spent the next half hour talking to those who were suffering worse.

As they screamed in pain, complaining about it being the worst thing to ever happen to them, he thought back to bleeding out on the floor of an abandoned building and understood why he was cut out for it all.

He was battle hardened.

He knew actual war.

The shower afterward had been the worst part; the toxicity of mixing it with water had caused a burning sensation across his entire body and now sat in his street clothes. The burning felt like a thousand needles being pressed against his skin. Just then his phone buzzed, and he smiled.

His ride had arrived.

———

'Man, that must have sucked dick.'

Sam laughed at Theo's reaction as he recounted the experience. They were sat in the beer garden of a local pub, their wooden table already stacking up a few empty glasses and an ashtray, which Theo was turning into a pyramid.

'It wasn't great, I'll tell you that much,' Sam agreed, tipping back the pint glass and letting the last remnants of his Moretti trickle down his throat.

'We were trained to not lie in wait. We attack,' Theo said, slightly merry from the booze. 'How did you control that urge to do that thing you do?'

'What thing that I do?' Sam questioned, smiling at the young waitress who motioned for two more beers.

'You know. Brutally kill people.'

Sam thumped Theo straight in the bicep, his knuckles hitting the hard muscle like a hammer hitting a brick wall. 'Fuck you.'

Theo knew Sam was mucking about, but instantly regretted it. No soldier needed to relive the horrors of war, and despite Sam building a career as one of the greatest snipers the country had ever known, there were times when he was racked with guilt for the things he had done.

The number of times he had pulled a trigger.

There were many drunken nights, especially since he was discharged after they had riddled him with bullets, where Sam would break into tears, relaying the guilt he felt when he held his son—that he was holding him with bloodied hands.

It may have been orders.

But death was still death, and it was a commodity that Sam had dealt in for a decade.

The moment soon passed as the waitress brought another two pints of Moretti to the table, the cold beer tasting sweet and satisfying as they both took a big mouthful. A white foam dusting stayed on Theo's moustache, much to Sam's amusement. The evening was cool, the sun escaping earlier than usual, but the air was light and a cool breeze danced between the tables. A double date was taking place a few tables down, young couples talking about holidays and reality TV. A group of young lads argued over Manchester United's chances in next season's Champion's League.

An older woman, wrinkled and covered in makeup, sat on her own, reading a novel as she sipped from a wine glass.

'So, how long until you become PC Plod, then?'

Sam smiled at the jibe and took another sip of his beer. Theo lit another cigarette, letting the smoke waft lazily into the night sky.

'About another seven weeks, give or take. They are doing another intake next year. You should apply.'

'No thanks,' Theo said instantly. 'I'm done following orders.'

'So what are you going to do? Join St John's?' Sam asked, alluding to Theo's career as a medic.

'I don't know, to be honest.' Theo took another swig of his beer.

'I'm thinking of doing something with kids, you know? There are so many of them running with gangs where I live, and I...I don't know, man...it's stupid.'

'The hell it is. Kids need guidance,' Sam said, the alcohol slowly wresting control of his speech. 'I'd be furious if my boy ended up roaming the streets.'

At that moment, one of the young men from the football enthusiast table said a loud goodbye to his mates before stumbling between the benches, to the jeering and laughter of his friends. Clearly drunk, he headed into the car park, frantically clicking the fob of his car keys until a blue Ford Fiesta blinked, chirping like a morning songbird. Sam watched with horror as the young man opened the driver's door and fell into the car, his mates laughing in disbelief. He turned to Theo, who had made eye contact with the pretty barmaid, who was smiling at the attention the strapping man was showing her.

'Theo, he's way too drunk to drive.'

Sam started to push himself up, struggling to negotiate the gap between the bench and table, when Theo shot an arm up, pulling him back down.

'One more drink,' Theo said, arching his head towards the barmaid. 'Besides, you're not a police officer yet.'

'Yeah, but...'

'Two beers please.' Theo flashed his best grin as the waitress obliged, returning with the drinks and a folded-up piece of paper with her number on it.

Sam congratulated his friend, feeling absolutely no ounce of jealousy for the endless pursuit of single life, and sipped his beer, hoping the alcohol would soothe his conscience.

———

That night would forever be burnt into Sam's memory.

It would haunt him more than the faces of the people he had lined up down the scope of his rifle, or those he had killed in hand-to-hand combat.

As he had stumbled away from Theo's goodbye hug, he had checked his phone, scowling as the battery had died. Lucy would have undoubtedly been chasing him, leaving adorably angry messages for him to not get too drunk, both of them safe in the knowledge that she found his drunkenness endearing. He rarely drank—usually only when he met up with Theo—and even she wouldn't begrudge him a drink after a face full of pepper spray.

As he rounded a corner onto the main road, the first thing he saw were the flashing lights. Two police cars were blocking a section of the pavement, the uniformed officers diverting horrified onlookers away with rushed voices.

An ambulance ominously sat between the cars, its lights blinking in unison with the police cars.

The paramedics were hunched over.

A blue Ford Fiesta was on the curb, its tyres twisted at a horrible angle, the driver's door open, a puddle of vomit beneath it. The drunken young man was sat in the back of one of the police cars, crying his eyes out.

Then he saw Lucy, sat stone cold, her eyes glazed and her skin pale. A police officer tried to speak to her, offering her a small brown bag to breathe into.

The words fell on deaf ears.

Her vacant stare was locked on the paramedics.

Sam felt his knees buckle.

Lucy had gone for an evening stroll to come and meet him, surprise him with their company and a possible trip to a takeaway shop.

He fell to his knees as he followed her stare.

Suddenly, the noise of the crowd, the surrounding traffic, and the police orders drowned out as he stared at the paramedics.

Jamie lay motionless on the pavement.

His small body was twisted unnaturally, his right arm locked underneath his broken spine. One of his legs was crushed, the blood already staining his jeans.

Blood trickled from his nose and his left ear, pooling around and matting his blond hair to the cold, hard concrete.

His eyes were wide open.

The life had left them instantly.

Sam tried to breathe, tried to move, tried to do anything, but all he could manage was flopping forward and emptying his stomach all over the pavement.

His little Jamie had been killed.

And he should have stopped it.

————

A few months after the funeral, he and Lucy attended the trial of the young man—a twenty-year-old named Miles Willock, who pleaded guilty, crying in the courtroom as his expensive lawyer spun a yarn of the horrors the young man faced, having to live with the guilt of killing a child.

Sam couldn't believe it.

At least Miles got to live.

It worked, and although Miles was found guilty, due to his age, regret, and the pity of the jury, he receive a reduced sentence of eighteen months.

Sam knew the boy would be out in less than a year.

A year.

For killing his son.

After that, Sam rejected the chance to pass out, handing back the police badge he had earnt and telling them he couldn't represent a justice system that couldn't deliver it.

The drinking stopped.

The ideas of having another family.

Everything stopped.

Lucy tried to connect with him, telling Sam that he didn't need to forgive Miles; he needed to forgive himself.

It fell on deaf ears.

Sam spent every evening sat in his son's empty bedroom, remembering the promises he had made to his boy.

That he wouldn't kill people anymore.

That he would read more books.

As the evenings passed, Sam sat on his son's bed, flicking through every book that Jamie had enjoyed, tears streaming down his face and his heart breaking further.

Eventually Lucy left, telling him that she couldn't watch him willingly spiral further into his grief. She thought he was a fighter.

But he had given up.

She left, finding happiness a year later.

Sam found his own method for dealing with his grief and guilt, and every criminal that felt his wrath was another step towards acceptance.

But whenever he returned to his empty flat, his knuckles split and the blood of a criminal spilt, he felt nothing.

Just a cold emptiness.

Nothing would bring his Jamie back.

Nothing.

———

Sam stood in the wreckage of Theo's house. The walls had been ashened black by the blast and ensuing fire, causing the surrounding houses to be evacuated until further notice. The rain lashed against the shattered shell of the house, his footsteps crunching over the charred remains of Theo's life. Sam had followed the back alleyways to the street, hopping over the fence to elude the police car keeping vigil out front.

He trudged through the broken kitchen, spying where the trapdoor was that had saved Amy's life.

The blood-splattered wood showed him where Theo lost his.

He looked away, the anger of losing another person

close to him again threatening to overspill in an avalanche of rage.

Slowly, he stepped into the garden, the rain welcoming him with a series of wet slaps.

He reached into his pocket, flicked the screen a few times, and lifted the phone to his ear.

'You have no new messages and one saved message. Saved message.'

Sam took a deep breath, the cold rain obscuring the entire garden.

The message played.

'Hey, Dad. I miss you. Mum says you are going to be away for a while. I understand, but I wanted to see you. I have some new books to read with you. I'll speak to you soon, Dad. I love you.'

Sam lowered the phone, the last message his son had sent him before he was snatched from the world causing his heart to break once more. Sam would never forgive himself for what had happened, for allowing a young man to drink drive.

It had ruptured everything he had fought for.

Everything he had killed for.

And whilst he couldn't keep his promise to his son, he knew that the same system that let it go unpunished would erase Amy and her husband from the world and no one would be able to do anything.

The same people who had brutally murdered his best friend.

Pearce was right: they wouldn't stop.

Gritting his teeth, Sam thrust his phone into his pocket and marched to the side shed, the wooden door heavy with rainwater. He wrenched it open and removed a shovel, laughing at the timing of the weather. It was pissing with rain and he was there to collect his 'rainy-day fund'.

Everyone brings a bit of war back with them. Theo had the safety bunker.

Sam had his fund.

He dug into the wet earth of Theo's garden, ripping it from the ground and piling it sloppily behind him. Soaked through, he dug for five minutes until he reached down and hauled up a thick metal suitcase. Without a moment's hesitation, with a huge clap of thunder roaring behind him, Sam entered the security code and flicked it open.

The array of automatic weapons, explosives, and body armour greeted him.

Everyone brought a bit of the war back with them.

Now, as he slammed the case shut and marched off through the rain, Sam was ready to bring the war to them.

CHAPTER TWENTY-SEVEN

The floor-to-ceiling glass panes framed the outside of the room, offering a lovely view of the city. Despite the torrential downpour, London was awash with the bright lights of its booming nightlife, the masses braving the elements for another night on the tiles. Howell stood authoritatively, hands on hips, staring out at the city that looked to him for protection.

The sixth floor of the High-Rise was the penthouse; the rooms on this level were beyond anything he had ever seen before. Sure, he had partaken in a few wild nights on Frank Jackson's tab—a group sex session with three Thai women and a gram of cocaine was a particular highlight—but even then, the apartment he had been afforded paled in comparison to the room he currently occupied.

Three leather sofas sat opposite each other around an oval glass table. Expensive art framed the wall above the roaring fireplace on the far wall. A TV the size of a small cinema screen was hoisted on the opposite wall. Below, a small oak cabinet filled with the finest spirits and luxurious mixers.

Beyond was an open-plan kitchen, fitted with black

marble countertops that Howell wanted for his own kitchen.

His kitchen.

Where Sam Pope was most likely dead.

'Jesus, what a mess.' His own voice rattled in his brain, copying the ice cubes that shifted in the crystal glass he held in his hand.

'It's over now.' Frank Jackson entered the room, speaking as if he had just read Howell's mind.

Howell snorted, shaking his head and sipping the expensive scotch he had indulged in. The High-Rise was built for that—pure indulgence—and Frank was proud of what he had built. Highly respected government officials, top-ranked members of the police service—hell, even well-known actors and musicians had passed through the doors, living out their fantasies or just basking in the opulence of the venue, women, and product he provided.

The more they came, the further they climbed into his pocket.

Frank knew Howell was aware of how much shit he was in. The entire plan had blown up in their faces, and Mark was in the basement as they spoke, ensuring Mayer paid the price for his failures. Frank wouldn't take the same approach with Howell. He had his reputation as The Gent to think of, but he needed to let Howell know he was taking over the operation and that any opposition would result in the end of Howell's career.

By the look on the man's face, he had already realised it.

'What's over?' Howell barked, staring out at the drenched city. He threw back the last of his drink and held out his glass. Frank smiled politely before pushing the offer away.

'I'm not a servant, Michael.' Jackson spoke clearly. 'In fact, considering the complete failure of your operation, I think it's time we made it quite clear the reporting line here.'

'I don't fucking report to you.'

'Language,' Frank warned, the menace of his words as clear and precise as his expensive three-piece suit. 'Let me make something very clear to you, Inspector. You came to me, wanting a cut and access to the services my High-Rise can provide for you. You bargained for that with your offer of being able to meet particular requests. Now, why on earth you entrusted that blithering idiot Mayer with this operation, only you will know. But right now, I have one of my closest allies lying in the morgue and a trail of bodies that, unless you intervene, could lead people all the way to my front door. And if they do knock on that door, Howell, I will string you up as their welcoming gift. Understood?'

Howell felt the power seep from his body, knowing he was too far gone to argue. The Gent was right. He had promised him he would handle the situation, but he couldn't orchestrate the murder of his own nephew. He had given Mayer the go-ahead, vividly remembering accepting the plan before emptying his guts in a toilet stall. Jake had been a good kid, hardworking, and had idolised his brave policeman uncle.

An uncle who was no better than a criminal.

Now, as he stood staring at the city he had betrayed, he wondered how easy it would be to hurl himself to the ground below. Frank stood next to him, absorbing his misery like a sponge.

At that moment, the door flew open and Mark stormed in, his white shirt unbuttoned at the collar, the sleeves rolled up to reveal his meaty, ink-covered forearms.

The entire front of his shirt was stained with blood.

Two other men entered, both of them holding handguns.

'Mark,' Frank greeted sternly. 'What's the matter?'

'I haven't heard from the boys over at his place' He jabbed a finger at Howell. 'Which means they're dead.'

'You sure?' Frank said, stepping forward with concern.

'Possibly. If Pope knows what's good for him, he'll flee, but I've called the boys in. I've told them to tool up and we're going to go hunting.'

'How many?'

'About fifteen or so. They're doing a quick sweep of the building as we speak.'

'What about Mayer?' Frank asked, arms crossed.

'Mayer? He's here,' Howell spoke up.

Mark smirked and tossed something across the room to him.

A human finger.

Howell dropped it in disgust.

'Jesus!' Realisation began to creep in. 'Wait…is that…?'

'Mayer. He effectively gave us the finger with his botched operation. So I decided to take it from him.' Mark spoke with no compassion. 'I'll be back later to finish him off.'

'Jesus,' Howell muttered, the colour draining from his face. Mark motioned for the two men to follow him as he headed back to the door. The men were nondescript, nobody that Frank would ever get to know on a first-name basis. They would do whatever Mark ordered, knowing that they would be rewarded and protected by the police. Frank trusted Mark to get the job done. They would head off into the downpour, scouring every street until they overturned whatever rock Pope was trying to hide under.

He would be dead by dawn.

Frank quickly scanned his watch. It was almost two in the morning.

Time for a nightcap.

Frank nodded his approval to Mark as he crossed the

threshold into the hallway and closed the door. He dropped two ice cubes into a glass and poured his expensive scotch over them, letting the liquid crackle in the cold.

Howell stood like a disobedient child outside the headmaster's office.

'See, Howell? That's a man who gets a job done.' He lifted his glass in a cheers. 'Consider this situation closed.'

At that exact moment, the building rocked as the booming sound of grenade echoed through like a roar of thunder.

———

Sam had parked the stolen car two streets away.

At two in the morning, Dulwich was a ghost town, and he walked through the streets carefully, the bulletproof vest strapped across his muscular torso. Two pistols were tucked into the back of his jeans, each one perfectly placed for a quick retrieval. On a Velcro strip across his armour he held two grenades, both of them primed and ready to cause serious damage.

Over his shoulder, tucked under his arm, was an M16A2, a light support assault rifle with a full magazine slammed into it. The rain lashed against him, providing him with even more cover as he walked through the streets.

Not one car passed by.

As he came to the corner, he saw the front gazebo of the High-Rise, the impression of class as tasteless as the heinous acts that were encouraged within. Squinting his eyes to focus, he could see that the front desk of the lobby was unattended, the girls clearly not needed to work nights. Most likely they were being strapped to beds upstairs so the rich and powerful could violate them even further.

Two silhouettes were moving in the lobby area, the very one Sam had stormed through a few weeks previously to get to Morton. Back then, he was armed with just a baseball bat. Now he was walking in as if he were walking through the gates of hell themselves.

He was about to go to war.

A brilliant flash of lightning illuminated the street for a split second before a roll of thunder roared like an angry god. Sam cast his mind back to his time serving, the adrenaline coursing through his veins as it did back then. He was trained for these situations; the very notion of kill or be killed had kept him alive in the face of death more times than he could remember.

Alive, to live a life that had been empty since the death of his son.

Since his wife had left him.

Now, as he stood in the pouring rain, his hands expertly clasped around an assault rifle, he realised why he had been doing it all. The attacks on the petty criminals who had beaten the system.

'The Night Shifts'.

The reason he had begun to investigate Harding's death. Why he had killed those two men to save Amy, and why he had been fighting the endless stream of corruption he had uncovered since then.

He was looking for redemption.

A redemption for not stopping the man who had killed his son. For not dealing with his guilt and losing the only woman he had ever loved.

Redemption for breaking the promise to his son.

Redemption for the death of his best friend.

Sam gritted his teeth and pulled a grenade from his vest, taking measured steps across the road to ensure he wasn't visible to any curtain-twitcher inside. He had heard the third man who had arrived at the house inform Howell that they were heading to the High-Rise.

This was where he would be.

Howell. The Gent. The other man who had killed Theo.

The men who had trodden over the justice system to line their own pockets.

They were about to experience war.

As the next bolt of lightning cast the street in a wild glow, Sam pulled the metal pin from the grenade and waited a few seconds. Sure enough, the thunder slowly built before it exploded loudly across the street.

He hurled the grenade.

It shattered the window, and instantly he heard two voices begin to question the intrusion. Just as one of them yelled out his realisation, the grenade detonated, the entire lobby area blasted clean open in a cocktail of noise and fire. The building rattled like a maraca. The glass windows shattered, the shards twinkling in the glow of the streetlight like fireflies. The alarm wailed in panic and the sprinklers burst to life, mimicking the outside downpour, trying their best to wash away the devastation.

The two men were scattered in various-sized pieces, the proximity ripping them apart and turning the majority of their bodies to paint.

Sam hopped over one of the broken window ledges and into the High-Rise, his shoes crunching on the broken, bloodstained glass. He whipped the rifle up, the stock wedged expertly into his shoulder, one eye closed, the other peering down the sight along the top of the rifle. Taped to the underside of the barrel was a torch, which Sam clicked on. The smoke slowly began to clear and Sam ventured in, passing the lifts which had automatically shut down upon the alarm.

There was no stealth mode now.

They knew they were under attack, and he had no idea how many people were waiting within the darkened building. The electricity had cut out with the blast, just the thin emergency lights giving each corridor a haunting glow.

Sam approached the door to the stairwell when he heard the frantic patter of footsteps approaching the bottom. He quickly stepped to the other side of the door, watching it almost thrown off its hinges as two men burst in.

They stopped dead, shocked at the devastation of the lobby, littered with glass and body parts.

Sam lifted the rifle and sent a bullet through the back of one man's head.

The other man turned, gun in hand, but Sam planted two bullets in his side, sending the man tumbling to the ground, wheezing in pain as the air whistled out of the exit wounds. Sam stepped over him, raised the rifle, and planted another bullet between his eyes.

He entered the stairwell.

A few emergency lights gave a dim view above and he carefully pressed against the wall, gun aimed up at all times, scanning the darkness of the stairwells. As he slowly ascended the first staircase, the door to the first floor flew open and a man decked in a black polo shirt and trousers lunged at him, knife in hand. Sam spun to the side, allowing the blade to swipe past his chest before raising a knee into the man's gut, drilling the air from his lungs. His attacker stumbled back, coughing, before sloppily slashing at him again with the blade. Sam, allowing his rifle to swing from the strap over his shoulder, reached up, snatching the wrist in his hand before twisting the man's arm. The man yelped in pain before Sam swung him round, slamming his head off of the thick metal banister and then redirecting the blade and plunging it into the man's chest.

The man gargled blood instantly, his eyes wide with realisation that he was on the verge of death.

Sam tipped him over the edge of the balcony, watching him drop ten feet into the darkness, the noise of his collision with the concrete below confirmation of his death. A gunshot echoed through the stairwell as a bullet drilled into the wall behind Sam. He instinctively dropped to his knee, whipping up his rifle in one fluid motion and squeezing the trigger. A burst of light lit up the corridor and he could see the stream of bullets strike the oncoming henchmen, a red mist spraying into the air as they fell to the floor.

Dead.

All of them dead.

As the dim lights of the stairwell struggled behind the smoke from his gun, Sam stepped through the door to the corridor of the first floor, sweeping his torch around from side to side.

Clear.

Spinning on his heel, he returned to the stairwell, slowly creeping up the staircase, taking extra care to plant his feet as silently as possible. The sprinklers were still firing on all cylinders, the water relentlessly coating the entire staircase, carrying the blood of the dead with it.

Sam pressed on.

The fire alarm died sharply, the inhabitants obviously keen to keep the authorities at bay.

Sam approached the door to the second floor and carefully pulled it open. The instant the door creaked on its hinge, two bullets erupted into the frame, causing him to spin back for cover, crouching beside the wall of the corridor. The door slowly swung shut and he drew his rifle up, waiting just a moment for the door to almost slot into place.

He slid his fingers into the frame, catching it before it closed, but only just. He could hear the approaching footsteps as he locked the rifle in place against his broad chest, steadying it.

He threw the door open.

A burst of ammo exploded from his gun with pinpoint accuracy.

The approaching assailant fell backwards, bullet-riddled, and he collapsed across the floor, wheezing as the life quickly escaped his body. The faded emergency lights barely reflected off the blood that pooled around the body, and Sam slowly stepped into the corridor. Like before, he drew his gun from left to right, scanning the corridor and making sure it was clear. Just as he cleared the left-hand side of the corridor, a large man, dark-skinned and at least twenty pounds heavier, leapt from a doorway, pushing his gun upwards and directing the fired bullets into the ceiling. The attacker, who Sam could see was missing an eye, the socket slammed shut and sealed by a brutal scar and prison tattoos, roared with anger as he clasped onto Sam's shoulder and shoved him hard into the wall.

Sam hit the bricks, feeling the air try to escape his body, but he shifted his body weight and caught the attacker with a brutal shoulder to the midriff before rocking him with a few hard rights. Sam reached for a pistol from the back of his jeans, but the large man caught him with a clubbing blow to the kidneys before charging at Sam, lifting him off his feet before both men dropped into the darkness of the corridor. Sam's ribs crushed against the assault rifle and he rolled over in agony just as his behemoth of an attacker lunged forward, a sharp, serrated blade in his hand.

Sam reached up, both hands wrapping around the man's forearm as he lay on top of him, using his extraordinary body weight to press the knife down.

Slowly, it began its descent towards Sam's neck.

Despite his best efforts, Sam knew the man would overpower him. Taking a deep breath, he shunted his body to the side and released one hand from the man's forearm.

The blade plunged into his shoulder, ripping through the Kevlar vest and pushing a few inches of metal into his shoulder. As he grunted with agony he focused on his movements, lifting his hip and sliding his hand beneath his back, returning with his hand clasped around a Glock 17. He placed the barrel against the man's temple.

He pulled the trigger.

An explosion of blood, bone, and brain matter sprayed the wall and the attacker slumped to the side, a hole burrowed through his skull like the Channel Tunnel. Sam shoved the rest of his dead attacker to the side, slowly sitting up and pressing a hand to the wound on his shoulder. The blade had pushed a few inches in, but he'd survive. With a hefty groan he pushed himself up, taking a quick glance at the dead body on the ground. The attacker's eye was wide open, his hand still clutching the blade that was stained with Sam Pope's blood.

The man's brain was splattered against the wall like a Jackson Pollock painting.

Sam reached down to collect his semi-automatic rifle, when the door to the corridor flew open again and another man stepped through, peering intently into the darkness. He noticed the dead body on the ground, gasped in horror, and then rested his eyes on Sam.

The man drew his gun, but Sam whipped the rifle up, swinging the butt into the man's wrist, shattering the bone and causing his gun to drop from his hands. The man yelped in pain, but Sam grabbed him by the scruff of the neck and pulled him close, ramming the barrel of the rifle into the man's gut.

He pulled the trigger, unloading several bullets into the man's stomach. Sam felt the warm blood pour out of the man, coating his legs as he pushed the man back through the door. The panic in the man's eyes soon gave way to acceptance and Sam shoved his bullet-riddled body over the banister.

He fell into the darkness, dead before his bone-crunching collision with the basement.

With his shoulder slowly pumping out blood, Sam gritted his teeth, ignored the pain, and slipped the empty magazine from his rifle. He tossed it into the dark, the plastic cartridge colliding with the wall. He pulled his final cartridge from his vest, slammed it into the rifle and, taking careful and considered steps, ascended the stairs once more, making his way to level three.

CHAPTER TWENTY-EIGHT

The room stank of vomit and urine, intermittently disgusting Mayer as he swung from the hook in the middle of the room. The blood loss had caused him to lose consciousness, his vision frequently blurring as the blood weighed heavy on his brain. The plastic that strapped his ankles together had cut into the skin, a trickle of blood oozing down his leg. A large meat hook swung between them, suspending him upside down in the plastic-covered room.

The sheets were stained with his blood.

Mayer could feel how sticky his naked body was, an amalgamation of his sweat, blood, and piss.

That animal Mark had rocked him like a punching bag, the skin darkening with oncoming bruises. Then the man had gone for his fingers, removing the middle and index finger of his left hand. As he had cried in agony, Mark had grasped his genitals, wrenching them in a circular motion and causing him to projectile vomit.

Laughing, Mark had then taken a pair of pliers and wrenched his front tooth from his gum, ripping it clean from the root.

Mayer had prayed for death.

Mark became distracted, radioing two men who had been left behind at Howell's house. Mayer, despite the pain, registered that his superior had been on the take as well, the man who gave the go-ahead for his own nephew to be murdered. He couldn't believe it, and it seemed like the only person who wasn't corruptible was the man everyone was trying to kill.

Pope.

Mayer shut his eyes and waited for his life to be ended, but Mark stormed out of the room, promising he would return to slowly end Mayer's life. The door slammed shut and Mayer swung, naked and alone in the dark.

He sobbed, regretting every step he had taken down the wrong path. He was head of the Counterterrorist Squad and had forged a wonderful career within the Metropolitan Police. He would have gone further, probably finally found a wife and settled down.

But greed had reared its ugly head and guided him on a journey that was to end with him being sliced apart in a basement.

Then he heard it: a loud roar that echoed through the building. The ceiling began to shake, the hook rattling as the entire building quivered at the mighty force of an explosion. Emergency lights flickered and then burst to life in the corners of the room, the power dropping.

As did Mayer.

The hook hadn't held, the vibration from the explosion shaking it loose of its bracket, and Mayer's body weight wrenched it free. He hit the sheeted floor hard but managed to get to his feet, woozily making his way to the bundle of clothes by the trolley.

His tooth lay on the metal, blood still clinging to it.

Mayer felt sick.

He picked up his bundle of clothes, and just as he was

slipping his legs into his trousers he heard the unmistakable rattle of gunfire. Panicked, he pulled them up, hurrying to the door. He poked his head into the stairwell before leaping back with fear as the gunshots echoed loudly in the narrow walkways. Gazing up through the dimly lit corridor, he saw more flashes of gunfire before he saw the barrel of a rifle peeking over the banister, heading upwards.

The fresh smell of burning dominated the air, the recently fired gun still red hot.

Now was his chance.

Quietly, with his shirt balled around his fingerless hand, he tiptoed up the stairs, listening in horror at the gunfire above, the bloodcurdling gasps of pain as metal ripped into flesh. Mayer stepped into the lobby and took a second. The entire ground floor had been demolished by a grenade; the fixtures and walls were charred and crumbling. Large clumps of human were scattered around the room like a horrific jigsaw puzzle.

Another blast of gunfire from above snapped Mayer out of it and he raced through the devastated doorway, into the torrential downpour and to freedom.

––––––

The sprinklers had stopped, the entire corridor smelling of damp. Smoke drifted from the end of Sam's rifle, the final bullet gliding through the air and catching the henchman in the throat. He had fallen to the ground, hand clasped around the hole as blood trickled through his fingers. Two feet to the left of him was his partner, his life escaping from the three bullet holes that riddled his body.

Sam eased the rifle over his head, the blood trickling from the gash on his shoulder. After taking four floors and killing eleven men, his other shoulder ached too. The makeshift bandage Pearce had applied had long since spoilt.

Sam had been through the wars once again.

And like before, he was walking on, a trail of death behind him.

Dropping the rifle in the empty corridor, his hand slid to the base of his spine, retrieving the Glock 17 pistol, and he instinctively slid his finger over the trigger. The other pistol had been lost on floor three in a brief struggle with another attacker. Sam had ended up snapping the man's neck.

Now, as he stepped slowly into the stairwell again, he imagined word was spreading and most of them would now barricade the penthouse until backup arrived. Although he was sure the reports of his entrance and subsequent gunfire would have been reported to the police, he knew they wouldn't be a problem.

The police didn't go to the High-Rise.

Sam made it up to the fifth floor and pushed open the door of the stairwell, creeping in, gun pointed out right as he stepped into the corridor. The higher up he had gone, the more pristine the interior. The fifth floor was painted a brilliant white, with a deep grey carpet that squelched underfoot. The walls were decorated with tacky art, paintings and canvases of little meaning but of extreme pomposity. The previous floors had provided a number of rooms, seedy areas for the depraved to indulge in whatever they wanted. A number of Jackson's loyalists even took residence in the High-Rise; the only price was their unflinching obedience.

They had run headfirst into a loaded gun for him.

Sam held the pistol with both hands, his left supporting the right, the index finger resting ready on the trigger.

He passed one of the luxury apartments. The door flew open and a half naked woman stumbled out.

She screamed as Sam swung round, the gun aimed directly between her eyes. Her top missing, she held one hand across her exposed chest, but before Sam could even bark an instruction, a right hook shot from the doorway with the accuracy of prize-fighting boxer.

He caught him clean on the jaw, rocking him off balance, and he stumbled back into the wall, the gun swinging loosely in his hand. As he tried to steady himself, he heard a gruff voice bark from the broad figure that stepped into the hallway.

'Get the fuck out of here.'

The woman nodded, her cheeks stained with mascara-heavy tears, and she scarpered towards the stairwell, unaware of the display of death she would soon witness. The cockney accent belonged to Mark, who slowly removed his black jacket. The tight-fitting T-shirt he wore was more than enough evidence he was a fighter, although age had turned the clear muscle into bulk. His chest was threatening to rip the shirt in two whilst his forearms, complete with incoherent tattoos, were as solid as tree trunks.

The fists attached to them were like sledgehammers, and Sam was soon reminded as another crashed into his side, drilling the air from him like a deflated balloon. Sam fell to his knees and quickly tried to regather his composure.

'You killed my oldest friend. I killed your oldest friend. You'd think that would make us even,' Mark said, sizing Sam up as he pushed himself to his feet.

'You killed Theo?' Sam spat, taking in a deep breath and feeling his body correct itself.

Mark waited, clearly wanting it to be a fair fight. Sam could tell he was a fighter, and the way he hit told him he didn't lose.

'Yup. Sorry, fella.' Mark smiled, pointing a meaty finger at Sam. 'But this…I'm going to enjoy this.'

A mere few yards separated the two of them, the walls of corridor feeling closer, and Sam remembered the fight with the bald man in the police station. Something told him this guy wouldn't be any easier. Mark grinned and then exploded forward, hammering at Sam with a series of thunderous hooks. Sam threw his arms up, deflecting each blow with his forearm, and then managed to lift a knee into Mark's gut. The solid muscle absorbed most of the impact, but it took a little wind out and Sam took the opening. He caught Mark with a dig in the ribs and then a few hard rights, drawing blood from his lip.

Mark stumbled back and Sam launched into a hard left hook. However, Mark caught his arm, locking it in, and then slammed his head fully into Sam's face. The impact was instant, blood shooting from his nose and all the sense knocked clean from his mind. As he swung woozily, Mark grabbed him by the scruff of his bulletproof vest and slammed him against the wall. The side of his head crashed against the plaster, leaving a deep dent and a trail of dust. Then, with the entirety of his weight, Mark turned and swung Sam, heaving him into the door to one of the apartments.

Sam's spine collided with the solid door, the velocity taking it clean off its hinges, and he landed on the hard wood as it crashed to the floor.

A woman screamed, stumbling off the sofa and doing her best to cover herself. An overweight man tried to button up his trousers, stumbling slightly and knocking a tray full of cocaine off the small table.

'Get out,' Mark commanded, watching as they ran past him out into the war zone, and he stalked Sam as he rolled onto his front, crawling towards the coffee table.

His head was spinning, and blood trickled down from

his nose. With every drag across the carpet, he felt his shoulders scream with agony.

'No one likes a fucking hero, mate,' Mark said, stepping forward and stamping down as hard as he could on Sam's spine.

Sam yelled in pain as he hit the floor, his back spasming in pain.

'And for all the good it's done, it got your mate killed, it's going to get that bitch killed, and it's going to get you killed. Worth it?'

Another boot cracked down on Sam's spine, the pain ricocheting off each vertebra on its way up to his brain. One more and his spine would snap. Mark smirked, watching the supposed killing machine writhing in pain.

The man responsible for killing his best friend.

The one who had caused all these problems.

Sam pushed himself onto all fours, defiant to the end.

Mark nodded in approval. 'I'll give you some credit though, son. You ain't half got some fight in you.' Mark lifted his boot once more. He drove it down, but Sam twisted his body, catching the boot with his hands. Caught off balance, Mark wobbled, and Sam yanked the foot to the left. Mark crashed through the coffee table, the paraphernalia exploding into the air like a class A firework. Sam quickly rolled on top of his brutish opponent and rained down three hard rights, each one crunching against the solid skull and cracking the bones in his knuckles. He pushed himself off and into the middle of the room again and began to pull himself to his feet. Mark stumbled out of the wreckage, the entire bottom half of his face caked in blood. His eyes were wild, the fury of being bested in a fight rising to the surface, and he drew a handle from his pocket and sure enough a knife flicked out of it.

'Come on, then,' he challenged, lunging forward and swiping at Sam's throat.

Sam stepped to the side, blocking the lunge and redirecting Mark's body weight and sending him stomach-first into the glass dining table. He grunted in pain before spinning back sloppily, slashing wildly in Sam's direction. Sam caught his arm by the wrist and wrenched it inwards, bending the arm at the elbow and then ramming Mark's own hand into his hip.

The knife plunged into his side and Mark roared with pain, cut off quickly as Sam spun him round and slammed him face-first into the thick glass table. Teeth shot across the glass, leaving a trail of blood in streaks. Sam hauled him up and spun him back into the centre of the room, blocking another lazy right and upper cutting him in the centre of the throat, crushing his windpipe and drilling the air clean from him.

Mark gasped frantically, patting at his throat as he struggled for air. The knife still stuck in his side, draining the life from him. With the final beads of sand descending in his hourglass, Mark stumbled to Sam, collapsing forward, and Sam caught him. Blood dribbled from his mouth, and with the light fading from his eyes, he gargled his final words.

'This was never your fight.'

Sam looked him dead in the eye; the only sound was the blood gurgling in the back of his throat. Mark smiled, a bloody, gap-filled grin, and Sam felt his body weight shift. Mark wrenched the knife from his own body, and in one final act of defiance tried to plunge it into Sam's chest. Sam caught it, pulling it from his hand, spinning it in one fluid motion before plunging the blade directly into Mark's eye.

As the blood squirted forward, Sam grasped Mark's collar and spun him round, ramming him face-first into the wall.

The huge body went limp, the knife ramming all the

way through to the brain, and he collapsed backwards on the floor. A fraction of the handle poked through the ravaged eye socket and Sam stared down at his fallen foe.

The man had killed Theo.

Now he had been added to Sam's ever-growing list of bodies.

Mark had come close to killing him, but had failed. And whilst his final words may have been hauntingly true, Sam knew it wasn't his fight. It belonged to two people who would never have been able to fight it themselves. He had a duty.

He was a soldier.

He had sworn to protect.

And as he stumbled out of the demolished apartment into the corridor, he headed back towards the stairwell. With blood trickling from his shoulder and a face that looked like it had been ten rounds with Tyson, he retrieved his pistol from the floor and set off for the penthouse.

The top of the High-Rise.

He slipped the clip from the bottom of the gun, checked the ammo, and slapped it shut.

Sam headed up the stairs, intent on adding a final few to his list.

CHAPTER TWENTY-NINE

Pearce cursed at himself as he navigated the corner, the back of his car swinging out, and he quickly realigned the wheel, pulling the car straight. The rain hurtled down, seemingly on a relentless mission to obstruct his vision. The windscreen wipers were on full power, swinging back and forth as if on fast forward, and Pearce pushed his foot down until it hit the floor.

His car roared forward, weaving in and out of the few cars that were navigating their way around the slippery M25. Water sprayed from the tyres like an ethereal mist and Pearce recalled his driving training. He cut through the sparse traffic as fast as he could, his eyes focused as his mind raced.

He had effectively sent Sam on a suicide mission.

Pearce knew what Sam was capable of. He had read the files, as well as watched the man willingly leap from the third floor of a building into the Thames. The body count was racking up, and regardless of the number, the High-Rise would be filled with dead men walking. Pearce knew he had given a silent order when he spoke of Amy's safety, especially as Sam was already seeking vengeance for his best friend.

But once he had finished the phone call and lit another cigarette with shaking hands, Amy had informed him of the tragedy that had dragged Sam to the edge.

The death of his son.

The failure of the justice system.

Sam may have been the most deadly soldier the UK had produced in a long time, but he had become a man with nothing to lose.

Which meant he wouldn't stop, even if death was the only outcome.

As the lights of an articulated lorry washed over his car as he rounded a corner, they reflected off the metal of the pistol he had checked out of the armoury. It had been a long time since he had broken down doors and fired on a target—back in the days when he wasn't treated like an unscratchable itch by his colleagues. Pearce had booked it out for protection, to keep the Devereux's safe whilst they figured out their next move.

Amy had begged Pearce to go, adamant that she could look after herself and her injured husband.

Pearce flashed a quick glance at the weapon, a knot tightening in his stomach at the thought of having to fire it.

Would he be able to?

With the searing doubt niggling in his mind and the adrenaline pumping through his veins, he turned off the motorway, splashing up the slip road as the bright lights of London rushed to greet him, and he prayed, to a God he had long since given up on, that he wouldn't be too late.

———

Sam pressed back against the wall of the stairwell as he reached out for the handle. The hallway was quiet, the drips from the wet bannisters after the sprinkler deluge echoing up to him. Gently, he pulled open the door a few inches, enough to lodge the top of his boot in. He could hear the low hum of the emergency lights, the smell of damp filtering from the drenched walls.

Wet footsteps echoed towards him; the final few guards were treading a slow, careful perimeter of the top floor. Sam deduced that there were two men in the corridor— one of them soon approaching, the other at the far end, presumably guarding the door like a bouncer. Sam slowly slid the gun into the back of his jeans, freeing his hands as the footsteps drew closer. Taking a deep breath to fight off the pain from his ascent, he waited until he caught a glimpse of the handgun the nameless man held nervously ahead. As soon as Sam saw a wrist, he shunted his foot, flinging the door open and he lunging forward, clutching the man's wrist and dragging him through the doorway. The man looked shocked, trying to free himself, but Sam dug his thumb into the wrist, digging into the pressure point that caused the man to drop his gun. With a lean build and piercing eyes, the man looked like he would have been a worthy opponent in a boxing ring.

But in combat, where strategy and training counted more, Sam had the upper hand. He spun the man around, locking his arm behind his back, and then drove him downwards, slamming his face into the metal guardrail. The impact shattered the man's nose, the cartilage exploding like a party popper, and both of his cheekbones cracked.

At that moment the door flew open behind them, the final henchman throwing it open and unloading two shots which amplified loudly in the enclosed stairwell.

Sam had already dropped to the floor, and the bullets ripped into the man's back, bursting out his chest in two crimson sprays and embedding in the far wall. The man slumped over the railing before gravity greedily pulled at him, and eventually he slid into the dark chasm between the staircases.

A moment later, a sickening thud echoed up.

In the split second that the gunman had fired, Sam had dropped to a squat and then propelled himself upwards, driving his battered shoulder into the man's stomach. They stumbled back into the opulent hallway, the wooden floor still slippery from the protective downpour. The man tried to recompose, but Sam charged at him again, driving him into the hallway wall before drilling a vicious right into the man's ribs.

In a final act of desperation he swung a sloppy punch at Sam, who ducked and slid behind him, wrenching his arm over his head and tightening it as it wrapped around the man's throat. The man struggled, his hands flapping, and he tried to ram Sam back into the wall. The sudden survival instinct had kicked in, but Sam would negotiate it. He tightened his grip, the throat closing, and soon the man's face turned a horrid shade of purple.

The man went limp, flopping forward, and Sam felt the strain in his shoulders, the dead weight pulling the gash on his shoulder wider. With gritted teeth he headed towards the door at the end of the corridor, dragging the dead body with him.

The entire High-Rise had been cleared.

There was just one room left.

Soaked through, beaten and bloodied, Sam approached the door, a trail of death left behind him.

———

Howell and Jackson had heard the commotion in the hallway and looked at each other with resignation. From the rumbling of the grenade that had shook the very foundations of the High-Rise to the endless echoing of bullets rattling from various points of the building, they had known what was coming.

Pope would make his way to them.

Fifteen men would have stood in his way, including Mark, who had excitedly headed to cut him off.

They were all dead.

Howell had berated Jackson for not being able to control the situation, for not being the imposing threat that he had portrayed himself to be. The Gent had defied his nickname in response, striking the inspector with the back of his hand and reminding him of the depth of the shit he found himself in. Howell had shrunk into himself, standing pathetically in the corner of the room, paralysed by fear. Jackson had massaged the pain from his hand and poured himself a drink, refusing to be intimidated in his own building.

He was one of the most powerful men in the city.

He had bought everyone from police inspectors to high-ranking politicians.

An ex-squaddie with a hero complex would have a price. Sadly, Jackson wasn't prepared to make an offer. Pope had destroyed his building and killed his two best men. There was no deal to be struck with this man. Sometimes there was no other way.

Some things just couldn't be pieced back together.

As they heard the collision of two men in the hallway outside, Howell had feebly asked Jackson to do something.

He did.

Jackson took a sip of his drink and then opened the drawer to his desk, pulling a Kimber Classic Carry Elite handgun from inside. The metal, embossed with a smooth, wooden finish, was light, despite being full with a twelve-bullet clip, with another already in the chamber.

At that moment, the corridor went silent.

The only noise was Howell's heavy breathing and the ice colliding in Jackson's drink.

The door burst open and Sam launched into the room.

Jackson unloaded the gun, four bullets colliding into the body as it hit the ground. He squeezed again, two more bullets bedding into the motionless body that was pumping blood onto the expensive white rug.

As Jackson realised it was one of his own men, a shot rang out, the bullet hurtling into the room and shattering his shin bone as it passed through. He fell to the floor instantly, blood erupting from his calf like a broken pipe, and he cursed loudly, dropping his own gun and clasping both hands around his destroyed leg.

Howell stood frozen in fear.

Slowly, with a slight limp, a swollen eye, broken nose, heavily bleeding shoulder, and soaked with sprinkler water and blood, Sam Pope stepped into the penthouse of the High-Rise, pistol in hand.

Howell locked eyes with him, the same man who, two weeks before, was just the quiet introvert who worked in the archive office.

Now there he was, an angel of death bringing an entire criminal empire to its knees.

Howell could have applauded the man, but was rooted to the spot.

Sam walked past the dead body of the man he had choked to the death, the rug beneath him staining red. Jackson sat up, hand pressed on the shattered bone in his shin and a look of terror etched across his face. All the power he had once commanded had been taken. Sam had destroyed his entire operation, killing his men, and now, as he cowered on the floor, exposing him as just another man.

A man afraid of his own mortality.

Sam raised the gun, aiming it squarely at Jackson's head.

'Sam, stop.'

Pearce's voice boomed behind him as the detective made careful steps into the room, his gun drawn and aimed at the rogue soldier. It was only a few weeks before that he had been sat opposite him in an interview room, trying his best to get a confession that he was a vigilante, a dangerous man who had taken the law into his own hands.

As he had made his way through the blood-splattered remains of the lobby, the dead bodies that littered the stairwell, and the corridors painted with death, he had all the confession he needed.

'This needs to end,' Sam stated, not looking back as the detective slowly circled him in the room, heading towards the inspector. Howell watched in shock, but then quickly recomposed.

'Pearce, thank God you are here,' Howell began, his lip slightly swollen from Jackson's strike. 'Call for backup and have these men arrested.'

'Shut up,' Pearce demanded, sending a look of pure disdain towards the inspector. 'You don't have the right to give orders anymore.'

'How dare you?' Howell snapped, the attack on his power bruising his ego. 'I am your superior and I demand…'

Another gunshot rang out, smoke trailing slowly from the barrel of Sam's pistol, and Howell hit the floor, his leg in tatters. He wailed in pain, tears falling from his eyes as he joined The Gent on the floor.

'Drop it,' Pearce demanded, his gun still fixed on Sam.

Sam turned, a look of understanding across his beaten face. Behind him, the two men responsible for the attack on London and deaths of Officer Howell and Officer Harding, Derek Earnshaw and his wife, and countless others, lay powerless and beaten.

'Pearce. Like you said, Amy will never be safe.'

'I can keep her safe,' Pearce assured. 'With this blown wide open, people will understand exactly what happened. She'll be safe.'

Sam drew his lips into a thin, frustrated line. Outside, the rain clattered against the large windows. The city would be a little safer, but both Sam and Pearce knew the reality of the situation: by removing a powerful criminal and corrupt senior officer, two more would just move into their place.

They would sprout up like weeds.

Sam didn't believe Pearce. Jackson quickly confirmed it.

'How safe do you think you can keep her? I'll go to prison, make one phone call, and I'll be back out in no time.' He chuckled, the colour drained from his face through the shock of his bullet wound.

'Stop talking,' Pearce barked. It was ignored.

Sam turned slowly, locking eyes with an irate Jackson who had long since lost any semblance of his manners.

'I'll get out, I'll find her, and I'll make sure she is passed around from whorehouse to whorehouse until she is nothing more than a...'

Sam unloaded the pistol. The final three rounds hammered into Jackson's chest, ripping through his major organs and sending a wave of blood shooting from his mouth. He fell back, eyes wide open and his entire front bathed in blood.

Sam dropped the gun, dropping to his knees. Pearce watched in confusion as Sam lifted his hands, interlocking his fingers, and placed them on his head.

Pearce stepped forward, pulling the handcuffs from his belt.

He stepped past Sam and wrenched Howell over onto his front, the man whimpering in pain as Pearce pulled his wrists together, snapping the cuffs around them and securing them tight.

Sam stood slowly, wincing in pain. Pearce approached, looking at him sternly.

'I need to call this in. This place will be crawling with people who want to put you away for a long time.' Pearce looked like he was struggling. 'I've been fighting corruption in this city for a long time. It never ends, and it will only get worse. I know it, the criminals know it, and the cycle will continue. We need someone like you, Sam. This city— hell, this country needs you. So why don't you get out of here while you still can?'

'Pearce, I...'

'Just go, Sam. I can give you one or two days' head-start. But they will hunt you and I can't stop that.'

Pearce extended his hand to Sam, who reached forward and took it.

'Why are you doing this?' he asked, his other hand pressed on the stab wound that had bloodied his shoulder.

'It's the right thing to do.'

Sam grinned, his own reason recounted to him, and then frowned at the sudden surge of pain through his body. They shook and Sam turned and limped towards the door, back into the warzone that was decorated with his handi-work. Just as he was about to cross the threshold, Pearce called after him.

'Hey Sam.'

Sam turned, witnessing the detective hunched over the captive inspector, applying pressure to the bullet wound in his leg. 'A hell of a night shift, huh?'

Sam smirked once more, raising his eyebrows in agree-ment before shuffling out into the corridor.

Pearce removed his blazer, wrapping it around the inspector's wound. Howell had passed out, the shock of his injury and the impending future behind bars proving too much.

Pearce surveyed the scene, shaking his head in awe at the carnage and destruction Sam had brought down upon one of the most feared locations in the city. An entire operation, one deemed too dangerous for the police to approach, had been completely dismantled by one man. Pearce raised his phone to his ear, preparing to call for backup.

Sam trundled back down the stairs, past the blood splatters and bullet holes. He stepped over the crumpled, broken bodies at the bottom and slowly shuffled through the dilapidated lobby.

He stepped out into the rain, raising his face to the onslaught, and let the cooling water wash over him.

As the sirens began to wail in the distance, Sam turned towards the alleyway opposite and disappeared into the night.

CHAPTER THIRTY

Adrian Pearce pulled his car to a stop, flicked his indicator, and reversed it in one movement, guiding it between the two stationary vehicles. As he killed the engine he took a moment, reaching up with his fingers and massaging the bridge of his nose. The summer sun was still out, the evening heavy with heat, and he could already feel his shirt sticking to his back despite the air-conditioning.

It had been three months since the fall of the High-Rise.

Pearce thought back to the chaos of that evening, of watching Samuel Pope leave the building, beaten and bloodied, with an entire criminal empire reduced to rubble. The following week had been a whirlwind, as Pearce was brought before every committee and senior officer, all of them demanding to know how the hell things had gotten so bad.

Pearce told them everything, from his suspicions of Pope all the way to helping him escape the police station. Despite Pearce's protestations for his heroism, Sam Pope was made public enemy number one, responsible for the deaths of over twenty men, including one of the most notorious gangsters in London.

It was easier for the Metropolitan Police to lay the majority of it at Sam Pope's door. He fit the profile: an angry ex-soldier with a dead child. Whilst that was what the narrative became and was fed to the press, the powers that be had worked with Pearce to identify the corrupt strains within their own ranks.

Howell was put front and centre, tried and sent away for eight years for his corruption. After two months of regular beatings, Howell was found hanging from his cell bunk, his eyes bloodshot and his life over.

Not many would weep for him.

Officer Khambay and his crew were all identified, but were given golden handshakes, much to Pearce's furious protests.

It was easier to sweep it under the rug than to air it in public.

No one had heard from Mayer, with the prevailing theory being that he had been killed by Pope on his murderous rampage. The reality was he had gone into hiding, a cowardly act from a weak man.

Amy Devereux left the Metropolitan Police immediately and was given a significant payout for what had happened. She had thanked Pearce personally, meeting him for lunch before she and her husband moved out of the city. She had sent him a business card in the post, having opened her own practice in Lowestoft in Suffolk. An open invitation was there for Pearce to visit whenever, but he was sure that she would rather put the whole ordeal behind her.

She had asked after Sam, who Pearce hadn't seen since he had hobbled from the war that night. She couldn't believe what he had done for her, the lengths he had gone to just to keep her and her husband alive.

Pearce couldn't answer, except to relay what Sam had told him.

It was the right thing to do.

Her smile was genuine when he had said that, and she had spoken of how she truly hoped Sam would find peace.

Pearce hadn't heard from her since.

As he looked out the window of his car at the building, he thought of Theo Walker. The man had lived a hero and died one too. Pearce had attended his funeral, watching as a packed room of friends and family mourned painfully at the untimely death of their beloved. Pearce had stood respectfully at the back of the crowd as the coffin was lowered slowly into the ground. Theo's mum, a large Nigerian lady, cried as she scattered dirt across the top, then stood proudly as the soldiers Theo had served with stood to attention, saluting as their comrade was laid to rest.

Pearce found himself crying as they did.

The rumours had swirled that Sam's ex-wife Lucy was in attendance, but Pearce didn't think it was the time or place to make an introduction or to try and find out any further information. As he had watched them grieve, he thought he could see a man across the cemetery and wondered if it was Sam, watching from afar as his best friend was enveloped by the ground.

Pearce didn't pursue it.

Theo Walker deserved more respect than that.

Which is what Pearce thought as he stepped out of his car and headed towards the Bethnal Green Community Centre. The derelict building had been given a makeover, the mayor deciding to honour Theo's hard work with the children and his bravery in death by renovating the centre. It equated to a lick of paint and new windows. But it was a start.

Pearce walked towards the doors, pushing them open

and stepping into the large hallway. Three months before, Theo had patched up Amy's husband in that very room.

Now, a table was set against the far room, with ice-cold jugs of water, canteens of hot water, and small baskets of tea bags and coffee sachets.

A plate of non-brand biscuits sat, half attacked by the other volunteers who had already arrived.

Pearce had taken it upon himself to volunteer twice a week, helping the centre run its new 'Childhood Watch' programme, a new scheme which encouraged the older teenagers who attended to look out for bullying and how to address the problems inherent with being a child on the streets. It had felt good to give something back, especially when he had seen how selflessly Sam and Theo had sacrificed themselves for the good of others.

With his senior officers badgering him to take a higher position, more from the fear of more corruption coming to light than to reward him, Pearce had found solace in his charity work. Whatever the future held for him, he knew that what had happened three months before had changed him irrevocably.

Despite the bloodshed, the carnage, and the sheer terror of how far the corruption of the city had spread, Pearce knew it had changed him for the better.

Sam Pope was still out there, and sooner or later the criminals of the city would know about it.

Until then, as he was warmly greeted by the teenagers, who thought his detective badge was the coolest 'bling' they could hold, he would do his best to make the world better any way he could.

————

Sam had watched as they had lowered Theo's body into the ground. From over two hundred yards away, the group of people were indistinguishable and he knew he was unlikely to be spotted. Sam felt the same fury he had felt when he had dug up his rainy-day fund as the dirt was dropped onto his friend's casket.

The ground was soon full and Theo was locked away like a secret. Sam had joined in with the salute, his fellow soldiers showing the respect a hero like Theo deserved. As the small crowd dispersed, the sun cut through the clouds and bathed the cemetery in a bright glow. The gravestones cast shadows across the grass, most of them faded with age.

Tributes to the long gone.

At the back of the group, Sam could see Pearce—the unmistakable authority that the man held himself by.

He was a good man. Sam respected him greatly and would be forever grateful for his intervention at the High-Rise. Pearce had given him the chance to escape, to begin a new life and embrace the newfound purpose that had begun to beat within him like a drum.

As he stood under the tree, cast in its shade, he adjusted his tie, cursing the formalwear he had forced himself into. He watched as a petite figure walked towards him, stepping respectfully around the gravestones, not wanting to walk over anyone's resting place. Her arms were folded across her body for extra warmth, her black cardigan pulled tight over her black dress.

Lucy.

Sam felt his heart begin to race as she approached, the love of his life who he knew had built a new one. Her bump was showing, the family life she had always dreamed of becoming a reality, and he remembered how radiant she had been when they were expecting Jamie.

Her beautiful face cracked into a loving grin as she approached him, her eyes moist from crying. She stepped into the shade a few feet from him. Despite her heart and love belonging to her new husband, she was happy to see him.

Silence sat between them, a gentle breeze carrying the smell of spring with it. Finally, after taking all of her features in, Sam spoke.

'Thank you for meeting me.'

'It's good to see you, Sam.' Lucy shrugged nervously. 'You look well.'

'You do, too.'

She stepped towards him as he spoke and wrapped her arms around him. He returned in kind, his muscular arms encasing her petite body, holding her close to him. He could smell her hair, remembering all the mornings he had woken up next to her. 'God, I miss you.'

'Look, Sam, I know it's been a while, but you know where things are now.'

'I know,' Sam said, nodding away the pain. 'I just needed to see you. I needed to see you.'

'Look, I'm really sorry about Theo. He was a great guy.'

'He was,' Sam agreed. 'A hero.'

'But Sam, I can't be a support net for you this time. I mean, I've got a family now and…'

'That's what I wanted to say,' Sam said, cutting her off. 'I just wanted to tell you that I am so happy for you, Lucy. I really am. I know that what happened to our baby boy was cruel and ripped us apart. But I also know that I didn't help. I left as soon as he did, and you needed me just as much as I needed you. I abandoned you, and for that I am truly sorry.'

Lucy shook her head and swallowed the lump in her throat. She dabbed at her watering eyes with a tissue. 'Goddamn you, Samuel Pope. I thought I'd done crying for today.'

They both smiled warmly and Sam stepped forward again, dabbing at her eye lovingly.

'I've finally found a way to make peace with what happened. A way to use the pain and anger I feel every day to turn it into something good. A way in which I can honour our son, and know that other people will never have to feel the same pain and torture that we did.'

'That's…great.' Lucy said, slightly astounded. 'What is it?'

'You're probably going to hear some things, and whatever happens, just know that I have loved you from the moment I met you. From then until now, and further still. But I have to go and I don't think I'll be coming back.'

Lucy looked at him, confused and teary-eyed. He offered her a warm smile and then took her in his arms once more. He squeezed, every fibre of his being reaching out to tell her how much he adored her. Finally he let go, holding her at arm's length and composing himself; the promise not to cry in front of her was getting harder to keep.

'Goodbye, Lucy,' he finally said.

'Goodbye, Sam.' She leant forward and kissed him on the cheek. 'Just remember, you are a good man.'

He smiled once more and Lucy took a deep breath. The finality in their parting was dawning on her and she nodded and turned on her heel. Just as she was about to exit the shade, she turned back.

'Just promise me you'll keep reading. For our boy.'

'I am. I just finished *To Kill a Mockingbird*.'

'How did you find it?' she asked, smiling warmly.

Sam held his hand out and waved it slightly, insinuating it was okay.

She chuckled and then gave him one last look, her eyes piercing into his own and telling him that despite everything, there was a piece of her that would always love him.

It was completely requited.

She turned and left, carefully plotting her way back to the cemetery car park and then off to the world, to bring a life into it with her new husband. Despite his heart breaking, Sam was happy for her and watched her until she became a small dot that turned past a large tree and out of his vision.

For the last time.

Stood, surrounded by the monuments to those they had lost, he reached into his pocket and pulled out his phone one last time.

As soon as he left he would need to disappear, to go off the grid forever.

Sam thumbed the screen to the voicemail option and clicked play.

You have no new messages and one saved message. Saved messages.

Sam took a deep breath and closed his eyes, imagining the beautiful smile of his son, the locks of blond hair that fell across his angelic face as he read from one of his books.

'Hey, Dad. I miss you. Mum says you are going to be away for a while. I understand, but I wanted to see you. I have some new books to read with you. I'll speak to you soon, Dad. I love you.'

Sam wiped a single tear from his eye.

'I love you too, son. I love you too.'

Sam clicked delete, finally accepting his son's absence in his life, and tossed the phone into the nearby bin. With one final look back towards his friend's grave, Sam marched down the gravel path, heading towards London and the dark underbelly he was about to be consumed by.

The sun cut through in delicate slices, lighting the pathway as he headed to the exit and disappeared, ready to begin his new life.

EPILOGUE

Colin Mayer hadn't shaved in over two weeks; his scraggly beard was itching constantly. His hair was the same, the thinning top made even more blatant by the contrast of the unruly curls that were sprouting from the bottom of his cap.

His appearance was the least of his problems, but as the sea air caught in his lungs and filled him with fresh hope, he thought back to that horrifying moment when he had thought he was about to die.

He had been strung up like a pig, stripped nude and beaten mercilessly. The ribs that were cracked were still trying to merge themselves back together. His entire rib cage was a dark brown, the bruises just beginning to fade.

Two fingers had been severed with secateurs; the cruel smile across Mark Connor's face as he had snipped them from his hand still haunted his dreams.

Mayer looked down at his hand. The cruel stitching across the two stumps was something he still hadn't gotten used to. He had made it to an A&E, the young nurse stitching up his fingers and then foolishly letting him go to the bathroom.

He had fled.

Left everything behind.

Colin Mayer had gone dark.

He took the cap from his head and wiped the sweat away. His new job working on the pier by Dawlish, a sleepy seaside town in Devon, was enough for now. He knew his photo would have been circulated, meaning almost every legal route out of the country was off the menu.

He had stolen a car and driven until the fuel gauge had hit empty and then stolen another. Eventually he had gotten to the coast, and after three nights of sleeping rough he had approached a local fishing hut, asking the trawler man if he could work for some food.

The man, sporting a thick beard and an even thicker waistline, was called Martin, and he not only opened his kitchen to Mayer, he offered him a shower and some accommodation. Clearly taking pity on the mutilated man, Martin was setting sail to Portugal in a few weeks to do three weeks' worth of fishing around the Algarve. Mayer had offered to help prepare everything in exchange for passage to Portugal.

When he couldn't answer Martin's questions regarding a passport, Mayer was relieved when his new saviour had shrugged and said a man's business was his own.

Now, as he heaved another large wooden crate across the storage cabin, he was eager to get back onto the deck and have a cigarette, and maybe even help himself to one of Martin's beers.

Then tomorrow they would hit the sea, and Mayer would have raised his missing finger at the country as he vowed never to come back.

With a feeling of undeserved smugness, he clambered back up the stairs of the fishing boat, hoping for the rays of the Dawlish sun to wash off his face in a warm greeting.

A shadow was cast across the entrance to the cabin as

Mayer emerged, following it back to its creator. A muscular man stood against the railing of boat, his arms folded, and the sun directly behind him, encasing his features in shadow. Mayer held up a hand to block the glare from above.

'Mayer. It's been a while.'

'Pope?' Mayer said, in a panic. 'Is that you?'

Sam stepped forward, marching across the ship and grabbing the feeble Mayer by the scruff of his checked shirt and slamming him back against the cabin door before hurtling him down the stairs.

Mayer crashed against the thick wooden steps, cracking his forearm and separating his shoulder. He collided hard with the floor, two teeth shooting from his mouth like Tic Tacs. He moaned in pain, and Sam, taking a quick glance over his shoulder, hurried down after him. Mayer, with both arms out of action, was struggling to drag himself across the dusty, dark cabin, weeping feebly.

Sam walked calmly behind him before reaching down and pulling him from the ground and slamming him into the large wooden crate. Mayer turned slowly, shaking with fear and ready to beg for his life.

Before he could even begin, he felt the thick, serrated blade burrow deep into his stomach, blood shooting up his throat like a burst fire hydrant, which he spat out onto the floor. The pain was excruciating, and he shook in agony as Sam slid the knife across his stomach, the warm blood crashing out like a waterfall as he dropped to his knees.

Sam stared at him coldly, watching Mayer feebly try to hold the contents of his stomach together with his broken arm. Spluttering through his final breaths, he looked up at Sam, who stared at him coldly.

'Help. Me.'

Mayer crashed backwards into the crate, slumped like a drunk on the side of the street. The huge gash across his stomach looked like an evil grin, the blood gently sliding to the floor and building a large puddle around him. Mayer had been the instigator in everything, which had seen innocent people killed, including Sam's best friend.

As the life left Mayer's body, Sam felt not one iota of sympathy.

A loose end.

With that tied up, Sam tossed the knife onto the crate and headed back up the steps, appreciating the fresh sea air which greeted him before stuffing his hands into his pockets and walking off into whatever direction would take him off the grid.

The waves crashed against the side of the ship and the cries of three seagulls overhead echoed loudly.

Moments later, Sam was gone.

GET EXCLUSIVE ROBERT ENRIGHT MATERIAL

Hey there,

I really hope you enjoyed the book and hopefully, you will want to continue following Sam Pope's war on crime. If so, then why not sign up to my reader group? I send out regular updates, polls and special offers as well as some cool free stuff. Sound good?

Well, if you do sign up to the reader group I'll send you FREE copies of THE RIGHT REASON and RAIN-FALL, two thrilling Sam Pope prequel novellas. (RRP: 1.99)

You can get your FREE books by signing up at www.robertenright.co.uk

SAM POPE NOVELS

For more information about the Sam Pope series, please visit:

www.robertenright.co.uk

ABOUT THE AUTHOR

Robert lives in Buckinghamshire with his family, writing books and dreaming of getting a dog.

For more information:
www.robertenright.co.uk
robert@robertenright.co.uk

You can also connect with Robert on Social Media:

facebook.com/robenrightauthor

instagram.com/robenrightauthor

Cover by Phillip Griffiths

Edited by Emma Mitchell